Three Floors Up

THREE FLOORS UP

Eshkol Nevo

Translated from the Hebrew by
Sondra Silverston

 Other Press New York

First published in Israel as *Shalosh Komot*
by Kinneret Zmora-Bitan, Tel Aviv, in 2015.

English translation copyright © 2017 Eshkol Nevo
Published by arrangement with the Institute of
the Translation of Hebrew Literature

Production editor: Yvonne E. Cárdenas
Text designer: Julie Fry
This book was set in Baskerville by
Alpha Design & Composition of Pittsfield, NH.

10 9 8 7 6 5 4 3 2

Library of Congress Cataloging-in-Publication Data

Names: Nevo, Eshkol, author. | Silverston, Sondra, translator.
Title: Three floors up / Eshkol Nevo ; translated by Sondra Silverston.
Other titles: Shalosh komot. English
Description: New York : Other Press, [2017]
Identifiers: LCCN 2017001627| ISBN 9781590518786 (paperback) |
      ISBN 9781590518793 (ebook)
Classification: LCC PJ5055.35.E92 S5313 2017 | DDC 892.43/7—dc23
LC record available at https://lccn.loc.gov/2017001627

First Floor

What I'm trying to tell you is that underneath the surprise, there was something else that Ayelet and I didn't dare talk about, that in the back of our minds we knew—okay, *I* knew—that it could happen. The signs were there the whole time but we chose to ignore them. What could be more convenient than next-door neighbors who watch your kids for you? Think about it. Five minutes before you have to leave, you just take your daughter as she is, no bags, no carriage, knock on the door across the hall, and that's it. She's happy to stay with them. They're happy to have her. And you're happy to be free to do your thing. And it's cheaper than a regular babysitter. Talking about stuff like this is unpleasant, but I don't have the energy to censor myself, so I'll just tell you everything and you promise not to put it in one of your books, okay?

A couple of pensioners like them have no idea what the going price for a babysitter is in the free market. They're not part of the babysitters' information network. Which means that you can tell them any price you want. So we did. Twenty shekels an hour. Nine years ago, that was reasonable. Low, but reasonable. In the meantime, the average price in our area climbed to forty, but we stayed at twenty. Every once in a while, Ayelet would remind me that we should pay them more, you know. And I'd say, yes, of course we'll pay them more. But we stayed at twenty. And they didn't say a word. Refined people, you know, like all those German Jews, the *yekkim*. He walks around the house in a suit and tie and she's a piano teacher at the conservatory, says things like "if you would be so kind." Even if they wanted to object, their *yekke* pride wouldn't let them. And we told ourselves—okay, maybe not out loud, but we thought it—what do they have in their boring lives, those people. They should thank us. They should be paying us for the privilege of being with Ofri.

I don't remember exactly how old she was the first time we left her with them, but she was pretty young. How long do you have to wait to have sex with a woman after she gives birth? A month? A month and a half? That's how it started. With sex. Ayelet had toxemia the last month of her pregnancy, so I couldn't touch her. A month after she gave birth she was still bleeding. And I was so horny I was practically exploding. It had never happened to me before—in the middle of a meeting I could stare at a woman client and think about dragging her to the restroom and ripping her clothes off. And the thing is, women pick up on that hunger. Loads of them came on to me during that period, loads of them. And it's not like I'm Brad Pitt or anything. I got a text from the spinning instructor that you wouldn't believe. I'll show it to you sometime. But I kept a lid on it. I bit my lips hard and Ayelet appreciated it. She didn't say, "I appreciate it," she wouldn't say anything like that. But she'd always tell me, "I miss your touch, I need it as much as you do." One night she suggested, "Let's leave her with Herman and Ruth for a few minutes." And she ran her finger over my shoulder, slowly. Which is a kind of signal we have.

It was her idea. Ayelet initiated the first time. Together we knocked on their door and asked if they could take Ofri for a few minutes. I think they understood exactly what was going on. What the urgency was. You can see that they're the kind of old folks who still have that spark between them. Herman's a tall man who stands very straight. Looks like a German chancellor. And Ruth has long white hair she always wears pulled back in a pony-tail, which makes her look more like a woman than an old lady. She asked Ayelet when Ofri ate the last time, and Ayelet told her that she shouldn't be hungry now, and in any case, it's only for a few minutes. She asked whether she took a pacifier and wanted us to leave a diaper too, to be on the safe side. Then Herman started making funny noises for Ofri and tickled her stomach with the tip of his tie. Ofri smiled at him. Smiles at that age are instinctive, not genuine, you know. But still I said to Ayelet, "Look at how she's smiling at him." And Ruth said, "Children are crazy about Herman."

Ofri wouldn't go to just anyone when she was a baby. She even cried when her grandmother held her. But the minute we put her in Ruth's arms, she snuggled up to her, put her head on her breast, and played with her long hair with her fingers. Ruth said, *sha, sha, sha,* and stroked her cheek. Ayelet bent down to Ruth's height and said to Ofri, "We'll be back in a few minutes, okay sweetie?" Ofri looked at her with that clever expression of hers, then moved her eyes to me. It looked like she was about to cry. But no. She only burrowed deeper into Ruth's chest and Ruth said, "Please, if you would be so kind, do not worry. I raised three children and five grandchildren." Ayelet said again that it would only be a few minutes, then stroked Ofri's cheek one last time.

As soon as our door slammed shut behind us, I grabbed her ass, but she froze and said, "Wait a minute, do you hear crying?" We stopped and listened, but all we heard were the normal sounds of the widow in the apartment above us dragging furniture. We waited another few seconds just to be sure, and in the end Ayelet took my hand and said, "Please, if you would be so kind, no foreplay, yes?" And pulled me into the bedroom.

Herman and Ruth's grandchildren are scattered all over the world. Two in Vienna. Two in Palo Alto. And the oldest, who lives with her mother in Paris, comes to visit every summer and drives the teenage boys in the neighborhood crazy with her miniskirts, her tanned skin and green eyes. They wait for her outside the building like cats in heat, and she toys with them. Touches them offhandedly when she talks but doesn't let them touch her. A regular little mademoiselle. Already in high heels. Wearing women's perfume. Last summer Ruth sent her to ask us for eggs and I answered the door without my shirt, so she said, in a French accent, "Monsieur Arno, put on a shirt. It is not very genteel to be like this in front of a lady." And she gave a flirtatious giggle. I brought her the eggs without laughing in return, thinking that you could tell the little minx didn't have a father. That if I were her father, I'd make her take off that mini. But never mind, we'll get to her later.

Herman and Ruth's other grandchildren also come to visit once or twice a year. And then their apartment, which is usually quiet except for the sounds of the piano and the voices on the German-language cable channel, suddenly becomes noisy and full of life. Herman builds the children slides and swings in the garden. Before he retired, he worked for the Israel Aircraft Industry, so he has the touch for things like that. He also makes them model airplanes they can fly with a remote control. If it's summer, he takes a pool out of the storeroom. A huge one, made of hard plastic. And he builds an aircraft carrier in the pool that they have to try and land the model planes on. Then he takes the carrier out of the pool and they change into bathing suits and climb inside, splashing each other. But they're not wild. They're well-behaved kids, not like the ones we have here. They eat with a knife and fork. Say hello to you on the stairs.

When their grandchildren fly back to their countries, Herman and Ruth are depressed. It's a regular routine. The day after the flight, their door is locked and you know not to knock. There's no way to explain it, as if there's a heaviness in the door that transmits the message: not now. Two days after the grandkids leave, they themselves knock on our door to say that if we want, we can bring them Ofri. Herman says to her, "Give Herman a kiss," and bends down so she can reach his cheek. She kisses him carefully so as not to be scratched by his bristles. Ruth says to Ayelet, "If you need to, you can leave her for a short time too, no charge." She adds almost in a whisper, "It's so hard for Herman when the grandchildren leave us. He hasn't slept for two days, hasn't eaten, hasn't shaved. I don't know what to do with him."

That business with the kiss, for instance. When I told you before that there were signs, I meant things like that. It started with asking Ofri for a kiss when she came in. One on each cheek. But this last year, he could suddenly open the door for no reason when we were on the stairs on the way in or out, bend down, and call to her, "Hey Ofri, give Herman a kiss."

Telling you this now makes me want to die: was the writing on the wall ever clearer? But we didn't want to see it, that's what I'm trying to tell you. Ayelet's mother is not the person you want to leave your kids alone with. My parents retired and are always taking long trips. South America, China. All of a sudden, they decided to be *muchilleros*. That's exactly when Yaeli was born. And she had that complication with her breathing. We spent weeks at her bedside in the hospital, Ayelet and I, taking shifts, and when you were on shift, you couldn't fall asleep because maybe the minute you closed your eyes would be the minute she stopped breathing. You went straight to work after your shift—there wasn't even time to go home and change. I'm not making excuses, I'm just saying that we needed Herman and Ruth more and more. In the afternoon, in the evening, on weekends. Sometimes we'd leave Ofri with them for just half an hour. Sometimes half a day.

Hey, I just remembered—how could I have forgotten—one morning, when Ayelet came to relieve me and start her shift at the hospital, she told me about a dream she had at night: We were both waiting outside the operating room. But the girl being operated on, the girl in danger, was Ofri, not Yaeli. And she wasn't nine in the dream, but a year old. And the surgeon, the one who came out of the operating room to tell us the results, was Herman. Except that instead of wearing a doctor's white coat, he was wearing a patient's gown, the kind that's open in the back. She couldn't see the opening in the dream. She just knew it was there. Then Herman put his finger between his eyebrows and said, "Ofri will live." And she was surprised that he was talking about Ofri and not Yaeli, but didn't want to ask because she didn't want to ruin the sense of relief she felt.

I didn't interpret the dream for her. When we first started going out in Haifa and I once tried to interpret a dream she had, she told me that I was terrible at it and I should just listen. But even if I had interpreted it for her, I couldn't connect it to what happened a year later. Sure, I would have told her something like: Maybe in your dream, only in your dream, you'd rather that Ofri was sick because she's stronger and has a better chance of fighting it.

That's how it is. Until you have a second daughter, you don't really understand your first one. Because of Yaeli, we realized how unusual Ofri was. How rare it was, that calmness of hers. Her backbone. All her teachers, even in nursery school, always told us that the child was mature for her age. But we needed to go through

Yaeli, with all her dramas, to understand what they were talking about.

I'll tell you something that sounds bad, but I don't care: in some way, it would have been easier if what happened had happened to Yaeli. With her, everything's simple: When she's sad, she cries. When she's frustrated, she lies on the floor and screams. Ofri doesn't scream. She absorbs. Ponders. Quietly considers things. And you have no idea what's going on inside her. Only sometimes, in the end, she says a few precise words. Then goes back to looking at the world, absorbing everything she can. I'm telling you, the kid's like walking radar. When she was little she could tell when Ayelet and I were going to fight just from the energies in the room, and she'd stand between us and say, "Daddy, don't fight."

She was also the first to see that there was something wrong with Herman. Even before Ruth. One day she came back from their place and said, "Herman's broken." What do you mean, broken? "He keeps forgetting things." What things? "Where he put his glasses, where the door to the garden is, his name." Maybe he's playing with you, Ofriki. Maybe it's a kind of game. "No, Daddy, he's broken."

One evening a few days later, they knocked on our door. Both of them. Herman went straight to Ofri, asked her for a kiss and then got down on all fours so she could ride around the living room on him. Ruth handed Ayelet a plate full of slices of her marble cake and asked if she could use our fax. Every once in a while, they used it or asked Ayelet to help them with their old computer that was always getting stuck. And we'd ask them for milk. Or eggs. Or onions. We don't have what you have in Tel Aviv, places open twenty-four hours a day, and if you're out of tomato paste for *shakshuka*, it means there's no *shakshuka* and you'll have to eat your eggs plain, with no tomato sauce. Sometimes they'd run out of oil or sugar too, but not as often as we did. It wasn't really balanced, but we never bothered to balance it. Just the opposite. We told ourselves that that's what made it great. They were neighbors like neighbors used to be. Before people had ulterior motives. I'll tell you even more than that: these last few years, every time we thought about moving to a larger apartment so the girls would have their own room and Ayelet could have a normal workroom, one of us would say, "But what are we going to do without Herman and Ruth?" And the discussion ended there.

So on the day that Ruth came in to use the fax, she didn't go straight to the machine in the corner as she always did, but stayed at the door. Her hair, which she always wore in a ponytail, was loose and she kept running her fingers through it. She said quietly, "Something's happening to Herman. Something's wrong with him. Yesterday, I came home from work and found him wandering around in the street, asking passersby where he lived."

Ayelet offered her something to drink and asked her to sit down, and Ruth sighed and sat down. Herman kept galloping around the living room with Ofri on his back. I took Yaeli in my arms so Ayelet could make Ruth a cup of coffee with milk.

"All those years alone in the house," Ruth said, "it hasn't been good for him."

"You can go crazy from being alone in the house all day long," Ayelet said.

And I said, "Yes, that's what finally got to me when I was running my own business from home."

Then Ruth said, "But what can we do, I have to keep working. His pension isn't enough for us."

"Tell me," I asked her, "don't we owe you money?"

Meanwhile Herman sat down on our couch, bounced Ofri on his lap, and sang to her *Hoppe, hoppe, Reiter,* which is the German version of giddyap. She screamed with pleasure. And I thought to myself, she's a little too old for these games. A little too old to be on his lap, too old for him to put his hands on her thighs.

Ruth said, "Don't be silly, pay me when you can. Your little girl is a source of joy for Herman. And that's the most important thing, especially now."

Ayelet said, "Drink your coffee, Ruth."

Ruth stopped to take a sip, then continued, "He was the most attractive fellow on the kibbutz. Those blue-gray eyes of his. Like a cat's. And he had that Israeli tan. I was new. Right off the boat. When they saw that I couldn't keep my eyes off him, they warned me, that one changes girls like they were socks. He's only interested in one thing when it comes to girls. But I didn't care what they said about Herman. I thought to myself, he's like that because he still hasn't met me!"

"And were you right?" Ayelet asked with a smile.

Ruth looked at Herman and Ofri with total serious-ness. "I was right and I was wrong." Then suddenly she was quiet, sipping her coffee and running her long pianist's fingers through her hair again.

Ayelet told her that if she needed help in the near future, we were there, and I added, "Don't be shy, really."

"Thank you," Ruth said. "Really, you are wonderful neighbors."

That night I said to Ayelet, "There's no way Ofri's staying alone with Herman anymore."

"Yes, you're right. And we have to pay them. It's not right for us to drag it out like this. Do you have any cash?"

"No."

"Take some out tomorrow?" she suggested.

"Yes, sure, how much do we owe them?"

"I don't know, a lot, at least six or seven hundred."

"Okay, I'll withdraw a thousand."

The week after that, we left Ofri with the Wolfs twice. Both times it was because we had to take Yaeli to the hospital for tests. Both times, Ruth was home. Both times, when we got back, there was nothing unusual in the hug Ofri gave us. She still talked about the ways Herman was "broken," how he put sugar instead of salt in the salami and eggs and tried to use the air conditioner remote to turn on the TV. Her eyes sparkled with happiness as she spoke. Herman, it seems, had managed to convince her that it was all a kind of game and she had an important part to play in it: to remind him about the correct order of things, to give him the right remote, to show him which plants he had to water, to tell him what day it was.

Ayelet said in English so that Ofri wouldn't understand, "She's so innocent. Smart and innocent."

"Soon she won't be innocent anymore," I said. "It's just a matter of time."

Ayelet, who's no fool and saw right away that I was heading for that let's-have-another-baby conversation, said, not in English this time, "Forget it, Arnon. Unless you're the one who's going to be pregnant."

"English, baby, English," I told her.

"Really Mommy," Ofri said, "boys can't be pregnant."

"I'm not your girlfriend, Ofri," Ayelet said, "so don't talk to me in that tone."

"What do you want from me," Ofri asked. "Why are you always mad at me?"

Switching back into English, I said, "She's right, you know."

And Ayelet told me not to mix in.

It's complicated between them, between Ofri and Ayelet. Always was. Maybe not the first year, when Ofri was nursing. But the minute she stopped and began talking, that tension between them started. One minute they were huggy-kissy best friends, and a minute later, they were swooping down on each other, claws bared. And the problem is that it has nothing to do with strength. Ofri's strong, very strong, but she has no chance when Ayelet tears into her with all that Ayeletness of hers. She calls it boundaries. The child needs boundaries. But from the beginning, I felt that there's more to it, that there's a kind of meanness in the way she talks to her. A kind of sting that's camouflaged really well with honey. What, for example? She can say to her, "Look at how many friends come to visit Yaeli. But you're buried in bed all day with your books. Isn't that a shame, honey?" Or: "Do you think that by tomorrow you can decide what to wear, pretty girl?" Or: "Earth to Ofri!

Earth to Ofri! Are you even listening to what I'm saying?!"
Even the pet names she gives her—astro, space girl, zippy
lips—they're really more critical than affectionate. And
sometimes, when she comes home late from the office
and Ofri does something smart-alecky that she doesn't
like, or is just off in her own world and doesn't answer
her, she can really lose it and say nasty things to the kid
like: "I'm your mother, so I have to put up with you, I have
no choice. Anyone else would just get up and leave if you
acted like this with them." Or—I swear she said it—"What
did I do wrong to deserve a punishment like you?"

It isn't just what she says. It's also the tone. Biting. Merciless. Why are they like that? I don't know. Ofri's pace is
slow, a little pensive. Sometimes she really doesn't notice
that someone's talking to her. If you try to rush her, she
deliberately slows down even more. And Ayelet's the
opposite, she's quick. Has no patience for anyone who
can't keep up with her. And she has a mother who's completely nuts. Maybe that has something to do with it. She
beat Ayelet when she was little. And in Ramat Aviv, that
upscale north Tel Aviv neighborhood, right? Not in any
of those poor south Tel Aviv places. In elegant Ramat Aviv
her mother used to beat her with belts and rulers. And
there was no father there to separate them. It just goes to
show you, by the way, that you can never know what goes
on with people behind their reinforced metal doors.

Before Yaeli was born, Ayelet and I used to fight a lot
about how to raise Ofri. She would say I was spoiling the
kid. And I would say, spoiled? The kid's perfect, an angel.
After Yaeli came into the family picture, things were a

little more balanced. A table stands better on four legs. But I still felt that it was crucial for me to be around to watch out for Ofri. To make sure Ayelet wasn't too hard on her. Wouldn't cause her the kind of damage that couldn't be repaired later on.

I'll tell you something that might sound screwed up to you. After Tavlina made it big, I had offers from Spain and Germany to go and design restaurants there. You wouldn't believe what kind of emails they sent me. "We admire your no-bullshit style of creativity." "The atmosphere you create makes people want to order the whole menu." I'll show them to you sometime. In any case, I turned them down. Even though it was an opportunity to go out on my own again. And a hell of a professional challenge. The real reason I said no—not the reason I gave Ayelet—was that in order to design restaurants in Europe, you have to stay there for long periods of time. And I didn't see myself leaving those two cats alone for so long. Do you see? I always felt a kind of special responsibility for Ofri. And that just makes what happened even worse.

Hey, tell me, is it okay to dump all this on you? You're sure? How are you anyway? I didn't even ask. I saw you on the best-seller list. How much do you make on every book? Is that all? They're fucking you, take it from me. You want me "to continue the story"? For you, everything's a story, eh? It's just too bad that for me, it's real life.

Forget it. Where were we? On Mondays, I have a double spinning class. It starts at seven, but you have to get there a littler earlier if you want a specific bicycle. Oh, you never did spinning? Okay, so you have good genes. In our family, all the men are overweight. So I have no choice. I have to take care of myself. The exercise bikes in our spinning class are arranged in a semicircle opposite the instructor. Numbered. I like number four. The farthest away from the air conditioner. Every Monday Ayelet takes Yaeli to Tel Aviv for a special yoga class for kids with respiratory problems, and they come home right afterward so I can leave for spinning at six-thirty.

That day, they got stuck in traffic. Ayelet called from the car to say they'd be a little late. I told her take Ayalon South. But she said she was already on Geha. That pissed me off. I always tell her to take Ayalon because there are fewer traffic jams, but she always insists on Geha. Because she's used to it. I could already see myself getting to class at the last second and ending up with bike number nineteen or twenty, which are behind a post. You can't even see the instructor from there. Do you get the picture? I wish I could tell you that I went to Herman and Ruth's because there was an emergency at work, or I had chest pains and needed to get myself to the hospital. But the truth is, that was the whole story: which bike would I ride in spinning class.

Ruth was at the conservatory. I asked Herman when she was coming back and he said he didn't know. I calculated: if I leave now, Ayelet will be home in ten or fifteen minutes at the most. What could possibly happen in fifteen minutes? In the meantime, Ruth would definitely be back. She usually gets home from work at six-thirty. And old people don't like to deviate from their routines. That way, Ayelet wouldn't even know I left Ofri alone with

Herman. And even if she did, so what, let her take Ayalon next time.

Ofri, of course, was in heaven. I explained to her that it was only for a few minutes, that Mommy would be home soon. But she was already riding on Herman's back, and he was shouting *Hoppe, hoppe, Reiter* (the German version of giddyap) and wasn't really listening to me. I wanted to warn him, but didn't know how I could phrase a warning without offending him, without his realizing that I didn't trust him. So I didn't say anything. I texted Ayelet: "Ofri's with Herman and Ruth." I changed clothes and left. I'm not sure it would've helped if I'd said anything to him. Even if I'd said, "In your condition, you shouldn't go out of the house with her," chances are that he would have answered, "*Yah!*" and forgotten it a minute later.

I keep my cell phone muted during spinning class. You can't hear anything anyway with the loudspeakers blasting. So it wasn't until the end of the double lesson that I saw that I had four unanswered calls. But I still thought that Ayelet just got stuck out of the house without her keys or something, and kept walking toward the showers. Next time she should listen to me and take Ayalon. That's what I was thinking. Let her learn her lesson. I took my time under the shower, do you see? I washed my hair. Raised the temperature higher and higher until it was almost burning my skin. You like to do that too? And here I thought it was my own private perversion. I didn't look at my phone again until after I'd toweled off. There were already twelve unanswered calls. I called Ayelet. And a few seconds later, I was on my way home.

How can I explain what a person feels at a time like that? Remember that first time on reserve duty when Ehrlich drove the jeep into that alleyway in Hebron by mistake? Remember when the concrete blocks started raining down on us? And that moron couldn't put the vehicle into reverse? Take that and multiply it by ten. By a hundred. A thousand. In Hebron, I was pretty calm. I had the feeling we'd get out in one piece. Most of the time, I'm calm under pressure. But here—I'll tell you the truth—I lost it completely. I yelled at myself while I was driving. Smashed my fists against the wheel.

Maybe the difference is that in Hebron, I was only responsible for myself. And here I was responsible for my little girl. I knew I screwed up. It was so clear that I screwed up that Ayelet didn't even waste time accusing me. The minute I got out of the car, she filled me in on the situation: The entire building was out searching, and there was also a police car on the way. They were combing our neighborhood. And the adjacent neighborhood too. I said, "I'll kill him if he did something to her, I'll just kill him." Ayelet said, "We still don't know what happened, maybe they just got lost." But I saw in her eyes that she was also thinking about the kisses and the *Hoppe, hoppe, Reiter.* I asked if anyone was searching the citrus groves, and Ayelet said no, they hadn't thought that far ahead. So I said, "I'll go there and take my gun."

"Why a gun?" she said.

"If he touched a hair on her head, that's the end of him."

When Ofri was in kindergarten, there was a kid there who hassled her. Saar Ashkenazi. She'd come home every day with stories. Saar Ashkenazi said this to her, Saar Ashkenazi did that to her. Ayelet spoke to the teacher, who said she hadn't noticed anything special and that at that age, they still can't always tell the difference between reality and imagination.

Our daughter could always tell the difference. And that was exactly what I said to Ayelet. Our daughter can tell the difference. So one day after I left Ofri in kindergarten, I waited behind a bush for the children to come out into the yard. At first, everything was fine. Ofri played with her friends and I felt pretty stupid. A forty-year-old man hiding behind a bush at nine in the morning. But then a boy approached them. From behind. I mean, Ofri had her back to him, And that little shit just yanked down her pants. And ran away. Then, from a few meters away, he laughed and said that everyone could see her underpants.

You know me. I'm not a violent person. During the Intifada, I used to stay in the kitchen to avoid going out on patrol, remember? But believe me, if you had seen someone pull down your Jonathan's pants, you'd react just like I did. It's a biological instinct. Out of our control.

What did I do to the kid? Exactly what had to be done. I climbed the nursery school fence, grabbed him, pushed him up against the wall and told him that if he ever touched Ofri again, I'd take him apart.

That evening, his mother called and said, "You started up with the wrong family." Turns out that Saar Ashkenazi's father is the protection king of the area. The police have been trying to nail him for years, without any luck. You don't believe there's a protection racket in the suburbs? Start believing.

To make a long story short, his wife told me on the phone that her husband, Asi, was out of the country, "checking out business opportunities," but when he got back and heard what I did to Saar—expect pain. Those were her exact words. Expect pain.

So I bought a gun and put it in a drawer. I put the magazine in a different drawer, then locked both of them with a key. I said to myself that if he shows up at my cave, that Asi, I'll have something to protect my cubs with.

A week later, an item in the papers said that Asi Ashkenazi had been arrested in Larnaka and was going to be tried and given a long prison sentence for drug trafficking. Saar Ashkenazi and his mother disappeared from the kindergarten right after that. The teacher didn't know where they'd gone. Or she didn't want to say. I think she breathed a sigh of relief too. And I—I kept the gun.

I only took it out of the drawer once after that—when we went hiking in Wadi Kelt. Arabs had killed two hikers there a few years ago, so I thought it was wise to be on the safe side. Ayelet said she really didn't like the idea, but her tone could have meant that she didn't like it in ideological terms, but did like it in practical terms. The night we came back from the trip, after the girls fell into bed and I went into the shower to wash all that desert dust off me, she undressed, pulled open the shower curtain, and said, "Is that a gun, or are you just happy to see me?"

Do you get it? Even strong women like Ayelet are looking for someone to protect them. It's a biological instinct.

So I took the gun and the magazine and started running toward the groves. You were at my place once, right? How could you not remember? A barbecue on Independence Day? Two years ago? That's it. So when you go out of the building, there's a path that leads to the synagogue, and after the synagogue there's a path that takes you to the groves in three to four minutes. For ten years already they've been talking about cutting down the trees and building a neighborhood for young families there, but I have yet to see a single bulldozer.

When Ofri was little, in fact, from the time she started walking, I used to take her there. If there were oranges or grapefruits on the trees, we'd pick ourselves a few, peel them, and eat them. If not, we'd just hang out. Someone had spread a mat on the ground in the middle of the third row of trees and put two old armchairs and a bamboo table on it, the kind you buy in the Druse markets. Probably some high school senior who went there with the guys to smoke a narghile before they went into the army. It's really beautiful in the groves at dusk. The sun sinks between the leaves and there's a breeze coming off the sea. I used to sit in one of the armchairs with Ofri, sometimes I'd tell her a story, sometimes she'd tell me one, and sometimes we'd just sit quietly and listen to the birds. I swear, I was never as relaxed as I was on those walks with Ofri. Even after Yaeli was born, I made sure to go to the groves with Ofri at least once a week. Listen, I'm an older sibling too. I know what a bummer it is when a little brother is born. Especially after seven years of being king of the world. It might sound funny to you, but to this day, somewhere inside me I'm still a little angry at my brother Mickey for stealing away my good life. So I said to myself that Ofri should have at least one hour a week when she can still be Daddy's princess. It didn't matter what we did during that hour, the main thing was to be together. Just the two of us. This last year, for instance, she started taking books with her to our hangout. Can you see it? She's sitting on the mat reading *Little Women.* I'm making orange juice with a juicer I bring from home. And then we drink it together from paper cups left over from her birthday party. Who needs more than that?

So I ran to the grove. To our hangout. Ayelet stayed home with Yaeli to man the phone and Ruth led a police team to places in the neighborhood where Herman liked to go. But I had a gut feeling. And I ran with it. It was dark already. The streetlamps lit the entrance to the groves, but when I was inside, walking down the rows of trees, I couldn't see a thing. A branch scratched me. I didn't even notice I was bleeding. Only later, at home, did I see it. I kept running. My nose filled with the smell of rot. All the fruit that the Thai workers hadn't picked in time was lying on the ground, attracting flies and worms.

When I reached the third row, I already knew they were there. I didn't see them, but I could feel it. I can't explain it to you. Maybe my nose picked up traces of the smell of Ofri's shampoo. Maybe it was just a kind of connection between father and child that lets you feel when your child is close to you even if you can't see him. I loaded the magazine, cocked the gun, and put my finger on the trigger. I had a picture in my mind—the minute I walked into the groves, I had a picture in my mind and I knew that if it was the true picture, I was really going to shoot, and Herman would get a bullet in the temple. Not in the back, so that the bullet, God forbid, wouldn't pass through his body into hers. I'd approach from the side, press the gun against his temple, and pull the trigger.

First I heard crying. A few seconds before I saw them, I heard crying. Even in a group of a hundred crying children, a parent can pick out the sound of his child's crying. So I realized right away that it wasn't Ofri crying. And I didn't understand what was going on. He'd abducted another little girl too? I kept my finger on the trigger and moved forward slowly. More cautiously. Even in a group of a hundred walking parents, a child can pick out the sound of his parents' footsteps. Then, as I was sneaking forward, I heard Ofri's voice very close to me, saying, "Daddy?" She sounded normal. Not hysterical. So I said, "Yes, honey, I'm here." I took another few steps, pushed away the last few branches that were concealing me, and saw them. They were on the mat. Ofri was sitting with her little legs stretched forward, and Herman's large white head was resting on her thigh. His tie had drooped to the side, onto her knee, and he was crying. Sobbing. And between one sob and the next, he raised his gray eyes to look at me and said, "I'm sorry, I'm so sorry."

It was weird. He said he was sorry, but the glint in his eye was something else, not the least bit sorry.

I told him to stand up.

He kept crying. And didn't move. I thought that he was crying like someone who'd done something he shouldn't have done. So I pointed the gun at him and said, "Get up, or I don't know what I'll do to you."

"He's broken, Daddy," Ofri said. "He can't stand up."

"No such thing. Sure he can stand up."

It made me crazy to see his head on her thigh. I grabbed him by the hand and pulled him up hard. I heard a cracking noise. Something inside him had cracked when I yanked him up. A bone or a joint. He fell back onto his knees, moaning with pain. I let go of his hand and let him collapse onto the mat. I asked Ofri, "What did he do to you?"

She looked away and didn't answer. Maybe if she had answered me right then and there, it all would have been different. But she didn't, she just looked away.

I persisted. "Answer me, Ofri, how did you even end up here?"

"We got lost," she said. And was silent.

Herman continued to groan with pain. There was a damp spot—I suddenly noticed—on the crotch of his pants. I wasn't sure whether it had been there before or had only just appeared. And his look—you know what? He had a horny gleam in his eyes. That's what it was. A horny gleam that hadn't completely died out yet.

My finger was still on the trigger. I felt like shooting him the way you shoot a sick horse. I swear to you.

"You got lost?" I asked Ofri.

"Yes. We were walking around the neighborhood and then Herman got broken and we didn't know how to get back because we were so far away, so we kept walking and walking, and his feet hurt him really bad and he needed to pee, and right when he said he had to pee, I saw that we were on the road to the groves, so I told him there's a place I know."

"It was your idea to come to our hangout with him? Why?"

"Because I knew you'd come here looking for me," Ofri said and hugged me. "I knew you'd find me, Daddy."

Now she was crying too. Into my pants. It didn't sound like she was crying with relief. No. There was something in the way she cried that first time that was too stifled to be tears of relief. I called Ayelet and told her I'd found them and needed someone to help me carry Herman because he seemed to have broken something and couldn't walk. She asked, "How is she?"

"It doesn't look good."

"What does that mean?"

"Are you sending me some people or not?"

It turns out that the police have a pretty standard drill for cases like that. I have to say that I was pleasantly surprised by them. Within a day, both Herman and Ofri were interviewed and had thorough physical examinations to—as the detective phrased it—"eliminate the possibility of sexual abuse." Herman was questioned and checked out in the orthopedics department of Assaf Harofe hospital. They examined Ofri at the station, with a social worker present. They had what they believed was a fair assessment of the situation: He had done nothing to her that could be considered an attack. There had been physical contact between them. They had walked through the neighborhood hand in hand. He had asked her to kiss him on the cheek once. Then, when it got dark and they realized they were lost, he felt humiliated by his help-lessness and cried, and she stroked his head and tried to calm him down. But that was all. There was no evidence of semen. No scratches. No bleeding. "I'm happy to say," the detective told us, "that there are no grounds for continuing the investigation."

But I wasn't happy at all. I had a bad feeling. Already then, I had a bad feeling. Why in the world had he asked her for a kiss while they were outside, walking? I can understand on the staircase, but in the middle of the street? What happened, he couldn't wait? And what about that glint I saw in his eyes in the grove? And all that wailing of his—a person doesn't cry like that just because he's lost. I don't know. Something just didn't jibe. But the detective sounded logical and Ayelet bought it, and for the first few days, Ofri acted normal, not like a girl who'd been traumatized, and I had no real evidence to the contrary. Just a feeling.

The symptoms began appearing two weeks later. Suddenly, the kid didn't want to go to her after-school activities. Didn't want to go to violin lessons, to comics class, to gymnastics. You drive her to a class and she just stays in the car. Won't get out. "Why don't you want to go, Ofri?"

"Because I don't want to."

"But why don't you want to?"

"Because I don't want to."

You let it go for the first week. The second week, you insist, almost drag her out of the car and put her in the comics class against her will. Fifteen minutes later, you get a call from the Arts Center secretary. "Your daughter won't stop crying. It's keeping the other children from concentrating. Come and get her." You go to get her, hug her hard, and ask, "What happened, sweetie?" She freezes in your arms as if the touch of a man suddenly repulses her, as if she's learned that the touch of a man can be dangerous, and says, "Nothing Daddy. I told you I didn't want to go to the class and you made me."

Her homeroom teacher calls Ayelet at work. You get a report on the conversation that night, only after you've made sure the girls are asleep. It seems that Ofri has stopped going outside at recess. She stays at her desk and reads books. She doesn't answer her friends when they ask her to join them in a game. And her schoolwork is slipping. She made six mistakes on the last English dictation. That's more mistakes than she's made in all the English dictations they've had this year put together. You try to talk to her. Feel her out. She says that the girls in her class are babies. That she's not interested in being with them at recess. That they do stupid things and talk about stupid things. You ask, What kind of stupid things do they do? She doesn't answer. You say to her, Maybe you can spend every other recess with them. She doesn't answer. In the morning, you see that her bed is wet. Her little sister has just been toilet trained—and Ofri's wetting her bed. She's not surprised. Not embarrassed. Doesn't talk. Goes quietly to the bathroom, washes and dries herself, takes new underpants out of her drawer and puts them on. You tell yourself that it's a onetime thing, but the next night it happens again.

About a week after the symptoms started, I said to Ayelet, "The child is falling apart right in front of our eyes and we're not doing a thing."

We were in bed, in the dark, open eyes focused on the ceiling, and in a small voice I've never heard her use before, Ayelet said, "I don't know what to do, Arnon, I've never felt so helpless."

I asked whether she'd noticed the look that Ofri has now.

"Her look? What about it?"

I couldn't tell for sure whether she was pretending or she really hadn't noticed, so I said, "She doesn't have that innocent look anymore. Listen to me, something happened in the grove that she isn't telling us. When I found them, I don't know, there was something in the way Herman acted."

"But the police—" Ayelet said in that new small voice.

I interrupted her. "The police are interested in closing cases, not opening them."

We called a psychologist. Ayelet's friend recommended her. You know what I think of psychologists, but when you're at your wits' end, you're ready to try anything. We went to her office, on a moshav. A small stone house in the backyard of a pricey private home. Separate entrance. To be discreet. A custom-designed door. And everything inside was upmarket too: the leather couch, the desk, the chairs. Each one cost about the same as our house did. Ayelet immediately launched into a how-lovely-it-is-here speech. When she meets people for the first time, she always compliments them.

The psychologist thanked her and asked us, "What brings you here?" When we finished, she said coolly, "I suggest a seven-session model. Two with you. Two with you and the child. Two alone with the child. And the seventh session, a summary of the process."

At the seventh session, she declared, "I don't think it would be right to look for a single factor to explain what Ofri is going through. There is a combination of factors here. A younger sister was born, school demands have increased, the gap in maturity between her and the other children is taking its toll in social terms. And there was, of course, the unfortunate incident with the neighbor, which definitely..."

Ayelet nodded in agreement. It seemed to me that I even saw the beginning of a smile on her lips. Not a smile of happiness. A smile of relief. After all, it was easier to live with "a combination of factors," right? You know what, maybe that's what pissed me off. That smile of Ayelet's. Or maybe it was the way the psychologist phrased it, "the unfortunate incident." Professional terminology. Cold. Or maybe it was the thought that we were paying five hundred shekels an hour for that bullshit. Five hundred shekels! No wonder she could afford couches like that. So I cut off that whole combination of factors in the middle and asked her right out, "Did Ofri tell you or didn't she? What did she say?"

Ayelet put her hand on my thigh as if I were a kid and said, "Arnon, let Nirit finish."

I shoved her hand away and started yelling at the psychologist. "I want to know if she told you what happened in the citrus grove. Because we, or at least I, haven't been sleeping for two months because of that question, and the way I see the dynamic here, you can talk to us about the combining factors for an hour and then say you're sorry, but our time is up."

The psychologist said, "I suggest that we all calm down—"

I slammed my hand down on the desk. "I don't want to calm down. I'm the client here and I demand to know if there's something you know and I don't."

The psychologist straightened her red scarf around her neck. She always wore colorful scarves, even though it was summer. I felt like grabbing the ends of the scarf and strangling her. She went on, "I'm not hiding anything from you, Arnon. The little I managed to get out of Ofri is quite similar to what she told the police. They got lost. It was dark. She took him to the groves because she was sure you would look for her there."

"Did she tell you that he asked her for a kiss on the way?"

"She didn't volunteer any more details. She didn't answer when I asked her for some. At our last session, I asked her to draw a picture of her family. Here, you can see what she drew. A girl leaning against her father, and her mother and sister standing close to them. There are none of the characteristics that indicate trauma of the sort you are afraid of. So it is my impression that nothing of a sexual nature transpired in the grove. I qualify it as an 'impression,' because in cases like this, there is a chance that what happened was so traumatic that it has been very deeply repressed and we still haven't been able to reach it."

"Still? That means you believe you'll reach it," Ayelet asked.

The psychologist played with the fringes of her scarf and said she didn't know.

I tried to make the point clear: "So what you're saying is that there's a chance we'll never know what happened there? That we'll never be sure?"

The slight nod of her chin that came before the word was enough for me. I stood up from her fucking couch, walked out, and slammed the door. Hard. I hoped it would make an ugly crack. Ayelet ran after me and caught up to me in the gravel parking area. "What do you think you're doing, Arnon, have you gone crazy?" I told her that I wanted answers, not a load of crap, and that I was going to the only person who could give them to me.

Maybe if Ayelet had come with me to see Herman, what happened later wouldn't have happened. But she didn't come. Because she felt uncomfortable about the psychologist. Do you get it? We pay five hundred shekels an hour and we're the ones who should feel uncomfortable?

She said, "Come on, let's at least finish the session, Arnon."

And I said, "Are you coming with me or not?"

"No. Just because you've lost it doesn't mean I have to lose it too."

So I got into the car and drove to the hospital. I knew that Herman wasn't in orthopedics anymore, that they'd transferred him to internal medicine. But I didn't know much more than that. If I was out of onions that week, I didn't make *shakshuka*. And they didn't knock on our door either. Their car wasn't in their spot most of the day, so I figured they were at the hospital. That Ruth was there with him. Ayelet bumped into her once at the entrance to the building—both were coming home from work at the same time—and Ruth told her that when he was in orthopedics, he suddenly came down with all the ailments of old age at once, so they had to transfer him to another department.

I asked Ayelet if Ruth had said she was sorry.

"Just the opposite."

"What do you mean, just the opposite?"

"From what I could tell, she's angry at us."

"What does she have to be angry about?"

"She says that you're the reason Herman was admitted to orthopedics. She says you pulled him by the arm in the grove. Is that true?"

"He couldn't get up."

"Did you pull him or didn't you?"

"Yes, I did."

"So from her standpoint, you and you alone are the cause of all his troubles."

"Did she say anything about the money we owe her?" I asked.

"No, but we really have to pay them."

That pissed me off. "You pay them if you want. They won't see a shekel from me."

I bought a large bouquet of flowers in the shopping center next door to the hospital. I said to myself, I'll come in peace. That's the only way Ruth will let me stay alone in the room with him. At the department desk, they sent me to room number 14. An old Arab man was lying in the first bed in room 14. He looked at me as if I were a soldier breaking into his house. I kept walking. I pushed aside the curtain and saw Herman and Ruth. He was lying in bed with his eyes closed, a tube stuck in his nose. She was sitting next to his bed, reading *Yakinton* to him. That's the German-Hebrew magazine the *yekkim* get in their mailbox once a week. On the small table beside his bed was a plate of thin, neatly cut slices of her marble cake. They both looked much older than I remembered. Her beautiful hair suddenly looked thin, as if half had fallen out. She looked up from the newspaper and said, "You." I handed her the bouquet. She said, "Thank you." But there was no thank you in her voice. I asked her how he was and she said, "Very bad." I asked what was wrong with him and she said, "Everything. Delirium, clogged arteries, a tumor in his colon. The doctors here say that it's been a long time since they saw such an assortment of medical problems in one person."

I didn't say anything. What could I say? She was silent too. That sometimes happens when two people have too much to say.

The old Arab moaned. Herman opened his eyes and looked back and forth from Ruth to me, lingering more on me than on her. Then he looked away from me and stared straight ahead. At the wall. As if the World Cup final game was being screened on it.

I said to Ruth, "I forgot, the nurse asked me to tell you that you have to go to the office. There's a form you have to fill out."

She gave me a look. So I said in the nicest tone I could muster, "Don't worry, I'll stay with him."

When she left, I closed the curtain around the bed. I waited until I heard the door to the room open and then close. So as not to waste time, I quickly bent over Herman, grabbed his chin and moved him to the left so I could look him in the eye, and said, "Now, Mr. Herman Wolf, you tell me exactly what happened in the citrus grove." He didn't answer. I pulled out his feeding tube and asked again, this time closer to his face: "What did you do to my daughter, Herman?"

He still didn't answer, but something in his expression changed. A spark flashed inside the grayness.

I play the idiot so I don't have to answer your questions. That's what the spark said to me.

And that's why I couldn't restrain myself.

I grabbed him by the throat with both hands and started pressing down from two directions. I said, "If you don't tell me now, I'll kill you."

My mistake was that I left both his hands free. I could have choked him with one hand and pinned his old hands to the bed with the other. After a few seconds he would have broken down and talked. I'm positive. But he reached out and pressed the panic button. I didn't even notice him doing it. I didn't hear the buzz. But suddenly someone put an arm around my chest and pulled my shoulders back, and someone else grabbed me from the front. There were elbows and fists and shouting and kicking. I fought like a lion, I'm telling you, but male nurses kept swarming into the room, and in the end, they pinned me to the filthy hospital floor, and one of them sat on my back and said in a Russian accent that the police were on their way and I should do myself a favor and stay quiet.

Ayelet came that night to get me released from custody. She came straight from work in her lawyer's clothes, and for a second, for a fraction of a second, when she came in, I wasn't sure whether that was my wife or a beautiful stranger I was paying to represent me. I pressed up against her for a tight hug. I wanted to feel her prominent hip bone. To know it was her. And she let me. Without speaking. She gave me that.

When we left the police station, she said, "You're very lucky. Ruth decided not to file a complaint. And without a complaint, the police can't do anything to you."

I was quiet until we reached the door of the station. The truth is that I was still in shock about being arrested. Tell me, in which of your books do you have a description of someone who was put in jail? The last one? That's it, I remembered something. Don't be offended, but anyone can see that you don't have the slightest idea what it means to be in jail. It's like a really hard slap in the face. What does that mean? I always thought that the world was divided into two kinds of people: normal ones and criminals. That you're either one or the other. There's no in between. But when you're lying on a smelly mattress in a cell, staring at the ceiling, at the things people who were there before you wrote on the wall, you realize that it's only a matter of how much pressure is put on you and about what. Everyone has a small criminal inside him that can come to life at any time, you understand?

When we got to the parking lot, Ayelet went to the driver's side. I told her I could drive, but she still climbed into the driver's seat, pretending she didn't hear me. When she started the car, I said, "You know why Ruth didn't file a complaint? Because she'd rather not open that Pandora's box."

"She didn't file a complaint against you, Arnon, because I begged her not to. I've been on the phone with her since noon. That's what I did at work today. I explained to her that you're going through a tough time. I reminded her of all the things we did for them. You know how much you could have gotten for an attack like that if she'd decided to file charges? Four years. Four years in prison! Four years without seeing Ofri and Yaeli!"

"The fact that she didn't file charges," I persisted, "only proves that something happened in the grove. You defend your husband and she defends hers. That's the deal here. It's just too bad that your daughter gets screwed in that deal."

That's when Ayelet raised her voice. "You're deranged, you know? No, really, I don't understand what else you want. The police said nothing happened there. The psychologist said nothing happened there. All you saw when you got there was Herman crying. So what's with you? Are you enjoying this?"

"What do you mean, enjoying this?"

"I don't know."

"You can't say something like that and not explain."

"I don't know, Arnon. I don't understand you, I don't understand why you yell at the psychologist, I don't understand why you try to strangle Herman, I don't understand what's going on with you."

"What's going on with me? My little girl went into a grove with an old man who likes kisses. At night. And when I found them, he had a stain on his crotch and the look of a pervert in his eye, and a month later, my little girl wets her bed every night. That's what's going on with me. What's not clear to you?"

"You know, Arnon, not everyone's a sex fiend like you."

"Sex fiend? Me?"

"Yes, you."

"What?!"

"You heard me."

"You know," I told her, "that of all my friends, I'm the only one, the only one! who never had anything on the side!"

"Wait just a minute, you're telling me that you want a prize for that?"

Don't get stressed out now, man. I've kept my mouth shut for twenty years about worse things you've done. And it's not only me. The whole unit kept their mouths shut. You should know by now that you can trust me.

Of course I didn't name names. Besides, no one would believe it about you anyway, not with the way you talk about Shiri and the boys in interviews. A model family man, that's what you are. And let's not get carried away: she was a German reporter and it was just a kiss on the cheek that was slightly off target. And don't forget, breaking a Nazi's heart is always a good deed.

Feel better now? Can I go on?

In every fight, there's a moment when you say something you shouldn't and there's no turning back. Know what I mean? So that's what happened. And what did I actually say to her? "If it was Yaeli, you wouldn't be so calm."

It isn't a...state secret, right? Just one of those little kinks that families have. Even in the Bible, in the story of Jacob and Esau, it's obvious that Jacob was his mother's favorite and Esau was his father's. The point is that it's natural for a parent to prefer one child over the other. Even love him more. What isn't natural—it turns out—is saying it out loud. Those little kinks are supposed to be transparent, invisible. But I just couldn't control myself. She was sitting there in her prim lawyer's outfit with her hair pulled back, talking to me in that patronizing way, like she was civilized and I was a savage. So I had to put her in her place. Every once in a while, you have to put them in their place.

Then she pulled over to the side of the road and told me to get out of the car. She stopped right in the middle of Route 4, not on some side street. Not near a bus stop. Or an interchange. But on the shoulder of a highway. I told her to keep driving, I wasn't getting out. And she said, "Either you get out or I do."

I've been with Ayelet enough years to know when she's serious, and she was serious. I said, "Keep driving." Then she said, "I'm getting out," and opened the driver's door. "Close the door," I told her, "it's dangerous." So she said again: "Either you get out or I do." And left the door open.

I got out. I couldn't let her get out of the car and be alone in the dark in the middle of the highway. And she's been with me enough years to know that.

When I was on the Mitzpe Ramon base, she came to see me one Saturday. Took a bus from Haifa all the way down to Mitzpe. None of the guys in the unit ever showed me the kind of respect I got from them that Saturday. They took me off all the guard duties and special shifts and left the room so we could have some privacy. And it wasn't because of me. I wasn't exactly Mr. Popularity there. It was because of her. All she did was show a little interest in them and laugh at their jokes at supper, and they were her slaves. That's how it is with Ayelet. I saw that she had the same effect on you at the barbecue. I saw the way you looked at her when she brought you the ice cream pops. You gave her that sensitive look of yours. That writer's look. It's okay, I'm used to men reacting to her like that. Besides, don't be insulted, but you're really not her type.

That Saturday night, I walked her to the gate of the base so she could catch the bus. We waited there for an hour, maybe an hour and a half. I have no idea how long it was because we were talking. And when you talk to Ayelet, time just flies by. She always has some new, surprising thought to share with you. Twenty years I'm with her, and I never know what she'll say next.

Anyway, no bus came. And finally, the guard at the gate came out of his little booth and told us that the bus we were waiting for didn't run on Saturday. That we had to walk to the intersection and hitchhike from there. She hugged me hard and said, "Bye, Noni." And I said, "No,

Ayelet, you're not walking alone in the dark." She was surprised: "You can leave the base just like that?" I lied to her and said, "Yes, of course." But not only was I not allowed to leave the base, we were scheduled for roll call in less than an hour and the chances of my getting back from the intersection in time were very slim. I'd be considered AWOL, and the punishment would be getting thrown out of the course. Automatically. Not even a trial. But the feeling was stronger than me. I just couldn't let her stand alone at the intersection in the middle of the night. Even if it meant I wouldn't be an officer.

There was that business now, you know, in the Carmel Forest? With the two Druze who attacked a couple in the parking lot? You didn't hear about it? They told the guy to leave and then raped his girlfriend. When they questioned him, he told the police that he heard her screaming for help but didn't go back because he was scared. So tell me, is that a man? It's a mutation of a man. I would have gone back with a big rock and smashed the heads of those Druze. You know what, I wouldn't have left the parking lot to begin with. I would have stood between the Druze and my girlfriend and said: If you want her, you'll have to kill me first.

Ayelet and I held hands and walked to the intersection that Saturday night. She told me about a soldier in her unit who everyone thought was having an affair with the commander, and from there, we jumped associatively to the Robin Williams movie she saw one Saturday when I didn't come home, and Robin Williams reminded her of *Good Morning Vietnam*, which made her say that she thought our generation, which never fought in any big wars, was most affected by the movie version of the Vietnam War, and I listened the whole time, occasionally throwing in an idea of my own and trying not to show how stressed I was.

Only after I saw her hitching with some normal-looking driver — the guy was wearing glasses, the car was clean — did I race back to the base. I'd never run so fast in my life. If they'd checked my time, I would've overtaken the three Ethiopians who took first, second, and third place in the all-time list of runners in the officers' course. In the end, I was five minutes late for roll call. But the squad commander was half an hour late. And I was saved from expulsion. After the end-of-course ceremony, I told Ayelet about the great risk I'd taken that Saturday. I don't like having lies between me and other people. She said, "You're crazy, I would have managed." I said, "If they had thrown me out of the course, I would have been miserable, but I would have gotten over it in a couple of months. But if, God forbid, anything had happened to you, I couldn't have gone on living."

I'm telling you all this, but honestly, it wasn't what I was thinking about when I was walking like a dog along the shoulder of the highway. Until I reached the main junction, I was thinking that Ayelet was a hard woman, too hard, and maybe I should find myself an easier one. After the junction, I was thinking about my father. Memories have a way of popping up at weird times. All of a sudden, I don't know why, I remembered something that happened with him once. My brother Mickey had a regular girlfriend from the time he was sixteen until he was eighteen. Dafi. A real sweetie. One of those good girls. Long, straight hair. Huge brown eyes. My parents were crazy about her. So one day, Mickey comes into the house with a different girl. Goes into his room with her and closes the door. And a few minutes later, we start hearing this giggling, you know what I mean, so my father gets up from his armchair—and it was in the middle of a Maccabi game, so you can imagine the drama—goes into his room, grabs him by the shirt, pulls him into the living room, and says, "What about Dafi?"

"What about her," my brother says, in that insolent tone his kids use today when they talk to him.

So my father slaps him and says, "If you don't love Dafi anymore, be a man and break up with her. The men of the Levanoni family respect their women. That's how my father was, that's how my father's father was, and that's how you're going to be. Understood?"

That was the thought that stayed with me when I turned onto the road leading home. And I was already planning how I'd use it to beat Ayelet in the argument, proving to her once and for all that I'm not a sex fiend. I had some really great comments ready on the tip of my tongue about the men of the Levanoni family, but when I opened the door to the apartment, the house was quiet, the shutters on the door leading from the living room to the garden were closed, and the couch was covered with a sheet and a thin blanket. A note was pasted onto our bedroom door with Scotch tape: *I don't want to sleep with you. You scare me. Take down this note after you read it (unless you want Ofri to see it) and sleep in the living room.*

Ofri woke me in the morning. She stood next to the couch and asked, "Daddy, why are you sleeping on the couch?"

"Because Mommy and I had a fight."

"Because we don't eat healthy food?"

"No."

"Your fights are usually stupid," she said.

"Yes."

"And in the end, you make up, right Daddy?"

"Right, little girl."

"Can I have chocolate milk, Daddy?"

Ofri and I usually get up first and leave early for school. Ayelet and Yaeli get up fifteen minutes later and leave for the nursery school. That's our morning routine. Ofri and I walk to school. Hand in hand. Along the paths between the buildings. On the way, she tells me about the book she's reading and I listen on and off. When we get closer to the school, she takes her hand out of mine. She likes to walk the last hundred meters on her own. I watch until I see her go through the main gate. Until I see her inside, I don't move from my observation point.

That morning, I suggested that we stop at the bakery in the shopping center and buy ourselves some rugelach. She was afraid we'd be late, and I said, "Does it matter?" "We have science and Galina yells at anyone who comes late," she said. I promised her I'd go to class with her and tell Galina that I made her late. "Okay," she said, "but don't embarrass me, Daddy!" I nodded and said I wouldn't embarrass her. Which meant no kissing her in front of everyone. No saying go-o-od morning to the teacher in a funny voice. No sitting down in an empty seat and pretending I'm one of the pupils.

We sat on a bench near the shopping center and ate rugelach. Each of us in his own special way. I take bites. She unrolls it layer by layer and nibbles each one separately. I said, "Mommy and I are worried about you. Lately, we see how hard it is for you. Lately means since what happened with Herman." She nibbled and said nothing. I said, "If you want to tell me what happened there, I'll be glad to hear it." She stayed silent. She looked away from me. She finished eating and now her teeth were biting her lips, as if they wouldn't let the words come out. I asked again, "Do you want to tell me what happened there?" I felt that if I pressed a little more, it would come out. But all she said was "I want to go to school."

I walked to her classroom with her. But when the door slammed shut, I didn't go. I stayed there to sneak a look inside. There's a wall between the hallway and the classroom, and it has three windows with curtains on them. The curtains block your view, but one of them was pulled aside slightly, and if you stand at a certain angle, you can see the back of the room, where she was sitting.

I looked at her and my heart shrank.

When an adult looks wiped out, that's reasonable. Life crushes us all at one time or another, but a child?

My little girl was playing with the zipper of her pencil case. She took out some crayons. Drew in her notebook. Put the crayons back in the pencil case. Occasionally looked up at her teacher. Then looked down again. Now that I'm telling you this, I realize that she wasn't doing anything unusual, but still, I started to cry.

I hadn't cried since I was about her age. I have nothing against crying—the tears just don't come. When Ayelet canceled the wedding and left me for six months because she wanted to be absolutely positive, didn't I want to cry? Sure I did. When I had to close my business because of the debts and went back to working for someone else, didn't I want to cry? Sure I did. Believe me, I did. You know how long it took me to get to the point where I could open my own business? Twenty years. And then in less than a month, three big clients left, and everything collapsed. Even so, when Iris from the bank told me she was closing my line of credit, my eyes stayed dry.

Why did I cry back then, when I was her age? Do you really care? Just kidding—I went out with my dad and asked him to buy me an ice pop. He gave me a lira and told me to hold it tight until I reached the kiosk, but when we were walking over one of the Carmelit air shafts—you know what I'm talking about, right? You have roaring air shafts like that up on the Carmel too, don't you—the coin fell out of my hand, through the grating, and into the shaft. It was deep, three meters at least. And on the bottom there were lots of other coins that had fallen there. I stood on the grating, stamped on it, and cried for my father to get the coin out for me. My father said—I remember the exact words he used—the shaft is too deep. And also, Arnon, learn to hold on to your money.

While I was standing there watching Ofri through the classroom window, I called Ayelet. She didn't pick up. I called again. I wanted her to leave everything and come to the school. I was sure that if she saw what I was seeing, she wouldn't call me a sex fiend anymore. But she didn't pick up. I called seven times and she didn't pick up. That's how she is. She once told me that when she doesn't answer my call, it's because she knows that if we talk, she'll say things she'll regret later.

I hate it when she doesn't answer. I hate it. But I learned to accept it. The way I learned to accept lots of other things I thought I never would. That's how it is when you love a hard woman. But that morning, it broke me. How can I explain it to you? There are moments when you really feel that blow to your chest that says, enough. So I stopped trying to call, left the window, and went home. Instead of taking the side streets, I walked along the main road, which is totally exposed to the sun. I walked down the middle of the road, not on the sidewalk. I think I had a small desire to be run over. For a car to hit me. Did that ever happen to you? I'm not talking about wanting to commit suicide. No way. When you walk down the middle of the road like that, you don't really want to die. You just want something strong to smash into you. Because that's what you deserve.

Why did I think I deserved it? Because I'm an idiot. That's why. Because I left her with Herman, because I wanted a better spot in the spinning class. And that's even though I knew very well that something was wrong with him. If I'd waited another twenty minutes—you know what, another *five* minutes—my little girl, the little girl I held in my arms right after she was born because they had to sew up Ayelet, whose first word was Daddy, whose every feeling I feel as if it was my own, that little girl would not have been sitting in class with that look on her face.

In our family pictures, Ofri never looks as good as she does in real life. The kid just isn't photogenic, Ayelet always says. But that's not it. It's that mischievous spark in her eye that even the most sophisticated camera can't catch. That's what makes her beauty special. And after she went into the grove with Herman, that spark was extinguished. Totally. Dead.

I walked down the main road that leads from the school to our house, punching myself hard on the forehead. I wanted, I really wanted, for a car to hit me from behind, hurl me a few meters forward and crush my bones, for an ambulance to come and take me to the hospital, to be put in the bed next to Herman...

But at that hour in the morning, after everyone has dropped off their kids in child care and school, the street is quiet and there are hardly any cars on it. So, I'm sorry to say, I reached our building's parking area in one piece.

And then I saw her. Herman's granddaughter. The mademoiselle.

She was just coming out of the building and sashayed over to me with that provocative walk of hers. She was wearing very short shorts and a white tank top with thin straps. Without a bra. One of the straps had fallen off her shoulder. She walked in my direction on platform flip-flops that made her taller. There was no avoiding her. Even if I'd wanted to. She walked straight up to me, and when she was close, she stood on the tips of her flip-flops, gave me a kiss on the cheek close to my mouth, and said, "Bonjour, Monsieur Arno, how are you? Maybe you are driving to Tel Aviv?"

I should have said no. But the truth was that I was on my way to Tel Aviv, to a meeting of Hungry Hearts. That's the NPO I founded. I mean, I'm not the only one there, I recruited another few colleagues. Seriously? I never told you about it? Wow. We've really been out of touch for a long time. We collect all the food left over in Tel Aviv restaurants at the end of the night, and instead of letting it be thrown out, we repack it on trays and transport it to needy children in the south. Nice idea, eh?

Anyway, I told Herman's granddaughter yes, I was driving to Tel Aviv. I didn't want to lie to her.

As soon as we started to drive, she took off her flip-flops and put her bare feet on the dashboard.

I should have told her to take them off. What the hell was she doing? But I have a weakness for small feet.

The scent of her perfume filled the car. It was the same perfume she'd worn last summer, but something had changed in the way it drifted from her body.

I asked her when she'd arrived in the country, and she said yesterday.

I didn't know what else I could ask her.

And then she said, "Tell me, Monsieur Arno, maybe you know what happened to my grandfather?"

"What do you mean?"

"My grandmother told me. I mean, she tells me one thing and I feel that she is hiding something else from me."

I asked her—casual like, you know—"What does she tell you?"

"That he was walking in the street and fell. And he dislocated his shoulder. Then, the tests they did on him in the hospital showed that he had other illnesses. It doesn't make sense to me. Besides, I can tell when people are lying to me. My father was a liar. My mother is a liar. I know all the signs."

I looked at her for half a second, then focused on the road again. I said, "I'd really like to know what those signs are."

"*Alors...*, first of all, the lips. This part"—I suddenly felt her finger touch my lower lip—"shakes a little bit when you are lying. And this part"—I felt a finger brush over my chin—"how do you say it in Hebrew..."

"Chin?"

"No..."

"Jaw?"

"Jaw, yes. It gets stiffer when you are lying. And of course, the eyes. It is not like people think, that when you are lying you do not look people in the eyes. That is actually when you do look them in the eye, so they will believe you are telling the truth, but there is a shade in their expression."

"Shade?"

"Shade is the opposite of sun, yes?"

"Yes."

"So yes, shade."

"And your grandmother had shade in her eyes when she talked to you about what happened?"

"Big shade. That is why I asked you, maybe you know something."

I thought to myself: I have to be very careful about how I answer her. She is a potential mole, and if I handle this right, she could get information for me. So I said, "I don't know any more than you do. But I think you should keep asking her."

"What do you mean?"

"If you feel that someone is lying to you, keep pressing them until the truth comes out. That's what life has taught me."

Then she laughed: "Oh la la, Monsieur Arno"—and pushed my shoulder lightly with her fist—"you are not only a hunk, you are smart too. How nice for Madame Arno."

"Where do you need to go in Tel Aviv?" I cut her off.

"To the sea. I am going to tan myself topless!"

I wanted to tell her to apply sunblock first. But I didn't want to sound like her father. So I didn't say anything.

She said, "I have a new tattoo. You want to see it?"

We were on the Ayalon Highway, where you shouldn't take your eyes off the road. Every second matters. But I couldn't not look. She lowered the strap closest to me, the one that was still on her shoulder, pulled it down, and exposed the upper part of her left breast. A Star of David rested there. A triangle lying on a triangle.

She asked me if it was pretty.

I said yes.

She rubbed her feet together on the dashboard. They really were very small. Not much bigger than Ofri's.

She said, "You know, there is one good thing about my grandparents being in the hospital all the time."

We were in a small traffic jam at a spot near the beach where the breakwaters look like a hyphen between Tel Aviv and Jaffa.

I looked at her. "Yes? What is that something?"

She laughed. "The house is empty and...I can bring anyone I want there."

I said, "Wow," and looked back at the traffic jam.

"When I enjoy myself, I mean in bed, I like the guy with me to know it. He deserves it. For the efforts he is making. And it makes me uncomfortable when my grandparents hear everything in the other room."

She looked at me when she finished the sentence to see what kind of impression she was making on me.

I didn't look back at her.

She opened the window and took a deep breath—you could actually hear her chest fill up. "There is nothing like the breeze in Tel Aviv. In Paris, the breeze is always...bad.

I dropped her off at the Frishman beach. She kissed me on the cheek, even closer to my lips than the morning kiss had been, and said, "You have another meeting in Tel Aviv tomorrow, yes?"

That was a week ago. And until yesterday, this was my life: every night after the girls went to sleep, Ayelet and I fought. About what? Ayelet said I'd lost it. That I needed therapy. That I'd been frustrated since my business collapsed and I had to work for someone again, and I was taking that frustration out on the whole world. She said I wasn't the man she'd married. That the man she'd married wouldn't have tried to strangle a sick old man. She said that I was imposing my view of reality on everyone. That I wanted them all to think like me, and anyone who didn't accept my crazy theories was wrong. She said that I'd always been a little obsessive, and that's why she took the six-month break back then, before we got married. This was exactly what she'd been afraid of. She said that my worrying so obsessively about Ofri was just a way of making her out to be a bad mother. And she was sick of it. Totally sick of it.

What did I say to her? Go argue with a lawyer. If I just try to say something, she crucifies me in the middle of the sentence. So I didn't say much. I pretended to listen, but I felt how every sentence she spoke pushed me further away from her. I heard the last few sentences of our fight as if I was in another country altogether.

Then I'd watch the panelists screaming at each other on *Grandstanders* until I fell asleep on the living room couch. In the morning, Ofri would wake me up and we'd go to school, with her reading *Anne of Green Gables* as she walked and I warning her every time she was about to walk into a tree. We'd stop at the shopping center every morning to eat rugelach. She'd nibble the layers, I'd take bites. I didn't ask her what happened in the grove anymore. I already understood that my questions upset her. And that I wouldn't get an answer. So I just sat close to her and loved her silently. I tried to give her as much love and security as I could without speaking. I couldn't hug or kiss her either—someone from her class might pass by and it would embarrass her—so with just my solid presence beside her, I tried to give her the feeling that there was at least one person in the world she could depend on. At 7:55, we'd get up from the bench.

Because after the first time she was late, she told me she didn't want to be late anymore. At 7:58, she left me after we crossed the street and walked to the gate on her own.

And every day last week at 8:05, I picked up the French mole and drove her to Tel Aviv.

When she got into the car, she would always put her feet on the dashboard—a different color nail polish on her toenails every morning—and she'd start to tell me about the guys who'd come on to her at the beach the day before.

One of them came up to her with paddles and asked if she wanted to play, but she said she didn't like paddleball and he got scared off. Another guy, a real hunk, asked if her father was a gardener, and when she said, "No, my father left the house when I was six and I have no idea what he's into now," he started stammering. And for her, there's nothing less sexy than a stammer.

Anyway, she has no idea what happened to the men in Israel. They used to be strong and tough like the outside of a seashell. Now they're soft like the inside. And they don't understand hints! Nothing! At the end of the day yesterday an older man asked her to have dinner in a restaurant with him. He poured her glass after glass of wine. She was sure they'd go back to his apartment afterward. She even said to him, "I'm dying to take a shower." In the end, he just took her to the central bus station, kissed her lightly on the cheek, and asked her if she wanted to go to a movie with him. "*Qu'est-ce que c'est? A movie, now? He does not understand that sometimes a girl just wants sex?*"

I wasn't really sure that all her stories were true. It's hard to explain. Something in the way she told them—some of the descriptions were too general. Too familiar. As if she'd read them somewhere.

But I listened to her patiently. And tried not to show her that I was waiting for her to talk about what I was really interested in.

Usually she'd get to it toward the end of the drive. Yes, she visited Grandpa Herman yesterday. And he was really fine. Made sense when he talked. So she took advantage of the opportunity and asked him what happened, how he got hurt, and suddenly the color of his eyes changed from blue to gray and he didn't say anything. Didn't answer. Her grandmother said, "It's not healthy for Grandpa to get upset now." And when she asked what she'd said to upset him, what was there to get upset about, her grandmother didn't answer her.

On a different day, Grandpa Herman felt a little better and went out to the department lobby to watch TV. The world artistic gymnastics championship was on and she sat down next to him so he wouldn't feel too alone. And all of a sudden, while he was looking at the screen, he started to cry. She asked me, "Don't you think it's weird that a bunch of girls tossing balls and ribbons in the air made him cry?"

"It's very weird," I said. "I think you should keep visiting him. From what you told me, I have the feeling you're right, Karinne. They must really be hiding something from you. And if you let it go now, you'll never know."

She rolled her eyes. "But Arno, what should I do?"

"I don't know, but you're a smart girl. I'm sure that if you think about it, you'll get some ideas."

She turned her body toward me and asked whether I really thought she was smart.

I said yes.

And then she said, "It's hot in your car. Do you mind if I take off my shirt and sit here in my bathing suit? I'm getting off anyway. I mean getting out. Of the car. Soon."

Her flirting was becoming more blatant all the time. During the day, it had no effect on me. During the day, I didn't react to the way she touched me or stroked the inside of her thigh while she talked, or how she kissed me close to my mouth when she got out of the car. During the day, I couldn't have cared less when she said, "I miss the vibrator I left in Paris. I don't understand how I could leave it there." Or "I can sleep with boys, but I come hard only with older men, with real men."

During the day, she seemed like a little girl in desperate need of attention who was trying to get it in the cheapest way possible.

But at night, on the living room couch, I dreamed about her. I slept with her in my dreams and I hurt her. I grabbed her by the hair and pulled, and I slapped her ass and choked her a little with my thumbs, and she loved it. When I hurt her, she said, *Harder, Monsieur Arno, harder.* Ayelet also liked it aggressive when we first started having sex. And then, one day a few years ago—just like that, no explanation—she stopped liking it. It didn't work for her anymore at all. And I accepted it. I'm not the type to force a woman to do something. All the pleasure I have in bed comes from the pleasure the woman with me is having. If it didn't work for her anymore, that was fine. And I didn't even miss it when we let up and were, you know, gentle with each other.

Do you mind if we move to another table, bro? No, because that couple who just sat down next to us is a little too close for what I want to tell you now. Is it okay with you? I want you to know that I really appreciate your listening to all this crap I'm dumping on you. But order something, really. On me. I get a discount at the bar here. I designed the place. From the ceiling motifs to the beer coasters. Beautiful, right? What can I get for you? A drink? A steak? They have fantastic entrecôte here. Nothing? You're sure?

It's better here, isn't it? More discreet. Where were we? So the day before yesterday, in the morning, she got into my car. The mademoiselle, who else? At first, I was still a little excited to see her because of what I'd dreamt about her at night, but then she started making up stories about the guys who'd hit on her at the beach the day before and I reminded myself that she was a pathetic little girl and that turned me off completely. Then all of a sudden—relatively early for her, we still hadn't reached Herzliya—she stopped the *Baywatch* stories and said, "I think I found a way to find out what really happened to Grandpa."

"Great," I said, trying not to sound too enthusiastic.

"When Grandma comes home from the hospital, she writes emails to Elsa. She's her best friend. She lives in Zurich. She writes her really long emails. I'm sure she tells her everything that happened. So yesterday, I stood behind her when she was typing her password and wrote it on my hand."

She showed me her small arm, with "WOLF 1247" written on it. It looked a little like it belonged to a Holocaust survivor.

So I encouraged her: "See? I told you you're a smart girl. You found an excellent way to find out what you need to find out."

She looked unhappy. "But I'm flying back to Mama tomorrow night."

"So get into her email tomorrow morning."

"I don't have the courage."

"What do you mean, you don't have the courage?"

"I don't have the courage to read Grandma's emails. I'm also a little bit afraid of what I will find there, Arno."

We were both silent. She bit her nails. I ran my hands over the bristles on my cheeks. My beard's been growing quickly this week. Two hours after I shave I have to shave again.

And then she asked me what I myself wanted to ask, what I was afraid to ask: "Maybe you'll come with me? Grandma goes to the hospital on the 8:20 bus. Pick me up tomorrow like always, and instead of going to Tel Aviv, we'll wait in the groves until she leaves the house and then we'll go back inside and read what she wrote to Elsa."

"Not in the groves," I tell her. "We'll wait in the parking lot of the squash court. There's no one there at that hour."

"Whatever you want."

So yesterday morning I took Ofri to school. She was reading *Anne of Avonlea* and I held her hand and pulled her back every time she was about to walk into a tree. At the place where we always separate, she kissed me on the cheek and said, "I love you, Daddy." Since she went into the grove with Herman, she hasn't told me that she loves me even once. I thought it was a good sign. Maybe she was starting to get back to her old self.

I picked up the mademoiselle at 8:05. We drove to the squash court parking lot. There were more cars there than I thought there would be, so I drove a little farther, to where there's a bench the boys in the neighborhood sit on at night and drink the vodka they buy at the gas station. She put her small feet up on the dashboard and told me she once learned how to play squash, but her instructor hit on her and her mother got angry and stopped the lessons. Then she met him without her mother knowing. In his studio. He was married. There was a picture of his wife and kids on the table at the entrance to his studio. But that didn't bother her. In Paris, nobody makes a big deal about things like that.

I counted the songs on the radio while she was talking. I didn't want to look at my watch because she might get insulted and cancel everything, so I counted songs. One song is about three minutes long. Five songs, fifteen minutes. I waited through one more just to be on the safe side. "Free Fallin'" by Tom Petty and the Heartbreakers. Great song, eh? It's just too bad that now it's fucked for me and I can't listen to it without remembering what happened.

The judge who lives on the third floor was just coming out as we were pulling up to the building. I thought, that's all I need now. And even though we hadn't actually done anything bad yet, I said to Karinne, "Crouch down." And with both of us hunched over like that, we waited for her to disappear around the bend in the street. Only then did we get out of the car and go inside.

We knocked on the door to be 100 percent sure that Ruth wasn't home. There was no answer. The mademoiselle put her key in the lock and turned it, and we went into their house.

There's a piano in the living room with a bust of Mozart on it. I felt like he was staring at me, Wolfgang Amadeus, so I turned him so he was facing the bookcase. They have hundreds of books, Herman and Ruth. Most of them are old, in German, by writers that you must know. The bookcase has glass doors. They're usually very clean. That day, they were full of dust.

The mademoiselle asked if I wanted something to drink. I said I thought we should do what we wanted to do as quickly as possible and started walking toward the computer room, but she stood in my way, actually blocked me with her body, and said, "I also think we should do what we want to do as quickly as possible." And then she took off her shirt. And her bathing suit top. And her mini. And her bathing suit bottom. She did it almost in one fell swoop, as if she'd practiced the movements earlier. And before I could say stop, she was standing in front of me on the Persian rug, totally naked.

The reading lamp illuminated her. Her skin was smooth,

no scratches, no wrinkles, no marks except for the Star of David on her left breast. She had a perfect body. A girl's body. And I felt dizzy. Not a good kind of dizzy. More like the kind you get in very high places. When you make the mistake of looking down.

"Get dressed," I said.

"But Arno, I thought that—"

"It's . . . it's not okay, Karinne."

Then she snapped. She folded into herself, stark naked, and collapsed to the floor near the armchair and started to cry. She cried like a child too. Lots of sniffling. And between sniffles, she said things like, "I'm ugly. You don't want me because I'm ugly. I repulse you. I'm fat. My legs are crooked. You don't want me because my legs are crooked."

I sat down close to her on the rug. I told myself that I had to calm her down or she wouldn't want to get into Ruth's email. And I'd never know what happened to Ofri in the grove. I stroked her hair. I said, "You're very attractive, Karinne, very, very attractive. Your body is beautiful. And your feet are small and lovely. I dreamed about you every night this week."

She said I was lying. Her fine hair hid her face and her voice seemed to purr as it passed through it.

I told her that I never lie. And kept stroking her hair to the place where it met her suntanned shoulder.

She said, "What you're doing, it feels good."

If I was a character in one of your stories, it would have ended there. With you, everyone always stops at the last second. Before the abyss. But in real life, it's not like that. Because at that stage, I myself was already convinced of all the things I said to her. And I was already stroking the length of her naked back, and she raised her head, took my hand and put my finger in her mouth. And sucked. And I got a hard-on. In real life, when a man passes a certain point, it's hard for him to stop.

I'll spare you the details. Actually, there's not a lot to describe. Let's just say that it was very far from my fantasies. Everything was very slow, but not sexy slow. Kind of clumsy. It didn't flow. Without the flip-flops and clothes, she looked small and vulnerable, and that made me cautious with her. I didn't really know what to do with my big body, how not to crush her under me. Don't forget that I hadn't been with another woman for twenty years. And when I took my prick out of her, I saw that it was covered with blood. I wasn't really surprised. From the way she froze when I entered her and the way she tried to fake an orgasm without even knowing what she was supposed to fake. It was easy to guess that it was her first time.

After she wiped herself with her shirt, I asked her why she didn't tell me she was a virgin.

She stroked my arm and said, "Because I . . . didn't want you to think I was a little girl."

All of a sudden, I had this idiotic but strong fear that my father would walk in and drag me out of the living room into the hallway of the building and ask me, *But what about Ayelet?!*

So I asked her if the door was locked.

She said yes, sure.

I asked whether I'd hurt her and she said a little, and kept stroking my arm. It was annoying. Ayelet always gives me these little kisses on the neck after we fuck. Suddenly I missed that. So I sat up and said, "Come on, let's go to your grandmother's computer."

"There's no reason to go to it," she said.

"What do you mean, no reason? What about your grandmother's emails to Elsa?"

"There is no Elsa."

"There's no Elsa?"

"No."

I wanted to slap her, but I fought to control myself. I actually pressed my hands on my thighs so that neither of them would fly out toward her cheek. Or grab the Mozart bust and throw it at her. Get up, I told myself. Wash off. Get dressed. And get the hell out of here. She's flying to Paris tonight, and until then, all you can do is minimize damages.

So that's what I did. I stood up. Washed her blood off me. Got dressed. Said that I had to go to work. I told her she was very beautiful. That she would make a lot of men happy someday. I asked her if she wanted me to bring her a glass of water. Or make her some coffee. I gave her respect. And she was silent the whole time. She leaned against the armchair and watched me wherever I went. She hugged her knees close to her body. Curled her hair around her finger. Even when I bent down and kissed her goodbye on the cheek, she didn't say anything. At the time, I took that as a sign of acceptance. Of maturity.

But just to be on the safe side, I came back from work as late as I could. So I wouldn't bump into her by accident.

There was no note waiting for me on the bedroom door. Ayelet had taken it down. Even so, I exiled myself to the living room voluntarily. I watched *Grandstanders* twice. The rerun too. In the rerun, you could tell that the panelists weren't yelling out of real anger. That they were faking it. That the director was telling them to raise their voices every time the program started to drag. Then I lay down and stared at the ceiling, rerunning the events of the day in my mind, and I said to myself, What did you do, you moron, what did you do? But I also said to myself, Calm down, she must be in Paris by now.

That's when I texted you the first time. I knew you were the only person I could talk to about this. Even though we haven't been in touch for a long time. My other friends are too new. Too connected to Ayelet. I don't trust them not to sell me out. You would never sell me out. I know too much about you.

Just kidding.

You don't have to apologize, bro. I knew you wouldn't answer right away. It was four in the morning. It's just that I remembered your telling me once that you write at night, so I tried. I doesn't matter.

In the morning, I walked Ofri to school. She finished the last few pages of *Anne of Avonlea* as we were walking and stopped to put the book in her bag. Then she told me about the little fights the girls in her class have. Alma said this, and then Mayan got insulted, and then Roni told all the girls not to talk to Alma. And then Alma got insulted. I couldn't believe it was happening. She hadn't mentioned anyone in her class for five weeks on our walks to school.

At the spot where we separated, she said again, "Daddy, I love you." I waited a few minutes after she went through the school gate and then followed. I climbed to the third floor and peeked into her classroom through the opening in the curtain. She was sitting there doing the same things she'd done the last time I looked in at her. Playing with the zipper of her pencil case. Taking out crayons. Drawing in her notebook. Putting the crayons back in the pencil case. But then the teacher asked something and she looked up and raised her hand. That's when I saw her eyes. The mischievous, curious gleam was back.

I restrained myself from racing into the classroom and hoisting her into the air with joy. The gleam was back! I stood at the curtain for another few minutes and waited for her to look up again. So I could be sure I hadn't made a mistake. Then I texted Ayelet: "I'm sorry for the way I've been lately. I really did get carried away. Want to make up?" And I went home. This time I walked on the sidewalk, not in the middle of the road. My life was suddenly precious to me. On the way, I stopped at the shopping center to withdraw cash. The widow from the floor above us was at the ATM. I waited for her to finish. She's not really a widow, but her husband is always out of the country and she has the eyes of someone who just got back from a funeral and she always wears black, so Ayelet and I call her that just between ourselves. But even she was smiling that morning. And she was wearing a yellow blouse for a change. When she finished with the ATM, she said, "Good morning, Arnon." And I said, "An excellent morning." Then I withdrew the thousand shekels we owed the Wolfs and walked home, taking long strides, and for the first time in five weeks, I was breathing normally and wasn't constantly holding the air in my chest, and all the problems about everything suddenly seemed small and solvable.

But when I reached the building, she was standing outside. The little mademoiselle. She started walking toward me. On her platform flip-flops. I couldn't avoid her. Even if I'd wanted to. She was coming straight at me, and when she was close, she stopped and said, "Hug me."

I took a step back and asked, "Weren't you supposed to fly to Paris?"

She moved closer to me. "My grandfather...he died."

"What?!"

"Last night." She took my hand and put it around her waist. "Hug me."

"I'm sorry for your loss, but...it's not a good idea to hug here in the middle of the street, Karinne, it's really not a good idea." I moved my hand away as gently as I could.

She pressed her pelvis against mine. "We must go away together. I want you. I need you."

"I can't. What happened—it was a onetime thing. I'm married. I have two daughters. I can't. I'm sorry, Karinne. But it's not right."

And then, all at once, she turned into a different person. We're standing in the middle of the building parking area at 8:30 in the morning, and she starts punching me in the chest. "All of a sudden you're married?" she screamed. "When you had sex with me yesterday, you didn't care! You're a bastard! That's what you are. A bastard!"

Luckily, the city cleaners were working on the garden with leaf blowers, so it muffled her screams a little. Even so, I thought I saw the judge on the third floor peering out of her window. And it was clear to me that if it went on like that, there'd be more people peering out of windows.

Somehow, I managed to grab her elbow and push her into the car. She kept cursing me in Hebrew and French, but at least now it was with closed windows. I tried to calm her down on the way to the parking lot at the squash court. I lied to her. During a two-minute ride I told more lies than I'd told my whole life. She screamed, "I'll knock on your door and tell your wife everything. I'll do it because you're a bastard." That scared me. I promised her the moon and the stars. To gain time. I promised her I'd visit her in Paris. I promised her we'd rent a hotel room near the beach in Tel Aviv. Tomorrow. Day after tomorrow the latest. I told her that I had feelings for her too. That it wasn't only sex for me.

I know, man, I know, I should have put her in her place. But I was scared.

We sat in the squash court parking lot through ten songs. She cried in that runny-nose way of hers until the seventh song, occasionally mumbling that I was a shit and a liar, or a liar and a shit. The seventh song was Radiohead's "Karma Police," and at the chorus, out of nowhere, she started telling me about all kinds of moments she had with her grandfather. The stories weren't all neatly organized like the ones about the guys at the beach. They didn't have beginnings, sometimes they had no endings, and sometimes they disappeared in the middle: "And then he picked me up and held me high in the air in the middle of the airport and said, 'You're home.'" Where?

What airport? What home? It wasn't clear. And when the camp counselor asked him if he was Karinne's father, he said yes without batting an eyelash, and he signed all his letters to her, "With Eternal Love, Grandpa Herman." And once he said to her, "Your father might have gone to college, but he's an imbecile if he left a wonderful little girl like you," and after lunch, he would give her a second dessert when Grandma wasn't looking, and at bedtime he would make up stories for her about a girl named Karinna who was brave and kind and always helped animals run away from the zoo and back to their real home in Africa. They went to Africa for her bat mitzvah, just she and her grandpa—Grandma didn't like traveling—and she was hot for a boy in the tour group and spent the whole trip with him, and her grandfather didn't say a word, didn't tease her, also because he himself was flirting with the young tour guide, and once at a barbecue they had with friends, she saw him kiss Grandma's friend behind the storeroom in the garden, and he told her later, "It's our secret, we don't have to tell Grandma, it would only hurt her." They always had their secrets, she and Grandpa, and that's why it had been so weird this last week, because she felt that he was hiding something from her. That he was ashamed about something. He had never been ashamed before. Never. But it doesn't matter anymore. He's dead now.

"Yes," I said, and the picture of his head on Ofri's lap came into my mind. "Looks like your grandfather will take his secrets to the grave with him."

Karinne nodded, sniffled noisily and wetly, and asked me to take her home. She had to get ready for the funeral.

Pick a dress. I hugged her. Of course I hugged her after everything she told me. It sounded like she really loved her grandfather. That they had a special connection. And I also felt a bit guilty, you know. Not that he died because of me, but he was hospitalized because of me. There was no disputing that. So I hugged her. But a fatherly kind of hug, you know. Clean.

On the way home, she didn't talk. I thought that the anger she'd had before had passed. I thought that she had gone back to being herself. That she understood there was no point in knocking on the door across the hall, and for all our sakes she should put the whole thing behind us. But then, just when I'm pulling into the building parking area and taking the key out of the ignition, she turns to me and says, "Your wife will definitely come to the funeral, yes? Very good. So I will tell her everything there."

And before I could say anything, she opened the door and got out.

I stayed in the car. Stunned. I sat there for a few minutes and didn't know what to do. I couldn't breathe. I opened all the windows but I still couldn't get enough air. I felt a kind of pressure in my chest. Then I felt pressured because of the pressure. Then your text message came.

You always had good timing.

No, really, bro, I definitely don't take it for granted that you agreed to meet me at the last minute like this. We haven't seen each other for what, a year? You don't have to apologize. We're at that stage of life when everyone has his head up his ass. But you definitely came through.

You know, just telling someone the story relieves the...

I had some thoughts after she got out of the car. You don't want to know. Bad thoughts. The kind you want to stop the minute they start but can't. You just can't. It's a kind of loop you just can't get out of. And slowly those bad thoughts fill your whole mind. And in the end, there's no room for anything but them.

Forget it, you don't really want to know.

I thought about chasing her. Grabbing her before she punched in the code at the entrance to the building. Dragging her to the car by force. Taking her to the beach, swimming far out with her after the lifeguards leave their stations and drowning her there, holding her head underwater until the bubbles of her breath stopped.

And she's small. It shouldn't take more than a minute.

I don't think I'll do that. I'm just giving you an example of the things going through my head so you can understand how low I'd sunk. You see, I am this close to losing everything I have. A few words she'd say to Ayelet at the funeral—and that would be the end. Everything I've built, everything would be destroyed.

Are you kidding? Ayelet would never give me a pass on it. Inside a week, she'd hand me the divorce papers. Believe me. Before we got married, she told me what was what. She said, "I've been through a lot in my life. I can take tough blows. And pull myself up again. But I'm not willing to accept infidelity. That's my red line." She said, "I'm telling you this now so you'll know in advance. So you won't be surprised." And she's a lawyer, don't forget. She'd make sure that I never see the girls again. And that all our property goes to her. She'll drink my blood through a straw, I'm telling you. Not to mention that according to the law, the mademoiselle is a minor. I can already see the two of them sitting in our kitchen, and Ayelet is convincing her—in a show of female solidarity—to press charges against me. And then it's court. And the judge won't care that she's the one who seduced me, that she's the one who told me about the vibrator she left in Paris, that she's the one who undressed before I even laid a hand on her.

It's like with Gaza. No one in the world cares that they'd been firing rockets on us for years before we went in there.

I'd get actual prison time. And when I'd be released, no one would give me work. And Ofri, they'd harass her in school. The girls in her class would have a field day with it. *I saw your father in the papers, your father's a pervert.* They'd make her life miserable.

And for what? All I wanted was to watch over my women, to protect them. To make sure no one hurt them.

Everything I did, I did out of love. Do you believe me?

Maybe I love too intensely. Maybe that's my problem. People today don't love like that.

I'm not crying. Of course not. My eyes are burning a little, that's all. I think it's from the onions they're frying in the kitchen.

I'm sensitive to onions. I swear. I cut the onions for the Saturday morning *shakshuka* with my eyes closed. Here, look at the scars on my fingers.

Do I want a glass of water? What do I look like? Order me a draft beer. And a steak. I have to dig my teeth into something. You want one too? You're sure? You won't make a gesture and join me in my last supper?

I'm not exaggerating. That's how I feel. Like Jesus before they crucified him. No, like Jesus on the cross. The nails have already been hammered into my palms. And the blood is starting to trickle out.

Did you ever feel like you're living the last few minutes of your life as you know it?

Right, I forgot. How many years ago was that?

In the end it wasn't malignant, right? What luck!

You and Shiri have been together since the army, right? Listen, after twenty years with a woman, you're all mixed together. If she leaves you, she leaves with you. Or at least parts of you. Ayelet and I are Siamese twins. I haven't made a decision in the last few years without asking her first. I always tell people, Let me sleep on it. But actually, I'm waiting for the minute the kids fall asleep. I make her a cup of instant coffee with a drop of chocolate milk powder in it, the way she likes it, and then tell her about my hesitations. And she tells me what I should do. I don't always accept what she says, but she always makes me see the real dilemma I'm facing. Makes me see the heart of it, not all the stuff around it. And we're not the kind of couple who, with time, turn into friends. I'm just as hot for her as I was when we first started. I get turned on from just seeing her get dressed for court. I'm crazy about the way she looks, the way she smells, the way she dances with the girls to YouTube songs on Saturdays.

It's nice, the way I talk about her, right? But the problem is that all that talk won't mean a thing to her after the mademoiselle tells her what we did on Herman and Ruth's rug. She's a guillotine about stuff like that.

No, I can see it already. Karinne will go over to her at the end of the funeral. They'll straggle behind the end of the line of mourners, Ayelet because of the heat and Karinne because she wants to be alone with Ayelet. And then, in a quiet voice, Karinne will start to talk. And the worst thing is that I can't do anything to stop it. The guillotine is dropping with my neck under it and all I can do is watch it fall. The blade is already on my jugular and I'm paralyzed. Can't move.

What would you do in my place, bro? Now, after you've heard it all. No, really. Don't pretend to be neutral. I read your articles in the papers. You have an opinion about everything. Tell me what comes into your mind.

You're the only person I'm talking to about this, so you don't have a choice. I mean, the person I most want to talk to about it is Ayelet. But that's impossible. People don't understand how much infidelity isolates you.

Don't tell me you have no idea what you'd do.

Your friend is drowning, waving his arms, screaming help, help, and you just happen to sail by in a boat. Wouldn't you stop?

It's not true that you don't have a boat. You do. Anyone who reads your books knows that you do.

You know what, think of it as a story you're writing. Think of everything I told you until now as the beginning and middle and three-quarters of the story, and now comes the end. And the end has to be good. Because the protagonist has suffered enough and has made others suffer enough. Take your time, man. I'll polish off my steak and fries, and meanwhile, you think about what kind of happy ending this story can have, okay?

Second Floor

Hi Netta,

You're probably surprised to get this letter. We haven't spoken in a long time, and who even writes letters today? But email is too dangerous (you'll see why in a minute) and the truth is that I just don't have anyone else to confess to.

I actually tried to call my psychologist. The one I went to back then, remember? I had good chemistry with her. It all boils down to chemistry, even with psychologists. I used to go to the small basement under her house in Har Adar, crushed, and I'd leave just as crushed, but a little less confused. She didn't speak in the usual clichés: id and ego and your mother and how does that make you feel. She spoke simply to me, down to earth, and sometimes she would tell me little things about herself. If we went a bit overtime, she didn't make a big deal of it, and at the end of a session, she'd put her hand on my shoulder (she actually touched me!). And all those years, I told myself that if I ever lost my balance again, I'd have someone to call.

Her son answered.

I asked if I could speak to Michaela.

There was silence. A long one. And then he said that she had died. Two years ago. "Of what?" I asked.

"Cancer."

I didn't know what to say. So I said, "I'm sorry. I'm sorry for your loss."

"Yes."

"Your mother was a very special woman."

"Yes."

It was obvious that he knew I was a patient. It was obvious that he already knew how to handle calls like mine, from patients, and that he'd be happy to end the conversation as quickly as possible.

I remained standing there with the phone in my hand even after we hung up, listening to the beeps that came after the call was disconnected. What a nerve she had, I thought, to die on me like that.

For the entire week before that call, I imagined how I'd sink into the soft armchair across from her, the thick wine-colored rug at our feet, the spiral heater between us, with only one spiral working, as usual. In my imagination, I gave her a bit more gray (after all, fifteen years had passed), but I left her the frumpy brown sweater, the oversized glasses, and the Werther's Original candies she put in a small plate at the beginning of a session, saying that based on the number of candies I unwrapped during our hour together, she'd know how I was really feeling.

I had an opening sentence prepared. Something intelligent. I'd already imagined the way the conversation would go, the moments we'd be silent and the moment she'd make the connection between my mother and my anxieties about Lyri, and the moment I'd burst into liberating tears and she'd hand me a lightly scented tissue, and the moment she'd glance quickly at the clock behind me, on the left, and the moment I'd take out a check and ask her whether the fee was the same as it had been then. I imagined her hand on my shoulder, lingering there, before we said goodbye, and my brisk steps from the basement door through her blooming garden to the parking area, and the slow traffic around the hills to Route 1, with the radio playing a song I love (let's say, Neil Young, let's say "Out on the Weekend"), and I'm once again open enough to let the music enter me, flow through my blood.

Now there's no garden and no Neil Young. One phone call was enough to push me down the ladder right back to the starting point:

Something is happening, Netta, and I can't tell anybody. But I have to, I just have to tell it to someone.

It got so bad that yesterday I looked for a church with a confessional. I drove to the American Colony. Remember when Nomi—when she was working for the Society for the Protection of Nature and was always using the word "magical"—took us on a tour there, and we ended up at a foreign workers' church?

So I walked around there for about two hours this week and couldn't find a trace of it. Finally, I asked a guy who was riding by on his bicycle (exactly your type, bristly cheeks and broad shoulders) and he said that there really had been a church there, but it was bulldozed a year earlier and they put up an office building in its place, and there it is, right in front of us.

"I thought churches were supposed to be eternal," I said.

He nodded without understanding and pedaled onward (young guys don't even see us anymore, have you noticed? Wait, maybe they do see you) and suddenly, the energy drained out of me all at once.

That's not the Hani I know. I can actually hear you thinking that, maybe even saying it out loud in your living room in Middletown.

And maybe that's why I'm writing to you. Because you remember the good version of me. Just writing your name on the top of the page is enough to make me feel a tiny bit cleaner.

I have a lot of friends here, I don't want you to think I don't (I'm popular! For the first time in my life!), but I don't trust any one of them. I met most of them (the truth is, all of them, but "all of them" sounds pathetic) through the kids. That's the way you make connections in the suburbs. A short conversation when you're picking the kids up from preschool leads to playdates which, if they don't end in disaster, lead to other playdates, and while they're playing, you and the other mothers talk, first about the kids, how terrific they are, even though they can definitely wear you out, and then you gossip about the preschool teacher—don't you think it's a bit much that she takes two days a week off? I can understand one day, but two? And it's very nice that she reads to them from the newspaper every morning, but I'm not sure that kids that age need to know the difference between a Qassam rocket and a Grad rocket. By the way, they have a special in the park on Sundays — the kids eat for free — and it really pays if you order pizza, for instance, and have you heard that the new pool is going to open this summer? The mayor wants to score some points before the election, and there are no two ways about it, Dr. Caspi is the best pediatrician in the area, it's worth suffering the endless waiting and his grumpy receptionist just for that moment when you look at the pictures from the family trip to the Black Forest and realize how much they've grown . . .

At first I used to wait for the moment when some kind of truth would emerge from all that trivial chatter. We're just feeling each other out, I thought, testing the waters. In a another minute, one of us will break free from the need to present her life as perfect, and then a real conversation will begin.

With time, I realized it wasn't going to happen. It was going to stay the way it was. A flight to nowhere.

But it's up to you too! I hear you saying on the other side of the Pacific Ocean (or is it the Atlantic? I never remember which of them separates us). After all, Hani, you can guide the conversation to things that interest you more!

But that's just it, at first I tried. I tossed out the bait. But none of them bit.

I'd say things like, "Sometimes I have a really strong urge to get up and leave everything." Or "I haven't been able to read since the kids were born, and that makes me feel hollow." Or "My daughter still has imaginary friends. And I'm afraid she'll end up like my mother."

They responded with an embarrassing silence. Averted their eyes.

So after a few silences like that, you stop trying. And settle for the chatter. After a few years of it, when a new mother who doesn't know the codes moves into the neighborhood, and when you're both waiting for your kids to come out of the pre-judo class, she suddenly says to you, "I always feel sad and don't know how to stop, I'm afraid my husband will leave me if it goes on like this"—you give her that same silence because you're afraid that after all those silences, if you open your mouth now, lava will come gushing out of it and scorch everything.

(Remember that night in Guatemala when they took us to see the volcano that had been inactive for two hundred years, and suddenly it started to spit out lava? You know what, I think that was the only time in our friendship that I saw you scared. Really scared.)

*

The asterisk is when I get up for a nosh or to pee. Or when it's really hard for me to write something and I have to take a breath before I do...

I'm scared now, Netta. I'm scared that if I don't tell someone what's happening, I'll just go crazy. That's nothing new, Hani, you say. You're always afraid you'll go crazy. Right, I answer. But this time it's for real. One owl in the tree, okay. Two, fine. But what'll happen if one night, there are three?

But wait a minute, before the owl I owe you an apology. For the way I behaved when you were in Israel last time.

(Maybe you've completely forgotten about it? Maybe you didn't give it much thought to start with? Maybe it was only for me that our friendship is so alive, and for you, it had already faded and you don't have the slightest idea where all these parentheses are coming from now?)

It was a great idea to take the kids to the places where we spent our childhood in Jerusalem. Really. To show them where we played hopscotch, where we hid when we ran away from home, where we tried to ride our bikes without training wheels for the first time...

Except that I couldn't stand the jealousy.

I didn't understand it like that at the time. Only now, because of what happened these last few days, have I realized that the sudden pain I felt in my midsection that made me cancel at the last minute (it was, in fact, after the last minute, because you were almost there already, and maybe that's why you were so angry) was the pain of jealousy. Actually, of the premonition of jealousy. Of the knowledge that if I didn't back out of the meeting of our families in Jerusalem, I'd find myself in the same unbearable situation I'd been in when you came to visit us a few days before that.

And it wasn't because of how you looked (fantastic, by the way. It's incredible how you look more and more beautiful with the passing years). Or because of those touches of Americanness I could see in every movement you made: the way you sat, the way you stood up, the way you held your coffee cup with a finger raised...

It was because of Noam. I mean, not because of Noam himself. That is, yes because of Noam himself. But not because of Noam as a man. Damn! I'm making a mess of this! It's unbelievable how hard it still is for me to say this.

It's because of that equal parenting you and he have.

In simpler words: I could see that you're together about the whole thing with the kids. That he doesn't "help you," as men like to say, but that he's just like you. Involved to the bone.

In the simplest words: it was unbearable seeing such a good father, while Assaf was on another one of his trips.

And it's not like I'd never seen good fathers before Noam, but none of them was *your* husband. There's too long a history of comparing myself to you and coming out the loser most of the time. But that's okay, it always made me try harder, and maybe the fact that I've stopped trying has something to do with the fact that you're not here and I have no one to compete with (I remember your back before the 600-meter run—what kind of distance is that, 600 meters? Only in the Hebrew University High School could they have thought up something like that—and how it moved steadily away from me up the hill).

Don't get me wrong. I was absolutely thrilled to see your girls in my house. (Remember when your Alma and my Lyri drew a picture together so companionably, as if they'd known each other for years, and we both looked at each other and had the same, unspoken thought: Ladies and gentlemen, welcome to the second generation of the sudden, inexplicable, strong chemistry known as "friendship between girls"?)

And your Mia, she's gorgeous. And it makes me want to laugh out loud that she, who was given that Hollywood-like name, babbles only in Hebrew. And don't think I missed the way you restrained yourself when I told you that I hadn't been working since Nimrod was born (you could have pried harder, could have hurt me), or the fact that you avoided waving your wealth in my face (in small ways, like the kind of clothes you dressed your kids in, or by telling me that you didn't have any pictures of the new house you bought). Nettush, you were just as wonderful as I remembered you, the same old wonderful you.

But every time Noam went over to one of the girls to see why she was crying...

And every time they curled into his arms...

And when he took Mia for a walk in her carriage just so we'd be able to talk...

It made my insides constrict. It was an actual physical pain. As if someone had grabbed me by the spleen and twisted.

That's how it is. Sometimes someone who sprinkles salt doesn't know that it's missing the salad and landing on a wound. (I promise that my metaphors will get better as the letter goes on. I haven't written in a while.)

In any case, I'm sorry for canceling the nostalgic trip to Jerusalem at the last minute. And for not saying goodbye before you flew back. And for causing trouble between you and Ariela Klein in the tenth grade.

Do you understand? And forgive?

I'll assume you do. I have no choice but to assume that you do.

*

You can never know what kind of father the man you marry will be, but there are some instructive signs. Let's say, the way he acts with your younger siblings. (Omer and Guy adored Assaf. Every time he came over for dinner, they would jump on him and hang on his shoulders, and he'd play hide-and-seek with them before we ate. Then after the meal, he'd leave scavenger hunt clues for them all over the house, and while they were running from one clue to the other, giving the grown-ups a bit of peace, he would prepare the prize for them: strawberry Jell-O.)

Or the way he responds to small children who happen to come into his world. (On our honeymoon in Paris, we were in a restaurant next to a family with a little girl who wouldn't stop crying. Instead of getting annoyed and demanding that the waiter move us to a different table, he started doing imitations of vegetables for the girl to make her laugh. After his imitation of a squash, her parents invited us to spend the weekend with them at their summer home in Nice.)

And maybe the best sign: the way he reacts to the child inside you. Even the strongest woman has moments when she needs to be protected. It could be a flu that wipes you out. Or a boss who says something nasty to you. Or you have a small car accident. At the entrance to the city. Nothing really happened. The bumper got slightly bent. But it really shook you up. And you just need to hear his voice on the phone. But that's just it, Assaf was terrific in those kinds of situations. Protective, but not patronizing. He saw my self-pity, but he didn't wallow in it with me. That was one of the reasons I married him. (And there were others: the fact that he liked to talk during a movie and didn't shush me like my other boyfriends did. The smell of his scalp. The fact that he really and truly believed I was talented. The way he walked, which looked like he was dancing. The fact that he still collected stamps when I met him. That I believed he would never leave me. That he treated life like a scavenger hunt. That he would keep buying key chains from deaf-mutes even after our first date. That on our first date, he agreed to share my ravioli. Enough. I'll stop here. Because it just doesn't work, this list. I expected it to make me teary-eyed, but it's like I'm describing a stranger.)

I just stopped and read everything I've written so far, and suddenly noticed that everything is in threes. Three punctuation marks in most of my sentences, almost always three examples. Maybe it has something to do with the fact that I've become part of a triangle? Maybe when you're part of a triangle, everything that happens in the world seems to you to happen in threes?

*

But I'm not going to talk about Eviatar yet. If I talk about Eviatar now, you'll judge me harshly and I want you to understand the background first and then judge me (harshly, what else?).

So let's go back to his brother.

*

It started when I gave birth. Assaf was texting while I was in labor. Can you picture it? I'm being ripped apart by pain and he's happily texting away. It's true that the epidural slows things down. And we were into the sixth hour already. But even so—show a little sensitivity. I told him: This is not the place to be texting. I kept myself from yelling at him. So I wouldn't be the clichéd woman yelling at her husband during delivery. And what did he do? He left. And texted outside. I had a contraction right then. And screamed. It was really loud. I was sure he'd come right back into the room to see what was happening, but no, he stayed outside. Texting. And didn't come in for another minute.

And later, in the ward, he didn't want to hold Lyri. Said she was so small that he was scared she might fall out of his hands. Besides, he said, he thought that what she needed most now was her mother. What a demagogue. He was always a bit of a demagogue, but that trait of his got much stronger after he started demagoguing at potential investors.

By the way, he went back to work after four days. Okay, I didn't expect him to split maternity leave with me, fifty-fifty. This isn't Norway, after all. But not to stay home for a week, just in solidarity? Not to call from work at least five times a day to ask how I was? How it was going? Whether postpartum depression had already started?

I can give you many more examples just from Lyri's first month, but I'm beginning to sound petty. (Remember that last night of our school trip to Eilat? When we and Nomi wrote our "List of Things We'll Never Do"—never marry someone we don't love, never invite friends on Friday nights to talk politics, never decide for our kids what kind of after-school courses they should take, never force them to do homework during vacation, never work more than six months at a job we hate, never choose a meal at a restaurant over a rock concert, never steal each other's boyfriend, never stop being friends. Suddenly I think: because Nomi died young, she never had to break her promises. And I also think: we wrote that list too early. We still didn't know what was lying in wait for us, what we would really need to be wary of when we grew up. For example, Never turn into the kind of woman who brings one petty example after another to prove to her best friend that she has a husband who is not okay.)

Besides, it isn't a matter of examples. It's a matter of the abyss that opened between the father I thought Assaf would be and the father he actually is.

Tell me—I know it has nothing to do with this, but I suddenly have a burning need to know—do you sometimes hear Nomi's voice speaking inside your head too? I don't mean do you remember her, or do you think about her, but do you actually hear her voice speaking to you. I imagine you don't. After all, things like that only happen to me (and my mother). When it happened to me the last time, I was on a family trip to Mt. Arbel. This year, we joined a group of people who have nothing in common beyond the tedium of long, drawn-out Saturdays with their kids. The idea is that everyone puts in a little (a lot) of money to hire a guide to plan a trip for them and activities for the kids. You can't just let kids enjoy nature as it is, right? So we were standing there panting after a steep climb and the guide was telling us some legend about the mastic tree. I can never really listen to those legends. I always want to, I really want to, but at some point in the middle, my attention scatters like pollen. Maybe I should go for tests. Maybe they'll find that I have an attention deficit disorder specific to tour guides' stories and explanations and they'll give me an hour's extension on trips. In any case, I suddenly heard Nomi's voice inside my head, saying, *That's not even a mastic tree. It's a terebinth.* I nodded submissively. I thought that would be enough for her. But you know Nomi. *Tell him,* she says to me. *Tell him. He's misleading the kids!*

I won't tell him anything! I won't interrupt in the middle of the legend!! I told her.

The problem was that I said it out loud. And every head, large and small, turned in my direction. You probably would have found something clever to say to explain the outburst. I just smiled apologetically and silently counted to twelve.

Okay, they think I'm a strange bird anyway. A cuckoo. Who goes on a family trip without a spouse?

I'll grant Assaf this: he warned me in advance. He said, "The company's about to issue stock. There's a chance that I won't be in the country on some of those Saturdays."

I said, "If you're here, you'll come. And if you're not, we'll manage."

A mistake. It turned out that going on a family trip alone (or to any suburban social event for that matter) is a serious deviation. A crime against the bourgeoisie. An iceberg that destroys Noah's ark.

Because what happens? If we dissect it briefly, the men look at you differently if you're alone (even after you've had two kids, and you're wearing faded tights and the shirt Assaf got at the end of his combat training course). And the women, sensing that their men are pursuing you with their eyes, get anxious and tag you as a potential danger. They ask you questions about your husband in order to remind everyone who needs reminding that he exists. So when's he coming back? Isn't it tough on the kids that he travels so much? Hats off to you for coming on these trips anyway. I would have stayed home.

But at home, I scare myself! That's what I want to tell them. At home, I'm all rapid heartbeats! Electricity in my hair! Owls speaking in the trees!

*

Assaf's trips began, with perfect timing, right after Nimrod was born. The company he works for decided to open offices in Europe and the Americas, and he "had" to travel in order to supervise the process. The trips to America take between a week and ten days. The trips to Europe are shorter, three or four nights at the most.

And this is what he'd say about it if he had the right to answer this letter (I can picture a PowerPoint presentation. He's standing next to it, reading point after point, occasionally telling an anecdote to support his claims):

1. *I'm a demagogue? She's a demagogue. Focusing on only one aspect of our life and blowing it up so it hides other aspects. Among others:*
   a. *I call her from the traffic jams every morning and don't hang up until I've made her laugh at least once.*
   b. *In general, I'm the one responsible for the half glass of happiness in the house. Nimrod only dances with me. Lyri only allows herself to be a little less Lyri with me.*

c. Not to mention that, once a month, I go to the Mental Health Center with her to visit her mother. I wait outside on a bench for an hour, sometimes two, just because she needs someone to hug her when she comes out.

d. "What would I do without you?" she always says on the way to the car.

2. I don't understand what her problem is with my trips. They're not vacations. I go to work. I'm not the least bit excited when the taxi picks me up to take me to the airport. And in the duty-free shop, I mainly try to buy as many gifts as I can for her and the kids before they announce that my flight is boarding.

3. Yes, I could quit tomorrow. But how exactly would we pay for Lyri's horseback-riding lessons and Nimrod's swimming lessons and their mother's searching-for-herself classes?

4. It's my fault that she's frustrated? We agreed that she wouldn't go back to Verbin's studio after her maternity leave, and instead, she'd start working as a freelance designer. That's what she wanted. Because "I'm sick of taking orders from people who aren't as smart as I am." And I encouraged her. Because I saw that she wasn't happy. Again. And I wanted her to be happy. Because that's how it is when you love someone. You want the person you love to be happy. So she really didn't go back to the studio after her maternity leave. But she forgot to fulfill the other part of our agreement. Is it any wonder that I can't not text my bosses—yes, even when she was giving birth—or refuse to travel when they tell me to? Maybe they're not as smart as I am, but:

a. I didn't go to the Hebrew University High School, and no one led me to believe that I was the Crown of Creation.

b. *They pay me a salary at the end of every month. That salary pays for our part of the outrageous fee that tour guide charges the families.*

5. *It's so nice, by the way, to hear that the men "pursue you with their eyes" on those trips. I'm not surprised. Three expensive years at the fitness center, which she chose not to write about here, do the trick. It's just too bad that when we have sex once a year, that shapely body is completely turned off.*

6. *There's nothing more insulting than a woman who does you a favor when she sleeps with you.*

7. *Actually, there is: a woman who writes to her best friend that you're a terrible father.*

*

It's funny how understanding sometimes comes to you from the most unexpected direction. I took the kids to the old, run-down playground. The one you only go to when you really have no energy. The one where dead snacks are buried in its sandboxes. The swings squeak. And even the owls extend their talons.

The neighbor's little girl from downstairs was there. Ofri. Lyri's two years younger than she is, so they're not really friends, but intelligent kids can recognize the spark in each other. So they're happy when they meet by chance. Ofri's mother took their little one to the toddlers' slides and swings, and I stayed to watch the older girls. Then Ofri suddenly asked me, "Lyri's mommy, what's a widow?"

"Uh...a widow...it's a woman, uh, whose husband, uh...whose husband is dead," I stammered (oh, that fear of injuring their tender souls).

"So why do my mommy and daddy call you 'the widow'?" Ofri asked. "Lyri's daddy isn't dead!"

"I don't know why they call me that," I said. "Maybe you should ask them."

*

I opened the Mac that night, after months of not touching it, and designed a death notice.

In the center, in large letters, I typed Assaf's full name.

On the top I wrote: "Beloved Husband and Father."

And on the bottom: "Has passed away (that is, he's flown there business class) prematurely. The shivah will take place at the home of the widow. Please do not visit before ten in the morning."

I put a black frame around it. Then printed it out. I played with the fonts a bit, to make it look more terminal, and printed it out again. I planned to hang it on the door the next day after the kids left for nursery school, and then open the door a crack, as people do when they're really sitting shivah.

I would have done it. I swear. I was unraveled enough to do it. (I've done things that are just as crazy this year. For example, I drove two and a half hours to a restaurant in Biriya, sat facing Mt. Hermon, and drank one glass of red wine, then drove straight back so I would be home in time to pick up the kids. I called in to a radio program and made up a whole story about a father who ran off to America when I was five, leaving me so damaged that I haven't been able to have a serious relationship with a man to this very day. I argued in the middle of the night—loudly—with an owl.)

But then there was a knock at the door.

*

A word about secrets in the modern era before I tell you (thanks for your patience) my secret.

There are none.

There are no secrets in the modern era.

Everything is bared, aired, shared, Twittered, and Flickred; you can Snapchat and WhatsApp and Viber and Wiki. Nothing is secret, privacy is dead, and the funeral will be broadcast live on the Reality Channel.

Even so—if you tell anyone what I'm about to write here, I'll get my revenge by giving away all your secrets (hint: the Sinai, two weeks before your wedding).

*

Eviatar was standing on the other side of the door. Holding a small green gym bag. I hadn't seen him in more than ten years, so at first I didn't recognize him.

"Eviatar," he introduced himself.

"Assaf isn't home," I said without moving.

"I know," he said. "Otherwise I wouldn't have come."

*

I never understood when the quarrel between them began. And I wasn't really sure what the root of it was. Not that Assaf didn't talk about it. He did. But he told a different story every time. Once it had begun in their childhood. They were too close in age, only two and a half years apart. And Eviatar didn't get what he felt was coming to him as the oldest son. He always tried to please his father and did everything that Assaf did just to prove that he was better at it. Judo. Chess. Girls.

Later, each took a side when their parents got divorced. "I don't understand how he can take my father's side," Assaf said then. "After all, it's clear who the bad guy is here." I remember him standing in the kitchen one evening and screaming into the phone, "If you don't come to the Pesach seder at my mother's house, you don't ever have to talk to me again!"

Even so, Eviatar still came to our wedding. I remember him dancing with his friends on the sidelines. I remember Assaf whispering to me, "What a schmuck. Who told him he could invite them?" And me pouring him shots of tequila so he wouldn't make a scene.

When Lyri was born, he sent a check along with a greeting card: Congratulations on the birth of a daughter. The check was exceptionally generous. Six thousand shekels, I think. Maybe more. Assaf ripped it to pieces and tossed them into the trash can where we threw newspapers.

Pictures of Eviatar began appearing in those newspapers a few years later. The long, narrow face. The prominent nose. And you could tell, even in the black and white of the newspapers, that the eyes were blazing green. Under the pictures were captions like "Prince of the Bubble," "The Oracle from Maoz Aviv," "The Heavyweight of Real Estate." "What kind of sucker lets my brother manage his money,"

Assaf would say angrily. But he'd still read the article to the end. Including quotes from his brother. And then he'd mutter, always twice: "Unbelievable, unbelievable."

*

"I need a safe place to stay," Eviatar said.

"What happened?" I asked.

He was already inside the house, but still standing. The gym bag was in his right hand, hanging in the air. He scanned the living room like a water sprinkler: a slow look from side to side, and then a quick return to the starting point.

"I'm in trouble, Hani, I'm up to my—"

"Speak more quietly," I interrupted him. "You're waking the kids."

"Sorry, I didn't mean... That is, I forgot... I mean—"

"Coffee?" I came to his rescue.

"Wow," he said.

"What's wow?"

"It's been so long since anyone offered me coffee."

"Come in," I told him. "I feel uncomfortable with you standing there like that."

"But maybe you should first hear—"

"I'll be happy to hear what happened, but you can tell me sitting down too, can't you?"

(I'm making myself a bit cleverer than I actually was in real time, and I truly hope you'll be understanding about this bit of poetic license. But the fact that I wasn't feeling stressed for the first few minutes—that's pretty accurate. All sorts of reasons that could have made Eviatar knock on our door were running through my mind, but none of them came anywhere near the reason he was about to reveal to me.)

"I need a place to stay for a few days," he said after he sat down at the kitchen table. His voice shook slightly. "People are looking for me. But they won't look here. The last place they'll think to look is here, do you understand?"

"No. Start from the beginning."

"Sorry." And he looked like a scolded child. (In general, I think that the first emotion he arouses in me is my maternal instinct. Maybe it's always that way with men we want to sleep with later?)

"You know that I buy apartments as investments for people, right?"

"Yes. Of course."

"I have a reputation," he explained, even though I didn't ask for an explanation, as if he'd prepared the words in advance, "for being able to recognize market... trends. Clients come, deposit their money with me so I can buy an apartment for them and then sell it at a profit, and—"

"You're saying that they don't live in the apartment at all?"

"Usually not. Sometimes they rent it out. But most people who come to me only want to buy and sell. They know I'm an expert."

"Okay."

"As long as I focused here, in Israel, everything was fine. Everyone was satisfied. But then my competitors began to offer apartments abroad for investment, and my clients got itchy to invest in foreign markets too, so I went into a few countries in Eastern Europe and South America. And...I lost big time."

"You mean your clients lost."

"Yes. But the thing is that I couldn't...I mean, they couldn't know about it."

"What do you mean? Why?"

"Because if they all pulled out their money at the same time, I wouldn't have anything to return to them, you understand? You make most of the profits in this field by moving the money around."

"Okay, but what...what did you do? How did you hide the real situation from them?"

"People trusted me. I had a good name...They believed me. I fixed the numbers in the reports I sent them, and waited for apartment prices to go up again. Meanwhile, so I could have a cash flow, I made some small investments, the kind I hadn't touched before, all sorts of people with small savings of a few hundred thousand shekels who still wanted to join the party."

(Are you following, Netta? I picture you wrinkling your smooth forehead in your living room in Middletown. But maybe after you realized the direction this letter is going in, you went out to one of those beautiful parks on the grounds of that college of yours, and you're sitting alone with these pages on a bench that's still damp from the last rain, occasionally looking around to make sure no one is approaching.)

"Would you like something to eat?" I interrupted Eviatar. He was always thin, but now he really looked like a

Holocaust survivor. "There are vegetables for a salad. I can also warm up some schnitzels." (Funny, but every time I offer people culinary options, even if it's at home, I immediately stand straighter, a vestige from my Octopus Club period.)

"No, thanks. I...I don't really have an appetite."

"Okay. Continue. So what happened? I understand that you started to lose money and you gave your clients a false picture of the situation, but how—"

"Ever hear of loan sharks?"

"Of course." (It's true that I've been at home for five years already and I've gone a little crazy and I can't always distinguish between daydreams and pipedreams, but still, give me a little credit, bro-in-law.)

"You have to understand, I had no choice," he pleaded, sounding like he was standing in the dock, arguing his case. "I had to take loans so my clients would keep believing that everything was fine, and I couldn't go to the banks, so I said to myself, it's temporary. Just until the prices abroad start going up again. But—"

"They kept going down," I completed his sentence, sounding more teacherly than I'd intended.

"Yes. And now they're after me." He clasped his hands behind his head, something that Assaf also does, a gesture they'd both copied from their father. Originally, it was a masculine gesture, very self-assured, the elbows spread to the sides in satisfaction that bordered on arrogance. But with Eviatar, at that moment, the elbows tilted forward, neither in satisfaction nor in arrogance. They seemed to be trying to protect his head.

"Who exactly is after you?"

"Everyone. The thugs the loan sharks send. My clients. Even the police will be in the picture soon. I've been on the road for three days already. Sleeping in citrus groves. You see, I really want you to get the whole picture. So you know what it means to take me in. My quarrel with Assaf is no secret, so it's hard to believe that they'll show up here. But I want to be 100 percent open with you."

"How long will you have to stay here?" I asked. (At this point, you're probably pulling your hair out and screaming, are you a retard?!! But wait, Netta, in a minute, you'll be screaming even louder.)

"Forty-eight hours at the most. An army buddy is arranging for a yacht to take me to Cyprus the day after tomorrow, at night. From there, two flights he already booked will take me to Venezuela. Then some plastic surgery, and I start a new life."

I didn't say anything.

"I called Assaf," he said. "He hung up on me before I could explain. But I have nowhere else to go."

I didn't say anything.

"I'll pay back what I owe. To everyone. I just need a little time."

His lower lip trembled. His whole jaw trembled. I was afraid that in another minute, he'd fall to his knees.

"You can stay here until tomorrow morning at the latest," I said. "I won't throw you out now, but tomorrow morning, you'll have to find another solution."

*

Okay, Netta, now you can let me have it with both barrels.

And yes, I'm an idiot. Of course I'm an idiot. Always was. On school trips, I always lagged behind on the end of the line. In math class, I was behind in the material. I was the last one to lose my virginity (I know that your first time was terrible, but even terrible first times count), and the last one to speak at Nomi's funeral (the eulogy I wrote was too funny, and I didn't realize how inappropriate it was until the funeral was under way, so I had to edit it in my head before I could read it).

But I'm avoiding the subject—I know—and the question is, why? Why did I let him stay when the list of pros and cons that Nomi's mother told us to make every time we were undecided were all cons?

I know that 99 percent of women caught in a similar situation would have thrown Eviatar out, if only because of their simple concern for their children. So why was I in the remaining one percent? If anyone touches even the edge of the tip of Lyri's or Nimrod's fingernail, I attack them like a tiger. When Lyri was in the first grade, some kid named Itamar used to bully her at recess, so I went to the school at around ten, told the guard that Lyri forgot her sandwich so he'd let me in, went over to that Itamar and told him that if he bullied Lyri one more time, I'd make *shakshuka* out of him (that's the word that came out of my mouth, *shakshuka*).

So what happened that made me let Eviatar in?

The truth is that I don't know, Netta.

It's just that sometimes, all your insides scream the command at you: Do the wrong thing! Do the wrong thing!

Do you understand?

Not completely?

It's all right if you don't understand. I don't either. And neither do the owls.

And it's all right if you decide to stop reading this letter in the middle. After all, I'm turning you, against your will, into my partner in crime. Bonnie to my Clyde. As far as I'm concerned, you can throw all these pages into the blue trash can, the one for recycling paper, anytime you want. There's one not too far from you, if I remember your park correctly.

But I have to keep writing to you. I just can't choke it back anymore.

*

I told him he could take a shower. I said, "Listen, Eviatar— how can I tell you this gently—for the good of humanity, you should shower."

He smiled sadly. "But I have no change of clothes."

I brought him Assaf's tracksuit. (I left this out of the list of petty examples, but in addition to everything else, Assaf isn't at home on Saturday mornings because he's training for the triathlon, because he *needs* the adrenaline that races through his blood, understand? Without it, he *withers*.)

I put a sheet on the living room couch, along with a thin blanket. I took the pillow from Assaf's side of the bed and put it on the couch too.

He came out of the shower. Wearing Assaf's clothes, which were a couple of sizes too big for him, he looked like a scarecrow. A scarecrow dripping water. His legs were dark and thin. Almost reedy. If he had been a woman, they would have been sexy. But he was a man. And he had hair from his ankles to his knees. Ugly tangles of hair dampened with water.

"Thanks," he said, nodding toward the makeshift bed. "I haven't slept in seventy-two hours."

"That's understandable."

"I'm not sure I'll be able to fall asleep here either."

"So watch TV. But keep it on mute, okay?"

I handed him the remote. He hesitated for a minute.

"Take it," I encouraged him. "There's nothing like other people's troubles."

"You're an angel, Hani," he said, suddenly focusing his blazing eyes on me. "Assaf's lucky to have you."

"No, I'm no angel. And I'd like to remind you that tomorrow morning—"

"I'm gone. I haven't forgotten."

*

I didn't expect to fall asleep. After all, I had a criminal on the run in my living room. But I fell asleep quickly and slept fantastically. I dreamed about Monteverde. You were in the dream too, I think. We were in Andy and Sarah's house. Inside, in the house, it was raining cats and dogs and outside, in the yard, flames were dancing in a fireplace between the hammocks. It was weird, but in the dream, I treated it like another one of the many surprises we had on that trip.

When I woke up, Lyri and Nimrod were sitting in the kitchen eating cornflakes. They were both perfectly dressed, although I didn't remember leaving clothes for them on the railings of their beds, as I usually do. "Mommy, Uncle Eviatar's here," Lyri announced. Only then did I see him. He was standing with his back to me, making something. A few seconds later, he turned around, holding three closed plastic boxes, and said with a flourish, "The sandwiches are ready! Cottage cheese for Lyri. Tuna for…Andrea, right? And ham for you, Nimrod. Hani, I hope this is okay"—he turned toward me. "We wanted to let you sleep a little longer."

"But…how…what…?"

"This princess woke me up"—he pointed to Lyri—"and asked who I was. I explained to her that I'm her father's brother. She asked me how come she never heard about me. Then I explained to her that her father and I had a fight. A big fight. And that's why I never came to visit before now."

"I told him that Andrea and I fight all the time, Mommy," Lyri interrupted, "but we always make up in the end, and I told him that he should make up with Daddy!"

"So I promised her I'd do that the first chance I got," Eviatar went on. "And then she asked me if I could help them 'organize the morning.' She explained to me what I had to do."

"And I tied my shoelaces all by myself," Nimrod said.

"Yes, Mommy, he really did," Lyri said.

"That's wonderful, sweetie!" I really was thrilled. He's been trying for six months without any luck.

"Here are our schoolbags," Lyri said, and went over to Eviatar. "You have to put Andrea's lunch box in my bag. That's how she likes it."

I felt uncomfortable standing there in the shabby clothes I sleep in. Usually I'm too lazy to change in the morning, and drop the kids off in my baggy sweatpants and wrinkled T-shirt. Now I went to my room, undressed quickly, put on jeans and a black shirt, and looked in the mirror. Then I changed from the black shirt to a red one that's been hanging in my closet for a long time. And I put on heels. Not high ones. And went into the living room.

"Shall we go?" I asked so that no one would have to react to the way I looked (Lyri could easily say something like, "Mommy, you look so dressed up today!").

"You don't have to drive us, Eli's mother is coming to take us at a quarter to eight," she announced.

"Lyri said that instead of waking you, we should call her," Eviatar completed the picture. "I understand that you help each other with the driving sometimes."

"Yes," I admitted. "Our kids go to the same schools."

Eli's mommy (it's embarrassing, but I never remember her name. On my cell phone list of contacts, she appears as Elimom, and in every conversation we have, I find ways to avoid saying her name) called to say she'd already left the house. I zipped up the schoolbags and we were about to go out to the parking area when Eviatar said, "Wait, where's that hug for your uncle?" And my kids walked over to him and kissed him, each one on a different cheek (at that time, I still didn't see that Nimord resembled him slightly, that only happened later), and he hugged them. Like an experienced uncle. "Andrea wants to give you a hug too," Lyri said. And Eviatar played the game: spread his arms as if he were adding another child to the cluster and said, "Have a great day, Andrea."

When I came back from the parking area and went into the house, he was standing in the doorway, gym bag in hand, ready to move.

"Where will you go now?" I asked.

"I don't know."

How many really desperate people do we get to meet, Netta? People camouflage their desperation so well that we don't sense it at all. But Eviatar's desperation was totally exposed. It was in his eyebrows, in his stooped shoulders, in his spread fingers as they tapped his thigh in a slow, steady rhythm.

"So at least have some breakfast before you go," I said.

He put his gym bag on the floor.

*

Breakfast went on until noon. Surprisingly, we spoke mainly about me. Every time I tried to shift the conversation to his situation, he said, "Forget it, the less you know, the less you'll be involved." I leaned back in my chair, occasionally sticking my fork into a stray bit of salad left on my plate. He leaned forward, resting his face in his hands, one hand on each cheek. Gray stubble filled the spaces between his fingers. This surprised me — the younger brother isn't supposed to be the first to turn gray.

He asked me questions the whole time. Profound questions. No one had been that interested in me for a long time, Netta. So openly. First Nomi died, then you went away, and there was no one left for me to be that way with. You know, sometimes I spend entire mornings having conversations in my head with the both of you, playing Nomi's part, playing your part, I can get so into it that I forget myself completely. Not long ago I heard Paul Auster explain in an interview how the characters in his books talk to him while he's writing, argue with him, rebel against him. And it calmed me down to know that I wasn't the only hallucinator.

He (Eviatar, not Paul) asked, "So what do you actually do in the morning after they go? Being alone in the house doesn't drive you up the wall?"

And he asked, "How's your mother?"

And he asked, "That business with Lyri and . . . Andrea? Isn't she a little too old for an imaginary friend?"

There were many more questions, so spot-on that they hurt. And he didn't take his eyes off me when I spoke. Didn't look at his cell phone as Assaf does. Didn't keep his head in the same position, making you feel he's thinking about something else. It was so weird, that with that whole mess closing in on him he could still take an interest in me. It's like a prisoner being led to the electric chair taking an interest in tomorrow's weather. And suddenly—I was this close to telling him about the owl—it was 12:30, and I panicked because I still hadn't made lunch and I had to leave to pick up the kids in another minute, and he said, "I can heat up schnitzels too, and I'll make mashed potatoes. Do they like mashed potatoes?"

"Yes," I said. And I still hadn't gotten up from my chair. I should have gotten up from my chair already. But I wanted to enjoy the curious look he was giving me just a little bit longer. It had been a very long time since anyone had such an intense desire to know me.

"Fruit salad for dessert?" he asked.

I stood up and said, "Yes. I'll stop at the store and buy some oranges. You can't have fruit salad without oranges. It comes out too dry."

"Right you are," he said.

And that's how it happened that he stayed.

*

Are you still on the bench in Middletown? Or have you already gotten up and gone to teach your class, postponing reading the rest of this letter until later?

You know, of everything we saw on our visit to you, that's what made the strongest impression on me.

Watching you teach your class, I mean. I remember the classroom with the framed posters of Israeli films, new and old (right in front of me was *Saint Clara*). I remember specific students (the girl with the plunging neckline on the right who was trying too hard, Jonathan Safran Foer's double on the left), and I remember you. I was so proud of you, Netta, that I forgot to be jealous. It wasn't because of the brilliant lecture (and it really was brilliant. I'd seen all the movies you gave examples from, but I never thought of them in terms of gender). It was because of your pedagogical ethics.

And I shall explain. (Remember Rivka Guber, the grade coordinator, and her "I shall explain"?)

Throughout the lesson, it was obvious that you were

there not to talk, like most lecturers, but also to listen. That you really were interested in your students' points of view. And the nicest thing was seeing those Americans slowly emerge from their adolescent acne, from their pretended indifference, and begin to say what was in their minds, or actually in their hearts—at that age, the connection between the two is so obvious that even a passing visitor like me can see it, and you saw it, I'm sure of that, but you didn't try to call attention to the connection, as I'm sure I would have done, but integrated it into what they said with such elegance (elegance, yes! That's the word I've been looking for this entire paragraph) that there were moments when it seemed like a dance class. A dance of thoughts—and you the choreographer. And the way you played "The Snake's Shed Skin" from the soundtrack of the movie *Shuroo*, and explained the lyrics. And how, after class, you spoke patiently with everyone who went up to you. Including the annoying girl (there has to be one in every class) who wanted you to explain the lyrics again.

All your fantastic qualities were on display at that lesson. Charisma, intelligence, perceptiveness, subtle humor, and a sense of timing.

And along with them, an inner serenity. The serenity of someone who has found her place in the world.

I suddenly realize how transparent my maneuver is: to soften you with compliments so that it'll be harder for you to criticize me when you read the rest of this letter.

But my compliments are as real as they are manipulative, Netta. Because at the end of that lesson, I thought that if you weren't my friend, I'd be dying for you to be.

*

After lunch, he sat with Lyri and helped her with her homework. I didn't ask him to. He volunteered. She said, "Andrea needs help in arithmetic, Mommy." I didn't say anything, but he picked up on the twitch of my cheek when I heard the word "arithmetic" and said, "I'll help you, Lyri." They went to her room. I didn't hear what they were talking about. I only heard his tone. And I could understand why clients agreed to put their savings in his hands. (I know, Netta, I know that those people are penniless now, but just for the moment, can we put aside the moral judgment of what he did? We'll get back to it later. I promise.) Then he "practiced" basketball with Nirmod: took a pail from the laundry room, pulled a balding tennis ball out from under Nimrod's bed, where it had rolled, and made up an entire story in which Nimrod is the star whose perfect shots help his team of good guys beat the team of bad guys. They spent an hour and a half like that, which allowed me to sign up for all the summer camps in one fell swoop. Then he gave him a bath. You should know that bathing Nimrod is usually a nightmare. He screams every time I shampoo his hair. Before the soap even gets close to his eyes. He hates getting into the tub, then hates getting out of it. And in the middle, he always splashes me, making the grubby clothes I'm wearing even grubbier. That's why I was so surprised when the main thing I heard coming from the bathroom was silence. And the sounds of light splashing.

(Only later, before he went to sleep, did Nimrod tell me that Uncle Eviatar built him a paper boat and they sailed it together to "Sipress.")

When they came out of the bathroom, Eviatar was holding Nimrod, wrapped in a towel and dripping water, in his arms. "So where are his pajamas," he asked, and that's when I first noticed how much they look alike. The sharp nose, the slightly protruding ears, the eyes, the color of their eyes, the expression on their surface, the expression in their depths...

Do you get it? Lyri looks exactly like my mother. And Nimrod doesn't look like Assaf either. When I tried to explain to myself why he seems so cut off from them, this thought crossed my mind: maybe if one of them looked like him, it would be different. And now a new thought joined that one: maybe he too noticed that Nimrod looks like Eviatar. And that's what put him off.

I was so lost in thought that I didn't notice they were still standing in front of me, puddles forming at their feet.

"His pajamas are under his pillow," I said.

He told them a bedtime story.

That is, first he asked them what book they wanted him to read them, and they began arguing, as usual, but then, before the argument could escalate into insults and tears, he said, "How about if I make up a story for you?" The offer shocked them so much that it stopped the argument, making them silent with expectation.

I was silent too. I pressed my shoulders against the wall next to the bedroom and listened.

"A fire once broke out in a forest," he began.

"Andrea doesn't like scary stories," Lyri said.

"Tell her not to worry," Eviatar said. "It has a happy end."

"You promise?"

"I promise."

"Then okay."

"All the animals in the forest crossed the river that ran through the middle of the forest so that the water in the river would protect them from the fire. Only the scorpion stayed on the riverbank, scratched its head with its claw, like this, and didn't go into the river. Do you have any idea...why he didn't want to go in?"

"Because he's allergic to water," said Nimrod (who's allergic to chocolate, yogurt, bee stings, and spring).

"Exactly," Eviatar said. "Scorpions live on land. Their bodies aren't built for water. But this scorpion was very lucky. Because who happened to pass by at that very moment? The turtle. Hi, turtle, the scorpion said, is there any way you would agree to carry me on your back to the other side of the river? No, there is no way, said the turtle. You're a scorpion. You'll sting me. Why in the world would I sting you, said the scorpion. If I sting you, we'll both drown. But you're a scorpion to the core, you'll have to sting me in the end, said the turtle. I promise I won't sting you, turtle, said the scorpion. Swear it, said the turtle."

"He should swear to God," Nimrod said (his nursery school teacher's helper is religious).

"I swear I won't sting you, the scorpion said. And the turtle let him climb onto his back. The fire burning the trees in the forest was racing toward them, so they hurried—as much as a turtle can hurry—into the water. The turtle swam toward the other side, and the scorpion lay on his back the whole time so that the water wouldn't touch his claws, God forbid."

"This is a scary story," Lyri said. "You promised Andrea that it wouldn't be a scary story."

"So I'll hold your hands, okay?"

"Okay."

"When they were more or less in the middle," Eviatar continued in a slightly brighter voice, "the scorpion suddenly felt a kind of tickle through his whole body. He knew that tickle. It was the tickle that always made him sting. Yes, all of a sudden, he really felt like stinging the turtle. No, what he felt was that he *had* to sting the turtle. Otherwise, he wouldn't be a scorpion."

(I almost walked into the room at that point. It annoyed me that he was about to break his promise to Lyri, because the end was horrible, and Lyri couldn't always distinguish between stories and reality. Later, she might imagine that there was a scorpion creeping around in her room.)

"But then"—Eviatar raised his voice, for me, as if he knew I was waiting tensely on the other side of the wall—"without their noticing it, a huge, kindhearted crocodile approached them..."

"How could they not notice it," Nimrod objected, "if it was so huge!"

"An ex-cell-ent ques-tion"—Eviatar stretched out the words so he would have time to think of a good enough answer to the boy's objection. "So it's like this...First of all...despite their huge size, crocodiles can be very hush-hush when they move. Besides...the turtle and the scorpion were so involved in being themselves, in acting the way they were supposed to act, that it never occurred to them that a huge, kindhearted crocodile might come along and act like a kindhearted crocodile is supposed to act. And that's exactly what happened. He approached them underwater...very hush-hush, of course, then opened his huge mouth and...and trapped both of them inside."

"God help us," Nimrod said.

"All at once," Eviatar continued, "they found themselves in its mouth. And the inside of a crocodile's mouth is totally dark. Not a single ray of light can penetrate it. So what does a scorpion do when it's in such a dark place?"

Lyri and Nimrod didn't answer.

"What do you do when Mommy turns off the light and says good night?"

"We say mean things to each other."

"And then?"

"We fall asleep," Lyri said.

"Exactly," Eviatar said. "The scorpion fell asleep and snored through its tail on the turtle's back and forgot to sting it."

"But then the crocodile ate both of them, right?" Nimrod said, still rebelling.

"That's just it. It didn't. The kindhearted crocodile had no intention of eating them. He didn't particularly like the way they tasted. With the one eye that he always kept out of the water, he'd seen what was about to happen. He'd seen that the scorpion was going to sting the turtle and drown them both, and he figured that the only way to save them from themselves would be to approach from the side and...do something surprising. And that's why, right after he took them into his mouth, he climbed onto the opposite riverbank and spit them out. As they rolled around on the ground, they separated. The turtle walked slowly in one direction and the scorpion, who woke up slowly, walked quickly in the other direction, and the three of them—the turtle, the scorpion, and the crocodile—were saved from the fire, which didn't cross the river because fire, naturally, has to be fire, and it can't cross water. A happy end."

"A very happy end. Another story!" Lyri said.

"It's late," Eviatar said.

"So just say 'hush-hush' one more time," Nimrod begged. "Please?"

"Hu-u-ush-hu-u-ush," Eviatar said with such hush-hushiness that it wasn't only Nimrod and Lyri who laughed. I chuckled quietly on the other side of the wall.

"Okay, sweetie pies," he said, "I'm turning off the light now and you're going to do what you do when it's dark..."

"Say mean things to each other! Then go to sleep!" Nimrod cried, sounding very wide awake.

"Can you ask Mommy to come and wish us salty dreams?" Lyri asked (before they go to sleep, I always say: Sweet dreams, salty dreams, peppery dreams, punctuating each spice with a kiss).

"Sure," Eviatar said. "I'll call her."

As I walked into the room and he walked out of it, our shoulders brushed against each other. That sounds hot, but the truth is that he's so skinny that his prominent shoulder bone stabbed me.

The kids, on the other hand, were as soft as usual. Those are my favorite moments of the day, you know? I lie down next to each one of them. First I cuddle up to Nimrod under the covers, then I do it with Lyri. We hug, kiss, talk. Nimrod loves me to rub his back between his shoulders. Lyri loves me to stroke her hair. Both of them love it when I rub their necks with the tip of my nose.

If I'm permitted a moment of satisfaction, I think that one of the things I'm most proud of as a mom is that I've taught my children that the first way to show love is with physical contact. I see the way they say goodbye to other children. They're always the ones who initiate the hug. Sometimes it's funny because the other children don't always understand where it's coming from and just stand there with their arms hanging in the air—but still, the sight always fills my heart with joy. Why? Because at least in that, I've succeeded in breaking the chain: my grandmother didn't hug my mother, so my mother didn't hug me. But I hug Lyri. So she'll hug her daughter too.

Right before Lyri fell asleep she asked whether Andrea could stay over at our place. "She's afraid to go home in the dark," Lyri explained, "because there are lots of scorpions in the street now."

"No problem," I said.

"Will you tell her mom?" she asked. Responsible, as usual. Like an oldest child, like me.

"Yes," I promised.

Nimrod didn't say anything, even though I could tell from his breathing that he was totally awake. That's really something. He can snatch things out of his older sister's hands, scribble in her notebook with a marker, pull her hair, and repeat every sentence she says just to drive her crazy.

But he never teases her about Andrea. Only sometimes, when she's not around, he comes over to me and asks quietly, "Andrea isn't real, right? She's in Lyri's imagination, right?"

*

The doorbell rang not more than half an hour after the kids fell asleep, Eviatar was scraping the dishes and putting them in the dishwasher. Without thinking about it, I got up to open the door. But he hurried over and stood between me and the door, signaling me with his finger on his lips not to speak, and went to look through the peephole. Then he took a piece of paper and wrote, "It's them. Tell them that you're looking for the key." I did. I made searching noises. Meanwhile, he opened the sliding doors and went out to the balcony. I gestured for him to wait a minute, and wrote on the paper, "The neighbors across the hall are out of the country. Hop over the railing to their balcony and hide in the children's playhouse."

I opened the door, deliberately sliding the chain off its runner to show the confidence of someone with nothing to hide, smiled, and said, "Good evening. And who might you be, gentlemen?" (I was very good, really.) The loan shark thugs were short, but something about their haircut was violent. One of them was wearing a tight white T-shirt and had a wide chin. The other one was wearing a tight black T-shirt and had a pointy chin.

"We're looking for Eviatar Gat," the one with the pointy chin said.

"There must be some mistake," I said. "This is Assaf Gat's house."

"We know, ma'am," he said. And they began walking around the house, opening doors.

"Excuse me, what do you think you're doing," I objected angrily. I followed them. Tried to block their way. "There are children here! You can't just come in like this—"

They ignored me (only later did I understand how scary that was) and kept looking for Eviatar. Under the armchairs. In the crawl space above the ceiling. They opened kitchen cabinets, searched through the shirts in the closet, overturned the laundry basket. I protested, threatened to call the police, even took a picture of them with my cell phone. But they couldn't have cared less.

Nimrod and Lyri slept through the visit. Even when the men turned on the light in their room. Even when they opened their closet. (In that respect, thank heaven, the kids are like Assaf: nothing wakes them up.) I thought that if one of those thugs dared to touch my children, I'd put what I learned in that self-defense class to use, and was already tensing one foot for a kick to the balls of the one in the white shirt, but they finished searching the kids' room quickly. As if they didn't feel comfortable about being there either.

Finally, they opened the sliding doors and went out onto the balcony. Whenever anyone describes moments like that, they say, "I held my breath." I didn't hold my breath, but my thumb climbed onto my index finger and started tapping it, which always happens when I'm stressed.

They stayed on the balcony for a long time, then came back into the living room. The one with the white shirt said, "Sorry for the mess" (that's what he said, I swear). "We got some bad information." The one with the black shirt turned his pointy chin toward me and said, "A word of advice, ma'am. If Eviatar Gat happens to show up here, don't let him in. He'll just cause you trouble. You have kids, so think of them."

"Clean up the mess you made," I said.

"What?" They looked at me, shocked.

"You turned my house upside down. Now clean up the mess you made," I persisted.

They didn't. And I didn't really say that. But wouldn't it have been great if I had? As I write, I constantly feel the temptation to describe what might have happened instead of what really happened. I'll restrain myself for the time being, but consider yourself warned. I don't know how long I can keep the impulse under control.

*

This is what we agreed on in the hushed, inter-balcony discussion I had with Eviatar right after the thugs hopped into their car (the owl sat on a nearby branch, looking pleasant and saying nothing, but clearly disapproving): He absolutely could not stay with us any longer. It was too complicated. I'd unlock our neighbor's apartment with the key they left us before they went away and he could hide out there until the yacht that was supposed to take him to Cyprus was ready. Unless one of the chins came wandering around our building again. In that case, he'd have to leave.

"Of course," he said.

"I'm warning you ahead of time," I said, "the neighbors' apartment is a bit weird."

"Okay. I'm not exactly in a position to be choosy," he said. (I'm asking you, as a film expert: do you think there really is something sexy about people who keep their sense of humor even under pressure, or do we think that only because all the action-movie machos behave that way?)

The upstairs neighbor, a retired judge, opened her shutters. Not completely, but she clearly moved them. That's all I need now, I thought in horror—for a representative of the judicial system (retired, but she must still have connections) to see what's happening here right under her nose. I signaled Eviatar to wait and hurried to open our neighbor's door.

*

Our next-door neighbors' apartment is full of clocks.

When I say full, I mean exploding with them. They have clocks in the living room, in all the bedrooms, in the hallways too. In fact, there isn't a single space in their apartment that doesn't have a few ticking clocks. Hanging one next to the other. With only a very small space between them.

It started with the father's private collection. The mother—she talks about it as if it's furniture they buy in Ikea, as if it's totally normal—told me that he brought them with him to their first apartment, and since then, he's been adding a few more to the collection every year.

I don't know if I'm getting across to you just how crazy it is. They don't have even a single picture on the walls.

Just clock after clock after clock. Round clocks and ellipti-cal clocks, clocks with Roman numerals and clocks without numbers, cuckoo clocks and grandfather clocks, clocks that show the hour here and clocks that show the hour there. And they all tick constantly in every corner of the house, every second. Tick tick tock. They must be used to it, but every time I go in there, I get tics in my eyelids.

There are four kids in that family. The oldest is an eighteen-year-old girl. The youngest is a six-year-old boy.

I wonder what it's like to grow up with such a clear knowledge that time is running out.

And what makes me laugh is that they're a quiet family. Solid. Can you picture it? Apart from that clock fetish—they're terribly respectable. A clichéd cliché.

They always take their annual vacation in the same place too. Crete. And always for exactly ten days. They leave me their key so I can go in and air out the place for them every other day. Clocks need to breathe, the father explained to me once (I swear, that's what he said).

Usually, when I go in to air out their place, I walk around a little to see the new clocks that have been added in the inner rooms that visitors don't usually enter. Some-times, you can connect the clocks to various stages of life: in the teenage son's room there was a new clock that had a woman's legs as hands. And sometimes the connec-tion is extremely obscure: what does it mean that in the eighteen-year-old daughter's room, the insides of all the clocks are exposed?

In any case, I had no time for clocks then. I didn't even turn on the light.

I said to Eviatar, "Don't open the door for anyone. Under any circumstances. I'll bring you some lunch tomorrow, and I'll knock three times, pause, and then two more times."

"Thanks. I'm sorry about all this..."

His bottom lip trembled again.

"Be sorry at lunchtime tomorrow," I interrupted him.

*

That night, I dreamed that the two of us, you and I, were walking along the main street of Granada. The shop owners on the street devoured us with their eyes as we passed by. I thought they were looking at me more than at you, and I liked that, but then Rami Leider, who was my commander in the army, suddenly appeared and said that we had to leave that city as quickly as possible because civil war was going to break out the next day. I tried to argue with him, to tell him that a bullet hadn't been fired there in years, but he was very assertive and sure about his sources, and he took us to the central bus station. Except that as the bus was leaving the city, I remembered that I'd forgotten my lucky sweater at the hostel, the checked sweater I bought in the thieves' market. I wanted it very badly, so I stood up to get off the bus, but then your face, Netta, suddenly turned as white as the owl's and you pushed me firmly back into my seat and said that it was too late to go back and I had nothing to worry about, Andrea would get the sweater for me.

*

At 7:30 in the morning, I was already knocking on the neighbors' door. I knew it was wrong. I knew I was putting myself in danger. But the kids wanted, demanded to see Uncle Eviatar, each in his own way: Lyri went back to bed, surrounded herself with a fortress of pillows, burrowed under the covers, and said in a firm, quiet voice that she and Andrea were not getting out of bed until Uncle Eviatar came back. Nimrod stood in the middle of the living room and screamed, "Uncle Eviatan! Uncle Eviatan!" Lyri corrected him from her room: "It's Eviatar, stupid." And Nimrod shot back: "*You're* stupid!"

I stood between them with their clothes hanging on me as if I were a hanger, and knew exactly what I should do. I do it ten times a week: I flexed the boundary-setting muscle that every parent has, slightly below the diaphragm, and said in a no-nonsense tone, "Get up. Right now. There is no Uncle Eviatar now. We're late for school. If you don't get up—"

But for the first time in seven years, it didn't work. I tried to flex the muscle. But it just didn't respond (how strange it is when you command your body-soul to do something and it simply refuses to follow orders).

I went to the neighbors' apartment across the hall and knocked three times, paused, then twice more. Eviatar opened the door, confusion in his eyes, as if they still hadn't decided what their expression for today would be, and said, "Good morning."

"Good morning. I…need your help."

Within fifteen minutes they were dressed, combed, and toothbrushed. Waiting in their lunch boxes was the sandwich each one had asked for. On the way Evi-Poppins also managed to make a "tree" for Nimrod: he stood in the middle of the living room, bent his knees, stretched his arms into branches, and invited Nimrod to climb to the top. And he played the bead game with Lyri and Andrea (the first to use up all their beads lost). But it wasn't what he did with them, but how he did it. His complete and utter involvement. As if there were no loan shark thugs after him. You know what? That isn't even it (I'm saying these things to myself as I write, sorry if it comes out a little convoluted). It's that he understood (how? so quickly?) the kids' main problem: moving from place to place. From the living room to the bathroom. From the bathroom to the kitchen. From the kitchen to the front door. At every one of those points, they always get stuck. Can't seem to move. But Eviatar found ways to get them from place to place without their even noticing that movement had occurred. And I watched all that from the sidelines and felt (not necessarily in this order): that I was superfluous; that I could let go, finally let go a little after all those years; that I was so used to being tense, I couldn't completely relax; that something in me was start-ing to bubble as I watched Eviatar, a gentle bubbling, the kind that happens before the water actually boils, no big bubbles yet, but you can tell there will be; and that the owl was not at all pleased about it and I knew I'd hear from it that night.

Before I opened the door to leave the house, he bent down to Lyri and said, "Remember what we agreed!" (They already have agreements?)

Lyri nodded. Hesitantly.

"If Mica says she doesn't want to play with you at recess," Eviatar persisted, "what will you tell her?"

"That's your loss."

"And what does that mean?"

"That I'm a terrific girl and anyone who plays with me can only profit from it."

"And what does 'profit from it' mean?"

"That she'll have fun."

"Good. And you"—he turned to Nimrod—"give me a high five. Hard. Harder. The hardest. Now a hug. Tight. Tighter. The tightest."

"Mommy, can Uncle Eviatar drive to school with us?... Please, please," Lyri pleaded.

"No, Princess," he said before I could stammer out an answer. "I can't."

I was sure she'd protest. That she'd stamp her hands (that girl stamps with her hands: spreads them to the sides, then slaps them angrily against her waist), but something in his tone made her understand that it wouldn't help. So she just hugged him again. A longer hug. And then another long hug from Andrea. Finally she straightened up and said, "Uncle Eviatar, you're really nice!"

*

On the way back from the parking lot, I grabbed the newspaper from the mailbox. Eviatar's face was in the corner of the front page, younger than in reality. A brief headline referred readers to the financial supplement: "Real Estate Guru Vanishes. Clients and Police in Pursuit." I started reading standing up. Then I had the vague feeling that someone was watching me, so I went into the house with the paper.

There wasn't any fact in the article that he hadn't told me.

The thing was that the article was written from a different point of view (you wanted moral judgment? So here it comes): the point of view of his clients.

I think we (girls who grew up in Jerusalem and went to the Hebrew University High School) were brought up to think of money and emotion as contradictory terms. There are things we do for money and there are things we do because our emotions tell us to do them. Wrong. Money is emotion. It's anxiety. It's self-worth. It's jealousy. When someone entrusts you with his money, he entrusts you with all the hard work that has brought him that money, all the small, painful, humiliating compromises he's made along the way. And somehow, it makes him no less vulnerable than he would be if, let's say, he was in love with you.

There was a retired couple from Hadera, for example, who transferred all their savings to Eviatar, and now they didn't know how they'd pay their bills at the beginning of the next month. There was a picture of them sitting at a Formica kitchen table, holding hands. But their hand-holding didn't look romantic. It looked as if they were clutching each other tightly so they wouldn't drown.

And there was a couple with three kids from Kiryat Ono who said they would have to take all three kids out of nursery school and preschool at the beginning of next week, and they had no idea how to explain it to them. What do you say to a child suddenly torn away from all his friends? Your parents are fools and you're paying the price?

And there was the owner of a transportation company who bought two new minibuses with the money he thought Eviatar was holding for him, and now he'd have to fire employees—who also had mouths to feed—in order to cut expenses.

They all had the same story, with minor differences: recommendations from friends leading to personal meetings with Eviatar, after which he found an appropriate property for them. Clear, well-organized reports (unlike bank reports) sent to their mailboxes every three months. Excellent returns. On paper. And then, the last few weeks, suspicious signs: a new secretary, messages left with her that were never delivered, reports arriving two days late.

And we still didn't understand that we were being led down the garden path, the retirees said in heartbreaking bewilderment. He made such a nice impression on us.

Ten years of work down the drain, the young couple said.

The police investigator asked for the public's assistance in the search for Eviatar, adding that this was one of the most serious fraud cases he had handled over the last few years.

Horrifying, right? If this were an American movie, I'd take the paper, march straight into the neighbor's apartment, throw it in his face in a fury, force him to admit that he'd committed all the seven sins together, turn my back on him even after he got down on his knees, and say: Some things are unforgivable. Or: I want no contact with an unscrupulous bastard like you.

Instead, I went to the apartment to warn him that the police were after him too.

*

But before that, Assaf called.

Overseas calls always have a silent delay before anyone speaks, and this time it seemed especially long.

"Did you see the newspapers?" he asked.

"Yes," I said.

"You know he called me the day before yesterday, that schmuck? Said he was in trouble. Needed money. I hung up on him. Can you believe it? He wanted to drag me into it too! Just imagine if I'd agreed to help him. The police would be knocking on your door now."

"Sounds like he's in very big trouble."

"You know what? He made his bed."

"Yes."

"It's just like him"—Assaf was boiling over—"to sell people illusions. And run away when they shatter."

"The whole country's after him now," I said.

"I hope they catch him. And put him in prison for years and years. It'll teach him a lesson...You know what? It won't teach him a lesson. He's a lost cause."

"There's no such thing as a lost cause," I said.

"Are you defending him?"

"No"—I was alarmed—"of course not. He ruined his clients' lives."

"Exactly. My mother called a few minutes ago. She wants to bury herself. And if I know her, she won't go out of the house for weeks. It was always like that. He'd get in trouble and embarrass us, and I had to go food shopping for her so she wouldn't have to see the neighbors. You know what it's like to be a ten-year-old kid getting all those looks in the grocery store, convinced that it's *his* fault, that something's wrong with *him*?"

"Is that why you're like that with each other?"

"It's one of the reasons."

"You never told me about that business with the grocery store..."

"And he has the nerve to call me. Unbelievable."

"People do all kinds of things when they're in trouble."

"You're defending him again?"

"I'm not—"

"Forget it, I'm just upset and I'm taking it out on you. I've had to answer questions here all morning. As if I'm his spokesman. People know I'm his brother. They read the same sites I do."

"Don't worry. It's just a storm that will pass."

"Yes, you're right."

"It's a good thing you're out of the country while this is happening. Here, you'd have a much harder time responding."

"There's something to that. You're really smart, babe. I miss you."

"When are you coming home?"

"Day after tomorrow, in the morning."

"Weren't you supposed to come back tomorrow?"

"Yes, but they set up an urgent new meeting, something that could really help us make it big time."

"See you day after tomorrow."

*

And now, a short break for another lecture in our "Theory of Morality" course (imagine the Army Radio station, University on the Air, a young doctoral student with a nasal voice that's shaking slightly because it's her first time speaking on the radio):

"For the purposes of our discussion, we must distinguish between universal morality, that is, man's behavior toward all those with whom he comes into social or professional contact, and particular morality, that is, man's behavior toward the people close to him, family members and associates. We would expect to find coherence between both types of morality, but in practice, we find that frequently they are at odds with one another and we are forced to decide: Which of these moralities is more important to us? Which do we consider more valuable?"

*

Damn! I can't believe how much effort I'm putting into convincing you that I'm fine, Netta, that I haven't changed. That despite everything I've said here (and will say later on), I'm still the same Hani you know.

I can't believe how hard I'm trying to be cool. I just read the letter from the beginning. How many parentheses I've used. And how many calculated maneuvers I've made just to hide the fact that I'm not cool anymore.

I've been defeated. By the pregnancies. By the lack of sleep. By the fear that the resemblance between Lyri and my mother isn't just external. By the long days I don't speak to another adult, except for my morning conversation with Assaf, who always tries to make me laugh but just makes me feel more lost because there he is, on the move, while I'm rotting away at home. I know that people don't usually admit it, but being with children for so many hours dries you up. There might be mothers who are thrilled to build miniatures with their kids. Maybe you build miniatures too. I don't. I can't stand miniatures. I can't look at those creative materials anymore. During Lyri's first two years, there was something exciting about putting together a puzzle with her. But not later on. There are some happy moments, but for eight years already, I've been trapped—yes, that's the word—trapped inside my desire to succeed at the job my mother failed at, and meanwhile, the dust of time is covering me, Netta. And I'm letting it cover me. I know it's a trite metaphor, but I'm trite too. And I don't have the strength to fake the happiness that is no longer inside me.

*

I could have said all of this more simply: A guy with green eyes showed up. And something in the way he acted with my kids made me feel desire again.

Yes, desire.

Some of my feelings for Assaf died because of the way he is with the kids. It's as if fatherhood and sexual attraction occupy the same place in my mind. Or that they occupy different places that are connected by a switch: when one is turned on, it causes the other to turn on too. Maybe Freud was right, and all sexual attraction is a variation on that first desire of a boy for his mother or a girl for her father. Or maybe the fact that Assaf doesn't know about the owls, that he's just too normal for me to be able to tell him something like that, has created a barrier between us. In any case, there's no arguing with the facts: my body-soul keeps playing the same chord of reticence when I'm in bed with Assaf. (And it isn't that I don't come sometimes. He knows my body. But even my orgasms are a little reticent, know what I mean?)

*

If he were given the opportunity to respond to this letter, he would say:

1. *Reticent orgasms? What the fuck?*
2. *I try to get out of being a father? That from the woman who keeps her kids close and never lets them go. She always thought there was something wrong about the way I did things: the way I held their hands, the way I buckled them into their booster seats, the way I fed them. She was disappointed in me from the very beginning. And then she shaped reality to justify her disappointment. So Eviatar gave Nimrod a bath, big deal. I bathed Nimrod. I enjoyed bathing Nimrod. Very much. Until she walked in once and saw that the water level in the tub was higher than she liked—and then she screamed to high heaven: I can't be trusted, I'm drowning the child, what kind of father am I. And that was it. The last time I gave Nimrod a bath.*

3. *She doesn't let me get close to Lyri either. Not really. It's in the small things. Like when I text Lyri from abroad and she doesn't show Lyri my message, then says that she simply forgot. Or when she doesn't let her go to sleep a little later so I can see her when I come home from work. She thinks I'm damaging her because I don't respect her poetic soul. Excuse me, but imaginary friends at her age is not a poetic soul, it's a problem.*

4. *If Hani would just give me a chance, I could be a great father. When she has no choice and has to leave me alone with them for a few hours, we get along beautifully. Suddenly, Nimrod—who, by the way, doesn't look anything like Eviatar—hugs me. Snuggles up to me. And Lyri stops talking to Andrea because she knows that I, unlike her mother, do not go along with that craziness. But we almost never have time alone, the kids and I. Hani doesn't trust me. She says that being away from them for more than a few hours stresses her out, makes her feel she's abandoned them. Bullshit. She just wants to guarantee that the kids will be on her side. Wants them to call her, not me, when they're upset. Wants me to fail at one thing, at least. Yes, that's my real sin: that I'm doing great at work. That's what's really eating her. Not my trips. Not my fatherhood. It's my success that's eating her. She's the one who went to the Hebrew University High School. She's the one who was supposed to make a higher salary and take business trips abroad. And all of a sudden, this yokel from Nahariya comes along and passes her on a bend in the street. So he should at least be a terrible father. Then she can feel superior to him about something.*

5. *That mild snobbery of hers — there was something sexy about it when we met in college. Challenging. And the confusion that the snobbery concealed, the many times she changed her major, the endless Winona Ryder searching for the special thing she was supposed to do, the thing that would finally make her really, really happy — there was something sexy about that too. When we were twenty.*

6. *I'm still crazy about her. That's the truth. But I have to admit that being with someone who always wants to be somewhere else, who is never satisfied, is exhausting.*

7. *And to be totally honest, the only thing I still enjoy on my trips is a few days' rest from the feeling that I disappoint her. A few days of breathing air with no bitterness in it.*

*

After Assaf's call, I did what I've been doing every morning for the last four years: pick at my professional wounds. I read through all the newspaper ads to see if any of the logos I designed are still there, and which have been changed because the client decided to rebrand himself. It seems as if, during these past eight years, all the companies in the country have decided to rebrand themselves (instead of really changing itself, a company always prefers to change its appearance). In fact, of all my logos, of my entire "design legacy" (hah!), only my dairy logo is left. And on that day, it beckoned to me from the bottom of the ad. But instead of making me feel proud, it looked old-fashioned. Embarrassingly old-fashioned.

So I put down the paper and went to my clothes closet.

It wouldn't be accurate to say that I knew I was dressing to seduce Eviatar.

But neither would it be accurate to say I didn't notice that I was dressing seductively.

So maybe I'll just describe what I decided to wear: a gray skirt that fit tightly around my hips (I think I wore it when we went out to a restaurant in Middletown); a clingy, yellow, button-down blouse you've never seen tucked into it; matching yellow-orange shoes with relatively low heels. Makeup. Nothing dramatic, eyeliner and a touch of blush. And the chain with the octagonal pendant. Which might be the most telling accessory in this entire description, because I hadn't worn it since Lyri was born.

I knocked on the door with a box of warmed-up schnitzels in one hand and a newspaper in the other.

There was no answer. A bitter drop of hurt slid down my throat: the bastard, he left without even saying goodbye.

But a few seconds later, the door opened.

"I fell asleep," he apologized.

"It's about time!" I smiled.

"Yes," he said, smiling back. A haunted smile.

I closed the door behind me. There were more clocks on the wall than I remembered, more crowded together than I remembered.

He followed my gaze and said, "The ticking can drive you nuts. Makes you feel like screaming."

"Not a good idea in your case. The neighbor upstairs can hear. And in your situation, I wouldn't want to attract the attention of former district judge Devora Edelman."

"Thanks for the information."

"Turns out you're a celeb," I said, spreading the front page of the paper on the table. I sat down.

I watched his expressions as he read, looking for signs of embarrassment, of shame. But his eyes moved quickly across the lines, and mostly he seemed to be trying to gather details. To survive.

"Tell me, can't you sail earlier?" I asked. "You're putting us all in danger here."

"I can't board the yacht in daylight."

"That's really too bad."

He folded the paper, handed it to me, and said, "I'll return the money to each and every one of those people."

"I'm not judging you."

"Sure you're judging me."

I smiled. "Are you hungry?"

"Very," he said.

I brought dishes and silverware from the kitchen and set the table for us.

He said, "What about a plate for Andrea?"

I laughed. A surprisingly hearty, liberated laugh. I never dared—we never dared—to look at the funny side of that whole business with Andrea.

"What a lovely laugh you have. You should laugh more."

I didn't say anything. I didn't know what to say.

He said, "Hearty appetite."

And we started to eat.

Our hands didn't touch accidentally when I handed him the salt. Our legs didn't touch under the table.

He wiped his mouth with a napkin, looked straight into my eyes, and asked, "Why are you helping me, Hani?"

"What do you mean?"

"You don't have to."

"Because you're desperate."

Or maybe I said, "Because I'm the only one who will."

Or maybe I said, "Because Assaf wouldn't want me to help you."

Or maybe I didn't say anything.

"You know," he said, "I called my ex-girlfriend and she hung up on me."

"That's understandable."

"Yes, but still..."

"How long were you together?"

"Eight months."

I threw my head back and laughed.

"It's not nice to laugh at me."

"I'm not laughing at you, I'm laughing with you..."

"What can I tell you, things never work out for me. With women, I mean."

"So maybe you should try men."

Or maybe I said, "Too bad, because you'd make a great father."

Or maybe I didn't say anything.

(I'm not trying to be smart, Netta. I'm really not sure what I said. Or what I just wanted to say. What happened, or what I wanted to happen. Honestly.)

"You know...," he said, and bit his lip.

"What?" I leaned slightly forward.

"Never mind," he said.

I hate it when someone does that to me. I leaned back.

Folded my arms on my chest. Frowned. Put my entire arsenal of disapproving gestures on display.

"Okay," he said, alarmed. "The chances are I'll never see you again anyway, so what difference does it make if I tell you."

"Tell me what?"

"But it's embarrassing, I'm warning you." He raised his index finger at me.

"Don't threaten me."

Or maybe I said, "I'm not easily embarrassed."

Or maybe I said, "I'm listening."

Or maybe I didn't say anything.

He turned away from me to look at one of the clocks. And it seemed like he wasn't going to tell me. But then—

"When you and Assaf started dating," he said without looking at me, "you came to Nahariya for the weekend. Assaf had already moved out, so they asked me to give you my room so you two would have someplace to sleep."

"I remember. That was the first time Assaf took me to meet your parents."

"Yes, that was it. We talked about katushas. You wanted to know what it was like to live under rocket attacks."

"Right!"

"That's not the point. After dinner, I went out to the Kibbutz Evron pub. We spent a lot of time there when we were in the army. I drank a little. I danced. I made out with some girl at the bar. I remember how weird it was that I didn't get a hard-on. We were really going at it. And she was hot. But I didn't get a hard-on.

I thought maybe it was because of the liquor. So instead of going to her place, I made a date to see her on Saturday night and went home. I was a little drunk and could barely get my key in the lock. Finally I went inside and out of habit, walked straight to my room and opened the door."

"Oh boy..."

"You...were lying in bed next to my brother...and you were...so..."

"Wait a minute, was I naked?"

"Uh..."

"Was I naked or not?"

"Not completely. The sheet was between your legs...so one leg was covered and the other wasn't."

"And the top?"

"Pretty much out there."

"Oh boy..."

"The window was open, and the moon was full, or almost full, and the light coming into the room danced on your body, and I just...just stood there, unable to breathe at the sight of all that beauty."

"Don't exaggerate."

"I'm not exaggerating. The problem was that at some point, all the air I was holding in my chest burst out, and it must have sounded like a moan, so Assaf woke up."

"Boy oh boy."

"I took off, sure he'd come after me. But he didn't. Only the next day—you and my mom were in the kitchen—he grabbed me when I came out of the bathroom, pushed me up against the wall in the hallway, and told me I was a pervert. And that if I ever dared to get any-where near you or even talk to you, he'd kill me."

"That doesn't sound like Assaf."

"He had a box cutter in his hand. He flipped open the blade, pressed it against my jugular, and said, 'Hani is my once-in-a-lifetime girl. The girl I want to marry. And if you take her away from me too, it'll be the end of you.'"

"That really doesn't sound like Assaf."

"It's a side of him you don't know, Hani. But I'm sorry to say that I know it very well. That's why...I took what he said seriously. I packed my duffel bag and said I'd been called back to the unit."

"I don't remember that at all—"

"Well, I was nothing to you then. Air."

"That's not exa—"

"It's okay. Don't apologize. It's natural."

Suddenly I wanted a cigarette. No, I didn't want one, I needed one. When I became pregnant with Lyri I stopped smoking, and since then, sometimes, mostly at night, I'd feel the echo of a desire to smoke. Nothing more. Now it was a fire inside me. My fingers were aflame. I remembered that this year, the neighbor whose house we were in started smoking outside on the bench in the garden of our building, and that meant she might have a pack in the apartment. "Wait a minute," I told Eviatar. And went looking.

I found one in the den. With a lighter next to it. I never liked Winston Lights, but in a situation like that, you take what's there. I went back to the kitchen and offered Eviatar one.

"No thanks," he said. "I stopped smoking. It projects something unhealthy to the clients."

I lit up and took the first drag. I tried not to exhale in his direction.

That word, "unhealthy," flickered in my consciousness like the lights of a motel on the way to Vegas. It flashed on and off.

"That image of you with the sheet," he said, "stayed in my mind for years."

"Oh come on."

"I'm completely serious."

"Like you were with your clients?"

"That's not fair, Hani."

"I don't think you're the person to decide what's fair and what isn't."

"Okay, don't believe me if you don't want to. But it's the truth. I fantasized about you in all kinds of situations. I made up scenarios."

"Scenarios?"

*

I'm stopping for a minute. Writing you all this is making me blush. I remember that in our Octopus Club period, we talked about sex a lot. Guys were constantly coming on to you, so you had a lot to talk about. But sometimes they came on to me too: less-than-perfect guys who felt more comfortable with a less-than-perfect girl.

I remember that my favorite conversations came after the nights when we both lucked out. Because then there was no jealousy. There was only the sharing. And the joy of discovering the scandalous truth: every guy does it a little bit differently. (The ones who pop into my mind now are the formerly ultra-Orthodox Elida, who used to recite verses from the Talmud when you went down on him, and Yoav from Psychology who used to cry when you stroked his hair and directed his tears so they fell right on your nipples. But now it suddenly occurs to me that both stories are just too good and maybe you actually made up some of the bizarre tales you used to tell me then. Probably not, you're not a liar like me. I, after all, am capable of making up a complete Eviatar just to impress you.)

Then you met Noam. And I met Assaf. And those stories stopped. Maybe because it became less important. Or maybe because an intimacy grew between us and our men that we didn't want to violate.

Maybe that's why I'm embarrassed now. And find it hard to go on.

You know what, I'll take a break and do a flashback. Maybe I'll feel more comfortable writing about something that happened in the past.

*

The last time (before Eviatar) I was so horny and wild was after Nomi's funeral.

Actually, when I think about it, it wasn't right after the funeral because first we went to see her parents in Beit Hakerem.

I remember the death notices at the entrance to the building. I remember standing and staring at her full name and you pushing me to keep going. I don't mean you really pushed me, you just touched my back gently.

Then we went into the house, which was always our favorite. Being in my house was no fun because there was no mom. They'd already taken her. And my dad, no matter how hard he tried, couldn't take her place. You, on the other hand, had a mom, but she was always looking for reasons to criticize you. I feel like hugging you when I remember that. I think that as a child, I mean, now that I'm a mom, I understand how much power we have, how one nasty remark from us can…And I don't understand how in the world you came out of that house normal. So maybe that's your response? That's your true victory over them, Netta? Being so normal?

So that left Nomi's house. With her balding-with-a-ponytail father, Josh, who had that store in the Ben Yehuda pedestrian mall, "Mister Pop," remember? I don't think there's anyone our age in Jerusalem who didn't buy Michael Jackson and Police pins there.

And with her mother-who'd-been-at-Woodstock, Barbara, who used play Santana records for us (right?) and taught us how to dance when you want to attract boys' attention and how to dance when you just want to dance.

The two of them, Barbara and Josh, sat in the living room that afternoon and were happy to see us when we came in. Barbara hugged us and said, "How nice it is to see you. You haven't been here in a long time." Her hugs were looser than the ones I remembered from childhood. Josh said to me in English, "That was so beautiful, what you read at the funeral." I swallowed the thank-you that was on the tip of my tongue because who says thank you at a time like that? Barbara said, "Sit down, why are you standing?" She shook hands with Assaf and Noam and said, "Nice to meet you." And then said in a weirdly cheerful voice, "She loved you both so much, you know?" You said, "We loved her too, Barbara." I kept silent and thought (I always have to ruin things, if not by what I do, then by what I think) that it was always obvious that my friendship with you was stronger, and that we accepted Nomi happily, but with a tinge of scorn because there was something about her that invited ridicule, with all those flowers in her hair and her Palladium shoes, and all the guys she fell in love with who were completely wrong for her. She seemed to have been born in the wrong decade, but we still needed her with us because without her, we were too "Jerusalem," too square, not to mention the fact that without her, we would have seen each other less often because it was at her house that we met, and she was the one who had all the bright ideas — let's go to the Arad music festival, let's stay in Eilat after the school trip, let's go down to the Sinai, let's pick apples at Kibbutz Menara (thank God for that last one. Without Enrique the Argentinian volunteer there was a better than likely chance I would have gone into the army a virgin, and I was lucky enough to do it the first time with someone who thought my body was the most beautiful thing he had ever seen. Even if he did break my heart a week later).

Without Nomi, we wouldn't have gone anywhere. That's the truth.

Her desire to be part of us made us realize that there was an "us." And that it was worth something. So strangely enough, even though you and I were best friends, Nomi was the driving force, and without her—

Do you remember that at some point during the shivah, I gave you my hand? And you took it and squeezed it hard, doing exactly the right thing, as always.

I felt as if I was falling, Netta. Plummeting. As if there was no floor in Josh and Barbara's house. I felt as if my life as I knew it had ended with Nomi's death. And that now, something new was supposed to start, except that a chasm of confusion lay between me and that something new (that's actually what I feel now: on the edge of the terrifying chasm before the change).

So on the way back from Jerusalem, right before Shaar Hagai, I asked Assaf to turn right onto a dirt road that leads to the pilots' monument. There was still some light, but I couldn't wait any longer. I said, "I need to feel you." At first he didn't understand. He gave me a tight hug. A platonic hug. So I unbuckled my safety belt and pushed the back of his seat down. That he did understand, but I would be on top and that wasn't what I wanted. I wanted him to fuck me. So I tugged down my underpants, yanked up my dress, went back to my seat, spread my legs, and said, "Come on already."

There's passion and there's neediness. And what went on in that Fiat Uno was neediness. I needed someone to defeat me. Because someone who is already defeated is no longer afraid. Someone who is defeated doesn't care about the chasm. She simply lies down on the passenger seat, free of responsibility. Her legs are spread on the dashboard, waves of pleasurable pain surge through her body, and she believes, if only for a few seconds, that nothing is going to change, that time has stopped its silent movement toward the deadline and things can stay as they are. Forever.

By all calculations, by the way, we became pregnant with Lyri that night in the car. Even though we can never be completely sure. And it's a bit too symbolic.

*

"Yes," Eviatar said, "I made up stories that led me to you. That brought us together accidentally. And ended with…you know. I used to play those stories in my mind before I went to sleep. Sometimes even when there was another woman with me…in bed, I mean."

"I know you're lying, but it feels good," I said.

Or maybe I said, "Why are you telling me this? What's the point?"

Or maybe I said, "Give me an example."

"What do you mean, an example?"

"Tell me one of the stories you made up."

"It's too embarrassing."

"So I don't believe you," I said.

"Can I have a cigarette?" he asked.

"I thought smoking 'projects something unhealthy to the clients,'" I teased.

He reached out to take a cigarette. Not the least bit annoyed. And lit up. He could have leaned toward me to light it from mine. But he chose to light it himself. He had some ugly blemishes on the back of his hand.

He inhaled deeply. Then exhaled. My smoke blended with his in the air between us.

Then he said, "You have to close your eyes. It only works with closed eyes."

I closed them, only peeking to see if his were closed too, then shut them again. All I heard was his voice, which actually wasn't very different from Assaf's, except that it had an additional nuance of urgency.

"There's a café across from Yemin Moshe. That's where I hold all my business meetings in Jerusalem. One evening, you walk in. You'd gone to visit your father, and all he had was instant coffee, so you're there to get coffee and go right back. I've just finished my meeting and am walking the client out. And then I see you at the bar. I say hello and you don't recognize me at first. Then you do. You're wearing jeans and a sleeveless tank top with a scoop neck. Ah, yes, I forgot to say it's a summer evening. A deep blue evening. I ask you to have a drink with me. You say you can't, you have to get back to your father. I offer to walk with you and you say okay. We step outside into Yemin Moshe — that's where your father lives in the story, I hope that's all right with you — and walk through the alleyways and talk. The intoxicating fragrance of jasmine fills the air. As our conversation deepens, we walk deeper into the neighborhood. Until we reach a small park with a bench hidden from view, surrounded by houses no one lives in. We start to kiss tentatively, and then more deeply, but you stop me and say that someone might pass by. Just as you're saying that, a group of Japanese tourists comes into the garden. Their guide is explaining to them in English that

Yemin Moshe is the first Jewish neighborhood established outside the walls of the Old City, and also a well-known meeting place for lovers in Jerusalem. The entire group laughs at us in Japanese, and it's clear to both of us that we can't stay there. I lean over and whisper in your ear that maybe we should go to the Mishkanot Shananim hotel. You agree."

"I would never agree."

"I know, but this is a fantasy. Everything's possible."

"Okay."

"Should I go on?"

"Yes."

"You're sure?"

"No."

"Okay, so... We go into a room in the hotel. It's a suite, with two rooms. A living room with a TV, and a bedroom. You tell me to undress and wait in the living room while you go into the bedroom. A few seconds later, you call me and I go into the bedroom. You're lying on the bed with the sheet covering only one of your legs..."

"Like in Nahariya."

"Exactly. Only this time my brother isn't there. You gesture with your finger for me to come to you..."

"And?"

"And what?"

"And what happens then?"

"We have sex."

"That's it? Let's have some details."

"Details?"

"Yes, the first time you touch me, where is it exactly?"

He didn't answer at first. And I almost opened my eyes. But I knew that if I did, it would all vanish. Everything that had begun to flow inside me.

I heard the click of the cigarette lighter.

I heard piano études being played by one of Ruth's students.

I heard the owl speak inside my head: *What are you doing? What are you doing?*

*

"Where would you like it to be," he finally asked, "the first touch?"

"My neck," I said quickly. So my courage wouldn't fail me. I have a few sensitive spots there.

"Finger or lips?"

"Lips."

"Okay, so I...go over to the bed, put my hands on either side of your body and bend over you—"

"Slowly, don't rush."

"Ve-ry slow-ly. And kiss the lower part of your neck. Then I move up, planting small kisses on one sensitive spot after another until I reach—?"

"My ear—"

"As I come close to your ear, my stomach almost touches yours, my chest almost touches yours—"

"I can feel the static electricity—"

"I can too. And then I move even closer and—?"

"Lick my earlobe—"

"Okay—"

"And then—you put your tongue inside my ear."

"All at once?"

"All at once. All the way in."

"It's in. And you? What are you doing in the meantime?"

The moment he said "and you," I felt my thigh muscles contract. Ready to move. "I wrap my legs around you, and...pull you hard against me."

And we went on like that, Netta. With our eyes closed. And the table between us. At first, it's just empty words, and you hear yourself and want to burst out laughing. But slowly the words turn into images and the images into sensations. How can I explain it to you (maybe you did something like that once and I don't have to explain?), it's not like the real thing. But if you get into it (and I never had a problem getting into fantasies), the sensations are very real. Your body responds as if it's actually being touched. When you hear the word "back," you really feel your back. When you hear the word "fingernails," you feel the scratches.

We both came. Me before him, I think. "Wait for me," he said. But I couldn't. It was too intense. Too sweet. Too bitter. So I described it all to him as it was happening. The speeding up of my heartbeat, the inner flush spreading between my thighs, the ever-increasing contractions...I talked and talked, and my voice became hoarser and hoarser, until the moment came when every breath was an *oh*.

He got up to wash himself.

Ruth's student was still playing études. And I thought that maybe next year, I'd register Lyri at the conservatory.

The clocks ticked. I couldn't understand why I hadn't heard them before.

Eviatar came back from the bathroom smelling like our neighbor, and sat down across the table from me again.

I was glad he sat there. I didn't want him to be close to me. I didn't want him to touch me (I know it sounds weird, but if he had touched me, I would have slapped him).

I took two cigarettes out of the pack. One for me and one for him.

He ripped out the first page of the newspaper with his picture on it and folded it into an origami ashtray.

We flicked our ashes into a paper ashtray. Nonchalantly. As if nothing had happened (and in fact, when you think about it, nothing really had).

I watched him flick his ashes, noticing that his fingers were short and thinking that Assaf was much better-looking than him.

"I need a favor from you, Hani," he said.

"What?" I liked the way he said my name, slightly emphasizing the second syllable.

"I have to pay the Greek skipper who's sailing the yacht. And I don't have a cent. My account has been frozen, so I can't use an ATM either."

(I know, Netta, that's exactly what he does with his clients. I'm an idiot, but I'm not stupid. I got it. Of course I got it. But I still asked.)

"How much do you need?"

"Two thousand shekels. I'll pay you back when I get to Venezuela."

"No problem," I said. "Stay here. I'll be back in ten minutes."

*

I danced all the way to the ATM. I didn't really dance, you know me. Dancing was never my strong suit. But I felt as if my inner soundtrack had been changed. Someone had removed the Nick Cave disc that had been stuck in the player for years and replaced it with, let's say, a Black Eyed Peas disc.

Standing beside me at the ATM was the downstairs neighbor. Ofri's father. The one who, along with his wife, calls me "the widow." I was glad he was the one who saw me like that. After I'd been made love to. When I'd taken out the withdrawal slip I turned around and said, "Good morning, Arnon." I waited another second to make sure he didn't miss the change. "And a very good morning to you," he answered, and I saw his expression change from *I know exactly what I'm about to see* to *Well, what do you know.* That was enough for me. I didn't need any more than that. I walked past him, put the cash in my bag, and floated all the way home.

(Remember how we walked home from the Cinematheque on Independence Day, in the early hours of the morning, when the excitement of spending all night out was still flowing in our veins and our steps were longer than usual? So, like that.)

A police car was standing in the building parking lot.

*

My thumb did not climb onto my index finger while they were in the apartment. I felt like an old hand at this, used to the situation. And sexy. I felt as if I had power over them because they were men and I was attractive. And lying has never been a problem for me. That's how it is when you grow up with a father who says to you, That's not something we should tell your mother (usually meaning endangering himself for no reason, like driving the wrong way on a one-way street because it's a shortcut, or going into the sea when the waves are high and the lifeguard's station is empty). And a mother who says, That's not something you should tell your father (meaning capricious spending or men who came on to her in the street).

That's how it is when your mom is taken to a mental hospital a week after your bat mitzvah and the only way you can beat your brothers in the war for the attention of the only parent you have left is to invent tragedies: the boys in school harassed you; the scout leader humiliated you in front of the whole troop. I would always base my story on a kernel of truth so it would be believable, and blow it up so it was unrecognizable. My dad always bought it, time after time, just like the policemen bought what I told them: "If Eviatar gets in touch with us, I'll report it to you immediately. It's in my own best interest too."

*

To be on the safe side, I waited half an hour before knocking on the neighbors' door. Three knocks, pause, then two more.

He only opened it a crack. We started talking through the crack, which created an imaginary line that ran from his forehead to his nose to his neck. I could smell his fear.

Not all the words could pass through the crack.

"Sorry I took so long," I said, "the police—"

"I saw them from the bedroom window—"

"I told them I had no idea where you are—"

"You shouldn't be here, Hani, they could be watching the building."

"I wanted to bring you the—"

"It's not worth the risk, I want you to leave now, I— Wait, Hani." He opened the door a little more and touched me (the first real touch) on the arm. "Thanks for everything you did for me and…don't worry…about Lyri, I mean…she'll be fi—"

"How do you—"

"I just do."

"Thank you for everything you did for me," I said.

Or maybe I stood on tiptoe and gave him a real kiss, on the lips.

Or maybe I just stood there like an idiot.

Behind him, on the wall, a huge pendulum swung on a large grandfather clock.

I didn't remember that clock being there before. I wanted to ask him whether he also thought that the phrase "grandfather clock" was lovely, but I didn't have time.

Something is always lopped off at partings.

*

That night I dreamed that every person's life story was written in his own special font, and in the dream I asked the head of the font committee to change mine. He said that was impossible: a person's font is determined at birth and can never be changed. I stamped my hands the way

Lyri always does, but he stood there with his arms folded on his chest, adamant in his refusal.

There was another part to the dream, but it's escaped me because I didn't talk about it right after I woke up. (Remember how, on our trip to Costa Rica, we'd tell each other our Lariam dreams first thing in the morning? I really loved you for restraining yourself and not trying to interpret my dreams.)

*

I decided to tell Assaf what happened the minute he came home. I could never hide anything from him for long anyway, so I thought it would be better to get it over with as quickly as possible. But his trip hadn't been very good, so I took pity on him (there is something to what he says: when things aren't going well for him, I like him a little better) and decided to wait a day to tell him. It wasn't an emergency.

I woke the kids early and took them to school before he got up. To avoid the danger that the news might come from them.

On the way, they didn't say a word about Uncle Eviatar. So I didn't say anything either.

When I got back, Assaf was already sitting with the newspaper. There was another report on the search for Eviatar. Assaf said, "It's only a matter of time. What an idiot. He should turn himself in so they might at least go easier on him."

I listened to him and thought, *He doesn't know what happened he doesn't know what happened he doesn't know what happened.* And I thought, *Not telling him what happened puts another barrier between us.*

The children didn't say anything either when they saw him that evening.

Nimrod I could understand, but Lyri? She lives for dramas like that.

I tried to remember when Eviatar might have had time before he left to ask them to keep his visit a secret—but couldn't. He'd been locked in the neighbors' apartment, and as far as I knew, he had no way of getting in touch with them.

It was much more likely, I thought, that during the commotion of opening all the presents Assaf brought, they forgot about their uncle. Children are blessed with the ability to be totally self-involved.

Even so...

I knew that at some point, something would remind them of him, would stir some dormant association, and it would come out.

I also knew what would happen right after that.

Assaf doesn't yell. He deletes. When someone abuses his trust in them, he removes that person from his internal list of people who are in his good graces. And once you're removed from that list, there's no way back. I saw it happen with his friends, with his employees.

But I wasn't alarmed. Just the opposite. I was strangely calm for someone whose life was about to turn upside down. I had amazingly pleasant dreams that night: the Yemin Moshe windmill was blowing such a caressing breeze on me that it almost made me come; I met Eviatar in the Amazon, riding on a giant, kindhearted crocodile, and even though he looked different because of the plastic surgery, I recognized him right away because of his inner self.

As I loaded the dishwasher the next day, I thought, *This might be the last time I'll ever load this dishwasher.*

I moved hangers in the kids' closet and thought, *This might be the last time I'll ever move hangers in this closet.*

I was cool and collected as I did those things. Like an anthropologist observing her own life. Like the narrator of a disaster movie a minute before the disaster. Which is pretty weird, when you think about it. I'd invested so much effort in having a normal family, and now that real danger was threatening to destroy the great achievement of my life, I was shockingly indifferent.

*

But Lyri didn't say anything. And Nimrod didn't say anything. And Andrea didn't say anything. I waited for two days. Three. Four. Nothing happened. Eviatar had apparently reached Venezuela, but the police were still asking the public to assist them in tracking him down.

The kids continued to fight endlessly, as usual. Assaf made sure to come home from work later so he wouldn't have to deal with them. And I started thinking that I'd gone crazy. That the connection between me and reality—which had grown more tenuous this last year—had finally broken.

*

I've always hated books that have a crazy heroine. There's always an attic in those books. And if they're adapted into movies (admit that this is a great subject for your new course in Middletown), the woman's hair is always wild, she's wearing a torn nightgown, and she's so pathetic and hysterical that you think, why the hell don't the guys in the white coats come and take her away already.

So just to be clear: I will never wear a torn nightgown. And we don't have an attic. But even so...

*

It happened to me a few times this year. Always when Assaf was away on business. Always late at night. After the kids fell asleep. First I hear a shrill voice calling me: *Han-ni, Han-ni.* Then I go out onto the balcony and see an owl there. You know, with that white, heart-shaped face. And it's looking at me and talking. In a woman's voice. It has only bad things to say about me. About the kind of mother I am. About everything. And I keep defending myself until, sick and tired of it, it hoots in disgust and withdraws into itself.

I know it's weird. That's why I don't tell anyone about it. Not even Assaf. I remember how my dad talked to my mom toward the end. His tone. And I won't let Assaf talk to me like that. It took me an entire letter to open up to you about it. But now that I've told you, I'm not sure how to explain the feeling without sounding, you know, nuts. It's a little... It's a little like daydreaming. But without the pleasantness. There's nothing at all pleasant about being unsure whether something you just experienced really happened or not. And the really scary thing is that after Eviatar left, there was another owl perched in the tree. All year, there's only been one owl there, and all of a sudden there were two. One can be random. Two was already an event. Both of them spoke to me at the same time. Criticized me. And there's an essential difference between being put down by one owl and by two. It's hard to explain. There are some things you can bear and some things you can't.

*

But all those episodes with the owls had been very short. A minute. Two at the most. And here I'm talking about two full days that I must have imagined! Now that makes absolutely no sense, Netta, right?

I know, I know, I can just talk to Lyri, ask her if she remembers Uncle Eviatar's visit. But what happens if she looks at me with an I-have-no-idea-what-you're-talking-about expression in her eyes? How long will it take for the people in the white coats to arrive?

*

They came to take her on a Sunday evening. I know because at 5:30 on Sundays, *Little House on the Prairie* was on, and my dad turned off the TV in the middle of the episode and told us in a tone we'd never heard before to go straight to our rooms. His intentions were good: he didn't want either of us to witness what was about to happen, he was afraid that the sight would haunt us for the rest of our lives. But the result was that we had to imagine what happened based on the sounds we heard through the wall. And what you imagine can haunt you for the rest of your life too.

He did the right thing, by the way, by calling them. He had no choice. That weekend, my mother abruptly changed from depressing to dangerous. I would have done the same thing if I had been in his place. I'm not angry at him for doing it.

After they took her, he opened our bedroom door and let us go back to the living room. The smell of her perfume was in the air. We managed to watch the end of the episode. The Ingalls family sat around the dinner table. All the girls wore dresses. Charles closed his eyes, steepled his hands, and thanked God for everything he had put on their table that night.

*

I remember the last time I called you to rescue me (and you came! All the way to Kibbutz Malkiya! Three and a half hours from Jerusalem to Kiryat Shemona and another hour's wait at the Kiryat Shemona central bus station and another half hour on the bus that stopped at all the kibbutzim in the area!). There were no cell phones then. I didn't know whether you'd come or not. They allowed us one call to our parents on Thursday night to let them know we weren't coming home for the weekend. But I called you and said, "Netta, I think I'm losing my mind. Can you come here tomorrow?" And you said, "I'll try, I don't know how my mom will feel about it." When my shift at the kibbutz gate was over at two on Friday afternoon, I went back to my room convinced that you weren't coming. That there was no chance. And then, at 2:30, the guard at the gate called on the walkie-talkie to say that I had a visitor. I remember that I ran. I actually ran from my room all the way to the first roundabout. But I slowed down when I got close to the gate. I didn't want to scare you. You came toward me wearing civilian clothes (now that I think about it, why civilian clothes? Ah, of course. You weren't in the army yet!), and we hugged each other tightly. I think that was the tightest we'd ever hugged. And you said, "Hanch, couldn't you lose your mind somewhere a little…closer?" That made me laugh out loud. We started walking along the path that led to the dining hall, and just walking beside someone like you calmed me down. I was even a little ashamed for dragging you all the way to Malkiya, for having been so dramatic, so when you said, "Well, do you want to tell me what happened?" I said, "Never mind, it passed already." But you—only eighteen! How did you get so smart?!—insisted, saying, "It won't really pass until you talk about it." "Here's the animal petting corner," I said, "and this is the children's house. Did you know that they still haven't switched to letting the kids sleep with their families? And here's the pool, but it's only open from May till October, and here's their factory, a toy factory. It's so cool that they have a factory like this on a kibbutz…"

But you ignored all those distractions. You stayed politely quiet and waited for me to crack, and finally, at the entrance to the kibbutz store, it happened. We were about to go inside, I wanted to buy you something to drink after your long trip, but you stopped me and said, "Let's sit for a while," and we sat down on the curb and you put a hand on my shoulder, not a confident hand, but a wary, probing hand—how much experience did we have with each other's crises?—but it was actually the hesitation in your touch that made me dissolve into tears. Between sniffles, I tried to explain: "I don't know what's been going on with me these last few days, Netta, but it's really scary, it's as if…We have inside us, in our heart, our soul, something that connects all the parts of us, the part that remembers, that guides, that organizes. Everything comes from it and everything goes to it. It's like a kind of essence, the thing that is us, like a spine, but not of bones, of feelings, do you understand?"

I remember that you nodded. And that was very generous of you. Because you definitely didn't understand anything at that point.

"It's like self-confidence," I kept trying to explain, "but it's more than that, it's the confidence that you even have a self, that you have something stable inside all the…messiness of being a person, something you can depend on to see reality, to translate reality as it is, and for the last few days, that something…has been crumbling. I'm crumbling. Someone who is me sits in the guard booth and…We're not allowed to read, Netta. We're not allowed to listen to the radio. I have no friends here. This whole course was a mistake. And I don't know…don't know anymore…Look, you can see that it's crumbling, I can't even finish a sentence…My mother too, before she…before they took her away…her sentences stopped in the middle, as if, by the time she got to the middle, she forgot the beginning…or the end…I don't know…"

"But that, that thing, that spine you're talking about, still hasn't crumbled completely. You were sane enough to call me."

"True. I had . . . I had an idea."

"An idea?"

"I thought maybe . . . you'd tell me about me."

"Tell you about you?"

"Maybe that way I would remember myself."

"Okay." You turned sharply to me, took me by the shoulders, and made me look into your eyes, something I hadn't been able to do before then. "No problem, I'll tell you about you." And I could see that you were relieved that I'd switched from mental meandering to a concrete request. The kind that could be granted.

"Once upon a time there was a girl named Hani," you began. "And when Alon Geva, our Bible teacher, said in the middle of the seventh grade that he wanted us to put King David on trial for his part in the Bathsheba and Uriah the Hittite affair and asked who wanted to take part, only she and I raised our hands. So Alon Geva said, 'If that's the case, Netta will be the defense attorney and Hani the prosecutor.' 'What's a prosecutor?' the girl named Hani asked. And the whole class laughed, but I thought that this girl was really brave if she was willing to admit in front of the whole class of Hebrew University High School cynics that she didn't know something. So I invited her to my house to prepare for the trial. And we were the first prosecutor and defense attorney in the history of Jewish law to work together."

"Right!" I said, already drawn into the memory.

"We arranged to meet at my house the first time," you went on, "because Hani said her house was sad. I wanted to say that maybe it would be better there anyway, because my mother is nasty. But I didn't. The truth is that at the time, I didn't see my mother that way. Every family is a planet unto itself, and sometimes you need someone from another planet to land on yours in order to understand. That girl, Hani, made me understand. After her second visit to my planet, she said, 'You know, your mom treats you like she's your stepmother.' I choked. Because until then, no one had ever dared to say that so directly, without mincing words."

Then you said to me, "Oof, Hani, you're going to beat me at the trial. You're a really good prosecutor."

"Right."

"Sorry, Nettush, I interrupted you. Keep going."

"Is this helping you?"

"I think so."

"Okay, so once . . . that Hani we're talking about designed and printed a new menu for the Octopus Club without telling the boss and handed it out at one table only. At the end of the evening, she showed him that the table that had the new menu had brought in the most money, convincing him to let her redesign all the menus. Another time, not far from here, on Kibbutz Menara, in the middle of picking apples, an Argentinian volunteer named Enrique stood under a tree with a guitar and sang the Beatles' "Something in the Way" in a hilarious Spanish accent, and when he finished, everyone in the orchard applauded and he expected a kiss, but Hani never liked dancing to the music of other people's expectations, so she just gave him a charming smile and went back to picking apples, saving her kisses for that night, in his room, when and where they would be real and private, not on display for everyone. And another time . . ."

*

You kept talking about me until you saw that I'd calmed down. Then you got up and said that you'd promised your mom you'd be home for Friday night dinner. "But there are no more buses now," I said, and you said, "Don't worry, I can hitchhike." "But the road is completely empty at this hour," I said, and you said, "It'll be fine." When we reached the gate, someone from the toy factory was just leaving, and of course he was happy to take the pretty hitchhiker to Jerusalem, what a coincidence, he was going there too. Before you got into his car, you gave me one more hug, took me by the shoulders, and said, "Promise me you'll be okay?" I promised. And I was okay.

It's a little embarrassing that I need you again, exactly the same way, twenty-something years later, because I'd like to believe that the time that's passed since then had some meaning. That a husband and two kids and a room of my own have given me a certain stability. But apparently our soul doesn't move forward but only in circles. Dooming us to fall into the same pits over and over again.

*

I'll send you this letter. It's terribly annoying when stories and movies end and the letters aren't sent. It really sucks.

But you don't have to write back, Netta. Even though I've sprinkled a lot of question marks along the way, I don't really expect to get answers from you. I don't need a defense lawyer. And certainly not a prosecutor. What I really needed was a witness.

I had to write this whole story to someone, uncensored,

so I could believe that Eviatar really happened. Or at least believe that I really did imagine him. That I was desperate enough to invent him.

*

I just read the entire letter from the beginning. I tried to see it through your Middletown eyes and thought that in your place, it would worry me. It might even make me leave everything and fly here to hug me tight and ask me to promise that I'll be okay.

I don't know. Maybe I got a bit carried away while I was writing, maybe there's something about writing that makes me intensify everything, or maybe all the hysterical death announcements and parentheses were fine at nine in the morning, and the fact that I wrote to you, the fact that you were with me while I was writing, have already calmed me down a little. (That's what the fear of losing your mind is all about—it doesn't only stem from loneliness, it also creates it. Traps you in loops of bad thoughts that you have to hide from the world, loops of thoughts that coil around you tight enough to choke you.)

In any case, it hasn't been nine in the morning for a long time now. And in ten minutes, I have to pick up Lyri and Nimrod from school. If I don't bring my two little chicks back to the nest, no one will. No one! And that's unthinkable. I'll stop at the post office on the way, buy stamps, stick them on the envelope, and give the letter to the clerk. Then I'll go to the supermarket and buy chicken breasts to make schnitzels, which I'll freeze later and reheat after that. And I'll be fine. I think.

Assaf is going away tonight. A short trip this time. One night.

After the kids go to sleep, we'll probably have sex. It's a kind of tradition: I tattoo a memory on him that he'll carry on his body when he's not with me.

We have quite a few good moments that I kept from you in this letter. The truth about our marriage is much more elusive than what I described here. And then there's the financial truth.

In the morning, I'll call the Verbin Studio. Amicam has a weakness for me. Always did. He'll agree to take me back. If I haven't opened my own studio by now, I probably never will. And I think that what I need to do most urgently now is get out of the house before one night, there are three owls on the tree...

I suppose everyone has a certain amount of aloneness they can endure. And I forgot that with my family's history of hysteria, I have to be especially careful. I sank too deeply into myself and now I have to climb back out.

Cross your fingers for me? The walls of the pit are very slippery.

Yours,

Hani

P.S. It would be nice if you wrote me something. So I can see that you're still alive.

Maybe you can share a secret with me too.

It can't be that you don't have one. Every woman does.

Third Floor

I know it's ludicrous. Nevertheless, Michael, I must speak to you. There is no one but you with whom I can share this burden. For two weeks I have been trying to decide how to talk to you without feeling utterly ridiculous. After all, I won't drive to the cemetery to talk to your headstone like a silly old woman, or write letters and address them to Pure Souls Street, Heaven, or go to a medium who will make your face appear in a crystal ball or slide a glass along a Ouija board. That is not my way. It is not our way. Yet my need to talk to you is real. And recently, things have happened that have turned it into a powerful urge.

Several days ago, while I was sorting the things in your study, deliberating about which of them to throw away and which to put in a carton before the move (which I will tell you about later. I don't want to put the cart before the horse), I found an answering machine in a drawer. The layer of dust covering it indicated that it had long ago been retired from active use.

I stopped sorting—you know how easy it is to tempt me away from housework—connected the machine to the phone, and called our number. After four rings, the tape began to run and your warm, firm voice filled the house: "Hello, you've reached the Edelman family. Please leave your message after the beep and we will get back to you as soon as we can."

A year has passed since I last heard your voice. More than a year, in fact. Because the voice that came from your throat during the last weeks of your life was different: softer, less certain. The closer you came to death, the more willing you were to entertain the possibility that you were wrong. That you had been mistaken the entire time.

But it was your old voice coming from the answering machine. When you finished speaking, the beep sounded, followed by a long silence: a void asking to be filled.

•

I checked it a few more times, of course: I measured how long it took from the moment you stopped speaking until the three beeps sounded to signal the end of the message (two minutes). I counted the number of words it takes to fill two minutes (between 200 and 205, depending on the speed of the speaker. I've been speaking much more slowly since you left). But I had already made the crucial decision: This is how I would speak to you. I'd leave you message after message on the answering machine.

Of course, this method is no less farfetched than the ones I mentioned above. The average person does not employ it. But when I hear your voice, I can temporarily put off my inner prosecutor who says, "Devora, you're making a fool of yourself," and fill the void that asks, almost demands, to be filled.

●

My love—I called you that too rarely—before I tell you what is happening in my life, you will certainly want to know what is happening in the country. I assume you don't have news flashes on the dark side, and I know how much you like to keep abreast. "News!" you used to announce in the living room and raise the volume of the announcer's voice, and now that you're not with me, I'm the one who sometimes says: "News!" And my voice ricochets from the walls like an echo.

The country is overflowing with tents, Michael. A young girl set up a tent on a main street in Tel Aviv to protest against housing prices, inspiring others with different complaints to do the same. Each pair of tents gave birth to another tent, and now every town and city has rows of tents lining the main street, and every Saturday night, young people emerge from them and fill the city squares to demonstrate for social justice and a new country. I watch the demonstrations on live TV, sorry that you're not with me to watch the miracle. They're confused, those young people, their slogans are crude and their speeches unfocused, but they have a certain passion that reminds me of us during those years when you and I believed we would change the world.

About three weeks ago, I decided to take action.

After all, we had so often watched longingly as people gathered in town squares to call out messages that were important to both of us while we, owing to the positions we held, were forbidden to raise our voices along with them. But now that I have retired, the door to the cage is open. So why, I asked myself, do I remain behind the bars? Why not hitch a ride to the big city with a neighbor and join the demonstrators myself?

•

I began, of course, with the Raziel family. As always, Avraham said, "Come in, come in, why are you standing outside?" But he stood in the doorway with his arms folded on his chest, blocking any possibility of going inside. I told him that I wanted to ask if, by any chance, they were going to the demonstration. "What demonstration?" he asked.

I couldn't hide my surprise. "Haven't you heard the news?"

He answered dismissively, "Ah, that. We don't really believe in demonstrations. Besides, our friends come over every Saturday night to play poker. It's a regular thing and we can't change it."

"Poker?" I didn't mean to sound disapproving. But I did.

He was alarmed. "We don't play for money, Devora, it's just for fun. Everyone puts in a few shekels. That's all."

I couldn't restrain myself and said, "Well then, maybe if you win at poker tonight, you'll finally be able to pay what you owe the tenants' committee."

He looked right at me and said, "I've ordered some new checkbooks and the minute I get them, I'll knock on your door."

"Good." I turned to leave.

"Have a good week," he had the nerve to call after me.

How could he not be embarrassed to pull the same lie out of his bag every time, Michael? And how could I have been so naive as to think that someone who wouldn't pay his dues to the tenants' committee would want to show broader social solidarity?

•

I went down a floor. Behind the Gats' door I heard the loud voices of children. I wasn't sure I should knock. Perhaps it wasn't a convenient hour? But I was determined to go to the demonstration at all costs. Hani opened the door, her son in her arms and her daughter pulling at her skirt. I said I was sorry for bothering her at that hour, and she gave a weary smile and said that the situation hadn't been any better an hour earlier.

I began, "I wanted to find out—"

But then the little girl pulled Hani's skirt even harder and it slipped down a bit, exposing the waistband of her underpants. She scolded the child: "I told you *not to do that!*" She pushed her away, pulled her skirt up, bit her lip, apologized, and asked, "What did you start to say?"

"I wanted to ask...if you and your husband are going to the demonstration."

"As you can see, there is no husband here at the moment, it's just me. Asaf is out of the country. I actually would have liked to go. I think it's important. But I don't see how I can find a babysitter on such short notice."

"I understand."

"And tomorrow I'm getting up early. I've gone back to work. I'm sorry, Devora. Did you try the Raziels?"

"They're playing cards tonight."

"So try Ruth or her neighbors downstairs."

I pointed to the door across the hall. "What about Katz?"

"In Crete. I think they're coming back tomorrow."

"Strange, I thought I saw someone walking around in their apartment a few days ago," I said.

Hani suddenly looked startled—something different flashed in her eyes—and asked, "You're sure? What did he look like?"

•

She actually pleaded with me to describe the person I saw in the Katzes' apartment.

I tried to dampen her enthusiasm. I told her that the shutters had been half closed and I didn't see anything.

But she persisted. "Even so, what did you manage to see?"

I wanted to say that it was hot that day. Very hot. And that I wasn't sure it hadn't been a mirage. But it was clear that she wouldn't let me go until I gave her a full report, even if it wasn't reliable. So I said that I thought the man, assuming it was a man, was thin. And that at first I thought he had broken in and I considered calling the police, but then I saw that he was simply walking back and forth in the living room. With no intention of taking anything. He had a gym bag. And he didn't put anything into it.

Hani tensed. "A gym bag? What color?"

She put her son down and moved her daughter's hand

away from her skirt, which the child was pulling again. She seemed to prefer standing alone to receive the crucial information I was about to give her.

I said I thought the bag was green. Maybe. And then—she hugged me, Michael. I wish I could describe that hug in detail, but I'm afraid that the beep of the answering machine will interrupt me, and you cannot describe an ongoing experience like a hug in spurts. So I'll stop now, if you'll allow me, and call us again.

•

Hani and I do not have a hugging relationship. We've never even shaken hands. Which is why my first reaction was to freeze in her arms. I was so surprised that I couldn't move. But she wouldn't release me, as most people certainly would if their hug received no response. On the contrary, she increased the pressure of her hands, burying them deeper and deeper in my back, and then pulled herself toward me, or me toward her, until we were like a single person. Pressed up against one another. Slowly I felt my body melt toward her, felt my shoulders and chest begin to sink into her embrace, and all my restraint dissolved.

You see, Michael, since you've been gone, no one has hugged me. No one has touched me with such tenderness. And here was an unexpected opportunity to finally stop trying to bear my aloneness alone.

"Thank you! Thank you! Thank you!" Hani said, and broke away from me. Her hands still held my waist, but the hug ended as abruptly as it had begun. I was confused. Puzzled. Longing.

She continued, "You have no idea how important this is to me, what you just told me. For the last few weeks, I—I've been shaky, Devora, I—I've lost my self-confidence, or more accurately, the confidence that there really is a me. Do you understand? And the fact that you saw him too...do you understand? The fact that there was a green bag means that there's a chance there won't be a third owl, do you understand?"

•

I didn't understand. I didn't understand who that thin man was. Or what he was doing in the Katzes' apartment. Or what the connection was between him and an owl. Nevertheless, I nodded in understanding. After all, the feelings she described were not entirely foreign to me. I also felt that way at the end of my maternity leave. That was why I went back to work so quickly. I sensed that something was beginning to unravel inside me during those long hours at home. That feeling of giving up was starting to spread in the spaces between my organs. It was so frightening and made me feel so guilty, Michael, that I couldn't talk to you about it. But it was one of the reasons I didn't want more. Children, I mean. One look into the abyss as I stood on the tightrope of sanity that stretched across it was sufficient, and I was afraid that another look might end in a fall. So I returned to work because there, at least, the rules were clear to me.

Are you really surprised to hear all this, Michael? I don't think so. I don't think that anything I tell you about our years together can surprise you. I won't be revealing any secrets from the past in these messages I'm leaving for you. After all, what is the greatest secret a person can hide from the world? The secret of his vulnerability. And that is a secret I revealed to you day in and day out.

Regarding the things that happened after you went—here I think I'll at least cause you to raise an eyebrow. But the time for that has not yet come. You like stories to be told properly. Beginning, middle, and at least one end.

•

Hani said, "Let me make a few calls. If I find a babysitter, I'll come up to tell you."

I said, "All right." I wanted to say other things as well. For example: It's good that you went back to work. Or: If it attacks you again, the fear of the tightrope, you're invited to my place for a cup of tea. A cup of tea at the right time can work miracles. But Hani was already being pulled back into the house by her children, swallowed up by their many arms like a fish caught in the tentacles of a sea anemone.

So I didn't say anything.

And walked down another flight.

The shivah for Herman had only just ended, so I decided to knock on the door of the lawyer who lived across the hall from Ruth. But a fraction of a second before I knocked, I heard the sound of a man's voice that made my hand freeze in the air on its way to the door. It wasn't what he said. Most of his words were almost unintelligible through the reinforced steel anyway. It was the tone. You would have recognized it immediately: it usually comes from the mouths of defendants between the verdict and the sentencing.

●

The lawyer's husband was begging for his life. When women beg for their lives, they simply weep. When men beg for their lives before sentence is pronounced, their entire bodies contort in an effort not to cry, and their voices crack, shift from low to high, as if they were adolescents again.

The lawyer answered him. Her tone was cool. Steady. Merciless. He continued to beg for his life in a voice that was shriller, more desperate. I heard the squeak of a chair. Then his footsteps. That's how it always is. The person begging always has to be moving. And the one being entreated remains seated in place.

The lawyer's husband said, "But, Ayelet..." I couldn't make out the rest. It was swallowed up in ambient sounds. But it was enough for me. I dropped my hand and retreated. I knew that if I knocked then, I might find myself unwillingly involved in their private drama.

I've noticed, Michael, that when people are around me, they have an uncontrollable urge to plead their cases. I could imagine it: after the initial embarrassment, they would recognize the opportunity that had arisen, would invite me in, and present evidence and testimony. Obviously, he's been unfaithful to her. What else could cause a man to be so contrite, and a woman—any woman—to become a prosecutor? Or perhaps not. Perhaps it's something else. The stage of life they are at now, when the children are small and the man and woman have conflicting needs, the list of grievances each one keeps in the heart against the other grows longer each day.

In any case I knew that, in the end, they would ask me to deliver a verdict, and I didn't want to. One of the great advantages of being retired is that you no longer have to determine the fate of others. Besides, I was on the way to a demonstration.

•

I didn't try Ruth either. I knew that if I went into her apartment, I'd have to stay. Offer consolation. Look at their picture albums. She would probably make me a cup of tea and serve up a plate of strudel, and in the end, we'd sit there like two old widows and watch the demonstration on TV.

Instead, I called a taxi.

You wouldn't have agreed to pay a hundred shekels for a ride to Tel Aviv, I know.

But I would, Michael. And now I'm the one who makes those decisions in our house.

Calm down. I'm not accusing you of being stingy. You're not. I'm not saying you are. I think that in general, you always tried to be financially responsible. But now that you're gone, I no longer see any point in saving pennies. For what? For whom? Adar never asks us for help. And while our money is accumulating in the bank, the time to enjoy it is dwindling.

So I called a taxi. And to be honest, it cost 120 shekels, not 100.

●

Damn it, why is your opinion still so important to me?

●

The taxi I took stopped in front of the barrier on Ibn Gevirol Street and the driver said, "Sorry ma'am, you'll have to walk from here. The police closed off all the streets because of the demonstration." I told him to let me off there, it wasn't a problem, and joined the many people walking to Kaplan Street, where the main stage was supposed to be. I was glad to see a few gray heads among them. Occasionally, a young boy or girl burst into song, and others joined in. Words like "justice" and "equality" floated in the air, but there was also some small talk and a few frightened owls that didn't understand what all the commotion was about.

At that point, walking was still pleasant. There was a nice breeze coming off the sea. I walked down Pinkas Street, and childhood memories suddenly flooded me. Your childhood memories, of course. I always thought they deserved preserving more than mine. Here, where this building stands now, there was once an empty lot where you and your friends played soccer with a ball made of rags. You were the referee, naturally, the one whose calls were accepted by both teams. And on that tree on the corner of Dubnov Street, you all built a big wooden house — at least then it looked big to you — where you went after school. And here, on this corner, you once fell off your bicycle and crushed your shoulder. You didn't cry, of course not. Your father had drummed it into you that Edelman men didn't cry. You kept all those tears in your chest for twenty years, until you met me.

The closer I came to the corner of Kaplan Street, the harder it became to move forward. It was terribly crowded. And the breeze had stopped. There wasn't a crack in the crowd through which it could enter. I couldn't breathe and I felt that I had to find a bench to rest on. To get some air. I was angry with myself for not wearing more comfortable clothes. Who wears a jacket in the middle of summer? I turned, planning to walk west, toward the sea, to get away from the masses of people, but the pressure exerted by those who wanted to turn into Kaplan Street was fierce and I couldn't walk against the flow. To tell the truth, I couldn't walk at all. I was trapped in the crowd. My heart pounded, my throat was dry, people pushed against me, pressed against me from every side, crushed me. If you had been with me, Michael, you would certainly have forced a way out for us with your strong arms, you would have protected me from the crowd and revived me. But you weren't there. I was completely alone, Michael, and my knees shook, my legs refused to move, the air stopped flowing into or out of my lungs, I had no air . . .

The last thing I remember is the shaved cheek of a young man leaning over me, saying, "Are you all right, ma'am?"

•

I woke up beside a tent.

Several young people surrounded me. They looked worried.

A voice said, "She opened her eyes!" Another called, "Get her some water!"

They took off my jacket gently. Brought me water. Asked me to lift my head and put two pillows under it so I could tip the glass to my mouth. I drank a bit. And only then did my eyes open to see that I was lying in the middle of a makeshift living room—thin rugs, torn armchairs, several pillows—in the middle of Rothschild Boulevard.

I asked, "How did I get here?"

They told me that I had fainted on the corner of Kaplan Street. I had lost consciousness. Two young men had picked me up from the street and put me inside a rickshaw (it seems that there are rickshaws in Tel Aviv too). All the streets leading to Ichilov Hospital were blocked because of the demonstration, so they decided to take me to Rothschild Boulevard, and meanwhile, they'd called a doctor-demonstrator who came quickly on a bicycle, checked me, and said that all I needed was rest.

"Thank you all," I said, "I think I'll go home now." But when I tried to sit up, the dizziness I felt pulled me back down to the pillows.

"Take it slow, ma'am," a young girl whose hair was braided into dozens of tiny pigtails said as she put a hand on my shoulder. "You've had a traumatic experience. Give yourself time to get over it."

•

Yes, Michael, it turns out that of all the tents in the world, I had been taken to the psychologists' tent. Do you believe it?

When I recovered enough to raise my body into a sitting position, I noticed the signs that were hanging all around me: WE'RE ALL PSYCHED UP, DIME STORE PSYCHOLOGY, SOCIAL JUSTICE ON OUR MINDS. After I asked, the young girl with the braids explained that various groups had put up tents on the long boulevard. All were part of the protest, but each had its own cause. The tent I was in was occupied by psychology interns from the entire country who had come to protest the low salaries of professionals in the public service sector.

She poured me another glass of water and said, "Drink, it's important!" And as I drank, she continued to explain: "As part of the protest, we've turned our tent into a therapeutic center that provides free psychological support for everyone on the boulevard, a kind of first-aid station." She turned her head toward the rickety picnic table that had been placed a few meters from us and added, "All you have to do is sign up there."

I asked what happened after people signed up, and my voice sounded strange, like the voice of a different woman. She explained that after signing up, you're directed to one of the interns in the tent. On the first few days, not many people signed up, but for the last few days—she said proudly—they could barely handle the flow and had to work nights too. They had taken a few hours' break because of the demonstration, but the sessions would start again at midnight.

"You can stay here and rest on the mattress," she said. "It won't bother anyone. There's no real privacy here anyway."

•

I wanted to say, Look, you are all extremely nice. In my work, I encountered mainly rapists and murderers, so it's good to remember that we have young people like you in our country. Nevertheless, and with all due respect, it's late, and I have to get home to my—

But then and there, of all places, in that makeshift living room with the endless beeping of car horns all around us, something dawned on me that should have dawned on me a long time ago and I didn't understand how I could have kept it in check for more than a year: there was no one waiting for me at home.

•

At midnight the patients began to enter the tent. First they went up to the reception table where they were assigned a therapist and referred to one of the two tents or to a nearby bench on the boulevard. From where I was lying I could hear fragments of conversation clearly. Not just from the bench, but also from the tents themselves with their opened flaps and thin canvas, and someone had even cut a window in one of them to let a bit of air inside.

I didn't want to eavesdrop on those conversations. You know very well what I think, what we think, of psychologists. Especially after what happened with Adar. But I was lying there on the mattress and had nothing to do but eavesdrop (please, Michael, consider these to be "extenuating circumstances"). And I must confess that I was surprised twice.

Once I was surprised by the willingness, not to mention the desire, of the people entering the tent to expose their personal lives to a stranger in a place that had absolutely no privacy. Didn't those people have families or close friends they could talk to discreetly?

For example, the woman about fifty years old sitting on the bench near my mattress. She told the psychologist that she had been working in an office close to the boulevard for twenty years, and since the protest began, a burning hatred toward her bosses had been growing inside her. She told the psychologist that they earned a fortune and paid their employees peanuts. And then—even though she'd only met the psychologist a few minutes earlier—she added, "These last few days, I've been having really scary thoughts. I want to hurt them. Do something bad to them. Put rat poison or something in their coffee. I can't stop thinking those thoughts. And I don't know what to do."

I didn't hear the therapist's response. A group of about a hundred runners wearing shirts that said RUNNING FOR AN APARTMENT dashed across the boulevard. The therapist and the patient kept talking as if sweaty bodies running past them was perfectly normal. I, on the other hand, became frightened that one of the runners would trample me by mistake, and I didn't resume my eavesdropping until after the last one had raced past. But I'd lost the thread of their conversation, so my attention wandered to a conversation going on in another tent. The one with the open window.

A man, whose legs were the only part of him I could see, was telling the therapist that he had been married to a woman for twenty years, but was also attracted to men. His wife didn't know, his children didn't know, none of their friends knew—but every once in a while he went to places where he could indulge that tendency of his. "I don't expect you to give me a solution," he said, "I don't really think there is one. It's just that walking around with a secret like this for such a long time...it's so...do you understand? So just the fact that I can talk to you here...do you understand?"

The supportive conversations continued into the night, and I continued to listen in on them as I swung like a pendulum from astonishment to horror: astonished at how easily people reveal their innermost selves to anyone who will listen, and horrified by exactly the same thing. While the supportive sessions were going on, various and sundry processions walked past us, sometimes among us.

Drunks, homeless people, and just plain cynics burst into the unadorned, makeshift living room to say their piece. But that did not disturb the people who had come for support. At least from what I could tell, they had no problem sharing with the entire boulevard their sexual deviations, their addictions, or the lies they had told to the people closest to them.

Gradually, Michael, I found myself coming to a momentous conclusion: these were not simply a few isolated cases, but a common phenomenon. It seems that the line between "private" and "public," between "inner" and "outer," has moved these past several years without informing us. And perhaps it has been completely erased.

•

My second surprise was the way the people who called themselves "therapists" reacted, and here too, I shifted from astonishment to horror. Astonished at how young they were (they wore shorts, Michael! So different from the image of the older man with a pipe I pictured talking with Adar), at their ability to listen, really listen, in the midst of the constant pandemonium on the boulevard, and at their sincere desire to help the people who came to talk to them.

And what horrified me? The fact that not even once did any of those professional psychologists offer a moral opinion about the aberrant behaviors being described to them. Not even once! Perhaps the most infuriating example of that was a small-boned girl who sat down on the bench at around two o'clock and told the therapist about the powerful sexual attraction she felt toward her older brother. The therapist listened. And listened. And listened. And finally said, "It's good that you're talking about it. It can't be easy to walk around with feelings like that."

Good God! I wanted to scream. That girl is on the brink of committing incest. Aren't you going to warn her of the moral ramifications of that? Aren't you going to tell her that even among the remotest tribes in the Amazon, sexual relations between family members is absolutely forbidden?! That, after all, is what the girl really needed. That's what all the patients filling the tent and waiting on line outside needed. To be told what's good and what's bad. And you people, instead of telling them that, say that bad is also good and good is also bad. So yes, they leave the tent with a spring in their step. Someone listened to them without judging them. Someone supported them. Wonderful. We all want to be supported. But the next morning, the unsolved moral dilemma will return to torment them, and this time with greater intensity, because now it's out in the open.

•

I didn't say any of those things, of course. I didn't think my status as a guest gave me the right to offer an opinion.

There was something else that made me keep quiet: I hoped that the conversations I was eavesdropping on would bring me a little closer to understanding what I wanted to understand, to imagine what I wanted to imagine: what exactly happened in Adar's therapy. Why, after three months of sessions, did he decide that we, his parents, were to blame for all his sins and it would be best for him to stay away from us for an indefinite time. What is it about that kind of therapy, so foreign to both of us, that pushed him into doing something so drastic?

I know that you don't like me to talk about Adar. If you were here, you would certainly change the subject. Or withdraw into yourself to make it clear that as far as you're concerned, the conversation is over. But now you're dead, Michael. And that is why you have no choice but to hear me out to the end.

•

I didn't open my mouth until the next morning.

The residents of the tent got together to write a position paper they would present at a meeting with the representatives of all the tent camps scheduled for that afternoon on the boulevard. They began with something they called "social dreaming." Each one talked about a dream he'd had at night, and together they tried to find what they all had in common on a deeper level. The fellow leading the discussion explained the idea behind the activity: in addition to the personal content, people's dreams also contain things that can benefit the society to which they belong.

I was also invited to share a dream, but I said that I never remembered my dreams, a reply that met with meaningful nods from everyone sitting in the circle.

After they came up with the deep layer common to all the dreams—the Holocaust, what else, you don't have to be a great psychologist to know that it has been and will continue to be the eternal deep layer here—they went on to discuss their position paper. They spoke quite well, really. They listened to each other almost the way they had listened to their patients. And I must say that relatively speaking, they made very few mistakes in Hebrew. But the practical aspects were beyond them. In other words, they had no idea how to get what they wanted.

During a moment of silence, I asked if I could say something.

Of course, they said.

I straightened up. My body still hadn't regained its strength, but happily, my voice was as sharp and clear as it had been in court. I said, "You're dreaming. You think they'll accept your demands just because you're right. But it doesn't work that way. If you want to change something, you'll have to do it through legislation, through the Knesset. Soon enough, Knesset members will want to prove that they are in tune with the people, but in your entire discussion, you never once talked about the legal aspects of your concerns."

The girl with the mass of braids, the one who gave me water earlier, asked, "What experience do you have that makes you say that?"

I chuckled. "Experience? I was a district judge for almost twenty years."

●

After I helped the psychologists draft a bill, write two administrative petitions, and prepare an organized list of demands for improving their employment conditions modeled on work agreement precedents in other sectors, a rumor spread through the tents that a retired district judge was there, offering advice free of charge. And so, Michael, I found myself invited to similar gatherings of doctors, students, theater people, and residents of the southern part of the city and the southern part of the country. Their ignorance of all things related to the law was atrocious. None of them, without exception, knew anything about their rights, so it wasn't especially difficult for me to assist them by suggesting possible solutions to the problems that concerned them. I spoke and they took notes. And also asked questions, some intelligent, others less so. Wheat—and also chaff. I think that chaos was one of the organizing principles of life on the boulevard. Nevertheless, some things were consistent: the stagnant air, for example, that made you feel as if you were walking in soup. Or the girl with the mass of braids who stayed close to me all morning, accompanying me from tent to tent and occasionally quenching my thirst with water.

Walking from tent to tent was not difficult in and of itself. But the humidity was extremely high, and the soot rising from the vehicles that continued to drive along the boulevard stuck to your skin. After an exhausting meeting with a group of theater people (unbearable, Michael—all of them so full of hot air) I apologized to my escort and said that I had to go home as soon as possible to shower.

She protested loudly: "But Devora, they're waiting for you in the other tents! The revolution is calling you!"

I averted my eyes. Reprimanded. Then she said, "There's an apartment not far from here where we take showers. Come on, I'll take you there."

I picture you now running your fingers slowly along your upper lip the way you always used to do in court when you wanted to show disbelief, when an attorney or a defendant made statements that sounded groundless to you.

Would your Devora shower in a stranger's bathroom?

I never agreed to spend the night in other people's houses because I was used to my own private shower. And I always took a bag overflowing with all my soaps and cosmetics whenever we had to stay in a hotel.

So would I just go, in the middle of the day, without a change of clothes, to a stinking bathroom where the entire boulevard showered?

But it was like this, Michael: they needed me. And it had been a long time since anyone needed me. You are on the dark side. Adar—God knows where he is. The office has stopped calling me to ask where one file or another is. And there is nothing worse than feeling redundant, Michael. Redundant in the morning. Redundant at noon. Redundant in the evening. And now, that young girl tells me that I am needed, I am indispensable, people are waiting for me.

I followed her up the steps of a building on the boulevard, stopping on every floor to catch my breath.

●

In my imagination, I must confess, I saw an apartment for young people with walls pocked with nail holes and a filthy floor strewn with cigarette butts. But lo and behold, behind the plain, reinforced steel door was a spacious, tastefully furnished penthouse. A powerful air conditioner spread cold air through the rooms, but it wasn't too cold, and I could see the ficus trees on the boulevard through the sparkling clean windows.

An older man came over to us. The girl smiled at him: "What's happening, Avner, is everything okay?"

The man replied, "Everything's just fine, Mor. Then he turned to me, took my hand, kissed it, and said, "Avner Ashdot. With whom do I have the pleasure?"

I pulled my hand away and said, "Devora." I saw that he was waiting for me to continue, so I added, "Edelman."

"The district court judge Devora Edelman?" I couldn't decide whether he spoke with respect or ridicule.

"Excuse me, but do we know each other?"

He smiled and said, "Let's say our paths have crossed."

I couldn't decide whether his smile was pleasant or nasty.

Mor cleared her throat and said, "I don't want to interrupt this class reunion, but people are waiting for Devora on the boulevard. She's helping us with the legal side of our fight."

Avner Ashdot gave me a too long look and said, "Great, that's just great."

Then Mor asked if it was okay with him if I took a shower.

"Of course," Avner Ashdot said, "follow me."

●

You, Michael, always said that it was immoral to invest thousands of shekels in a bathroom. What does a bathroom need except running water, you'd say, adding another two-word phrase (in your verdicts, you also liked to use two-word phrases to express loathing): Outrageous waste. Pure ostentation. Revolting hedonism.

After showering in Avner Ashdot's computerized bathroom, I want to add to the list, if you will permit me, another two-word phrase: pure pleasure.

Buttons that regulate heat, cold, and water pressure in such a way that you can adjust them exactly, not approximately, to what you want. A steam hood that keeps too much steam from accumulating. Shelves overflowing with the best toiletries, including bath oils and natural soaps. Scented candles. Buttons you press that change the color of the water by activating underwater colored lighting. Velvety soft towels.

I know that you couldn't care less about all of this. It's clear to me that you consider these technical specifications irrelevant. But I really want you to understand, Michael, not only how much I enjoyed that shower—so much that I forgot I was supposed to step out of it at some point—but also why, for days after it, I couldn't stop thinking about it with longing. Actually yearning for it.

•

I said to Avner Ashdot, "Your bathroom is really wonderful."

"Any time," he said, and spread his arms to the side. They were long and thin. Very different from your arms.

I felt the need to say something else, so I added, "It's very generous of you."

"I can't sleep in the tents with you," he said, "because of my back, so at least this."

"It's no small thing."

"It's basic. Why not give if you have?"

"It's very generous of you," I said again. And was suddenly embarrassed. I never say the same thing twice in such a short period of time.

"Time to go," Mor said.

Then Avner Ashdot held out a business card and said to me, "This is for you." For a moment I hesitated. I had a strange, inexplicable feeling that this was a trap. That if I took the card, there was no going back. But Mor was moving around impatiently. For her, this wasn't the right time for hesitation.

So I took it.

●

The card was still in my pants pocket when I got out of the taxi that took me home. In response to your question: I spent another night on the mattress on the boulevard. I met with everyone who wanted my services. I discovered that the protesters were tragically at odds with each other. I made appointments for later in the week. I smoked a cigarette. I had a reflexology treatment. I played the guitar. I drank warm beer and ate mainly pizza with pepperoni. I know, you don't believe in quick metamorphoses of that kind. But first, quick metamorphoses can happen when something has been bubbling under the surface just waiting to erupt, and second, all of that did happen, Michael. And I have the pictures to prove it.

And after all that—I stood in front of our building, the building in which we spent twenty-five years of our life, and it suddenly looked, how shall I say it, pathetic.

Not pathetic. Maddening. That parking area. Organized. Numbered. Cars stamped with the names of the companies that provided them to their employees. The manicured front garden. The remodeled intercom. The mailboxes—not even one broken. Not even one labeled with more than two surnames. The bicycles lined up in perfect order. The chains perfectly locked. The quiet we loved so much. No loud music. No voices raised in argument coming from any apartment. How terrible.

An island of sanity, that's what you proudly called our suburb.

An island of dullness and conservatism is what it looked like to me at that moment. A kind of... bourgeoisville.

You always said: The day when the entire country is like this, clean, well ordered, law-abiding, levelheaded, we'll know that Herzl's vision has become a reality and Zionism has triumphed.

And my response to you is: Zionism is losing and the people in this building are asleep while it's happening. Until someone knocks these walls down on them and they wake up—there is no chance that anything will change.

•

And that's what I wanted to do, Michael: I wanted to bang on everyone's door, on Ruth's and Hani's and the Katzes' and the Raziels', and say: Wake up, residents of bourgeoisville. Wake up from your poker games and your excessive concerns for your children and your pathetic infidelities inspired by emptiness, not desire. Wake up from your too comfortable TV chairs and your investment advisers who tell you to take out a loan and buy another apartment in exactly this kind of building in exactly this kind of suburb. Wake up from your lack of faith, your lack of involvement, and your lack of caring. Wake up from your glut of vacations, cars, electrical appliances, and special after-school classes for your children. Not far from here, something very important is happening. And you are sleeping.

•

I didn't say any of that, naturally. I didn't knock on any doors. The minute I entered the building, I too became part of that "buildingness." The couple who live in the apartment across the hall from Ruth and Herman were still arguing. And someone suddenly laughed in despair. Or maybe cried. I wasn't sure. On the second floor, I stopped in front of Hani's apartment. I briefly considered knocking and asking for a hug, but something about the door seemed to say: this is neither the time nor the place for that kind of thing.

Nevertheless, when I went into our apartment, I took action: I photographed it from complimentary angles. And put it up for sale on the Internet.

•

Yes, Michael, on the Internet. We had to be careful when we were still working. We could have only one email address, the one at work. And we couldn't open a page on social media. But now, after retirement, why keep hiding?

•

And yes, Michael, I know: This is not a good time to sell. It was never a good time to sell, in your opinion. And I know that with the money I get for our large apartment, I can barely buy an apartment for dwarfs in Tel Aviv. And I know that selling an apartment isn't all that easy. There are lots of swindlers in the market.

I also know that it wasn't by chance that we moved to bourgeoisville. I too am aware that the big city is full of people who have a grudge against us. People we'd have to cross to the other side of the street to avoid if we saw them coming toward us. I've spent only two days there — and I've already met an Avner Ashdot, who seems sort of shady.

•

I can hear you say: What's the rush? Have a cup of tea. Consider the matter seriously. One should not make such decisions hastily, under the influence of a euphoria that has the most tenuous connection to reality.

But Michael, the day I spent on the boulevard was only the straw that broke the camel's back.

•

You must understand, Michael, I feel you in every corner of the apartment. I hear your footsteps behind me. One foot moving slightly faster than the other. At night I reach over to your side of the bed, looking for you. You speak inside my head when I'm watching TV. Giving your opinion, usually negative, of the quality of the program. For months after you went, I continued to buy pickles in vinegar. Yes, you're in the kitchen too. Your smell, the smell of your body, appears without warning in the mixture of cooking smells. Sometimes I still set the table for two by mistake. I say a silent goodbye to you when I leave. And a silent hello when I return.

But more terrible than those moments are the ones in which I no longer feel you. And they have been growing in number recently. Suddenly I can't remember the shape of your ears. Suddenly I manage to complete a crossword puzzle without you. Remove a blockage in the sink drain without you. That's when I feel an empty space where you used to be. I feel that this entire apartment is a space where we used to be. And if I stay here, I will become trapped in the cobweb of your death that is being spun around me, fated to die an insect's death.

In any case I will die, of course. The verdict has already been handed down. But I want to delay the execution, to live a little bit longer, if possible. I'm only sixty-six, Your Honor, can you understand that?

•

After you proposed to me, in the moonlight, and after I accepted—how could I not? I was a nineteen-year-old girl head over heels in love—you said seriously, "Tomorrow we'll ask your father for his permission." And I began to laugh, but not with happiness: my father? I don't need his permission. He doesn't have the right to permit or forbid us to get married. Both my parents should be grateful if they get an invitation to our wedding.

•

And now too: I don't really need your permission, Michael. I need you as a witness. The changes in my life the last few weeks have been so radical that sometimes even I find them hard to believe. Only when I speak to you, when I leave these messages on the answering machine, am I convinced that they are real.

•

Where was I? Ah yes. Thanks to the Internet ad, I have met a host of fascinating people in a very short time. I was so sorry that you couldn't observe with me the carnival of interested parties that passed through our apartment. Lack of space prevents me from telling you about all the thirty-two people who came, so I'll divide them into five groups: the insulters, the remodelers, the bargainers, the real estate agents, and Avner Ashdot.

The insulters storm into your apartment, and before they even shake your hand or mutter a hello, they're already criticizing: The building's old, right? Nobody builds like this today. Then they go from room to room, loudly listing the disadvantages of each one: The kitchen—small. The living room—faces the wrong side of the sun. The walls are thin. The bathroom is poorly planned. The bedroom is okay, but overlooks the street.

We actually enjoyed living here very much, you say, driven to defend the place where you spent most of your life.

Then the insulters give a restrained chuckle of disbelief: What is there to enjoy here?

The remodelers, on the other hand, are people with a vision. They don't see the apartment, they see its potential. Soon after they come in, tape measure in hand, they're already redesigning in their minds: Here we'll take down the wall. Here we'll put up a plasterboard partition. There we'll build a pergola. We'll have to join those two rooms together. And close off the back balcony.

As far as the remodelers are concerned, your presence is superfluous. A mild annoyance on their way to happiness. When you tell them that they can't close off the balcony because it's not legal, they say (to each other, they speak only to each other, not to you), It's okay, we know people in city hall.

The bargainers come to close the deal. They don't waste time. After a very quick look around the apartment—they don't even go into the rooms, just stand on the threshold and peer inside—they sit down in the living room, gesture with their hands for you to sit down too, as if they're the hosts and you're the guest, cross their legs, and say: So let's get the dirty stuff out of the way.

•

The first time, I didn't understand, Michael. Honestly. I checked my blouse: was there a stain on it that I hadn't noticed? When you live alone, that's liable to happen. No one is around to rescue you from your stains. Or maybe they wanted to talk about the sewage. Or the toilet. Or the sewage that flows from the toilet. And what do I know about that? But no. The "dirty stuff" they wanted to talk about turned out to be money. And to talk about money meant to bargain. And to bargain meant to offer a scandalously lower price than the one that appeared in the ad, along with a firm statement: That, Madam, is the going price for your apartment.

The real estate agents always have sweaty foreheads. Five of them came to see the apartment. They all had sweaty foreheads. And they all tried to convince me that I needed an agent. We'll do the screening for you, make sure that only serious people come to see the apartment, they promised. And by saying that, they sealed their fates.

You have to understand, Michael, that I had no desire to screen. Just the opposite. I'm a woman alone. I enjoyed all those visitors. Serious and not serious. Polite and vulgar. Anything was preferable to the echo of my voice bouncing off the walls.

And Avner Ashdot? Well, he definitely deserves a separate message.

●

Avner Ashdot made an appointment to see the apartment. But he didn't give his name. I knew that an older man would be coming, but I didn't expect him, of all people.

When he came in, I asked, "Why didn't you tell me on the phone that it was you?"

"I didn't think you'd remember me."

"Come in," I said, "I'll show you around." (You know me, Michael. I always channel my embarrassment into action.)

We walked through the rooms. He followed me into each one, penetrated the air with his glance and said nothing. I took him to the back balcony and showed him the view. And he still said nothing. When we went into the bathroom, I tried to break the ice: "Yes, well, I know it's hard to top your bathroom." But he didn't laugh.

He didn't have a pad in his hand, but he looked as if he had one in his mind and was taking meticulous notes on what I showed him. Finally he said, "The price you quoted in your ad is too low."

"Too low?"

"I'm prepared to buy your apartment for 20 percent more."

"That's very generous of you."

"It's not generosity, it's economics. The market is slow now because of the protests, but they'll be over in the end, and then the prices here will go up again."

"How can you be so sure?"

"That's how it is in Israel. The happy families and the miserable families are similar. They all want the same thing—their own home. And if possible, another one as an investment. But land is sparse. There isn't enough of it, so the prices have to go up in the end."

"Okay."

"I've also found you an apartment in Tel Aviv, by the way. For almost the same price. You'll even have some money left over."

"Wait just a minute, how do you know I'm looking for an apartment in Tel Aviv?"

•

You're right, Michael, I should describe him to you. When I used to tell you about defendants I was undecided about, you always demanded to know, But what did he look like, Devora?

Tall, that's probably the first thing you would say about Avner Ashdot. Tall, but not stooped. I would expect a man like that, at that age, to look like a crowbar. But no. He looked more like an arrow. Straight but not fast. I'd say his movements were measured. Every step carefully considered before taken.

But perhaps I should have begun with his clothes. Very elegant. So elegant that they didn't look Israeli. As if he had spent many years in Europe, came back not too long ago, and still hadn't reverted to the careless look so common here. A button-down shirt worn inside his pants, of course. A shiny belt with a large buckle. I wouldn't want to be the child beaten with that belt.

I don't mention beating for no reason. There is a suppressed violence about him. But where, you demand to know, Michael, where exactly does one see that violence? I'm trying, Michael. I really am. You can't always pinpoint such things. Sometimes it's just a feeling. The very slightest sense of menace in the air. Perhaps the eyes. They're a beautiful shade of blue. But they're not beautiful eyes. They don't make you want to look into them for very long. On the contrary. They make you not want to look into them for very long.

He fixed them on me and said, "How do I know you want to move to Tel Aviv? Let's just say...I have my sources." And a moment later he added, "I don't expect you to offer me your shower, Devora. But is it possible to get a glass of water here?"

•

And so—with each of us holding a glass of water as if it were wine—we began to talk.

We talked for a long time. Whenever I tried to channel our conversation back to the reason we were talking at all, that is, the purchase of the apartment, Avner Ashdot changed the subject and we moved further away from it.

It seems that he had worked in the Ministry of Defense for years, and as part of his job, visited many places in the world and was exposed to many different cultures. What impressed him most, what continued to fascinate him even after thirty years of travel, was the fact that every culture had its norms. In Paris, for example, it is quite acceptable to have an extramarital relationship. Part of his job was to plant eavesdropping devices in the homes of senior officials our intelligence people were interested in, and what did he learn? Most of the conversations those senior officials had, both men and women, were about their infidelities. In Italy, on the other hand, they were more conservative in their private lives, but the economic corruption there, the Mafia's control of daily life, was incredible. In Naples, you couldn't open a grocery store without the Cosa Nostra's permission, and what shocked him most was that nobody there thought that was strange. They accepted it as an inseparable part of life.

Avner Ashdot told me about the many places he had visited and the many transgressions he had witnessed there, and concluded by saying, "After seeing all of that, you realize that morality is completely relative. And you become a little more forgiving, of others and of yourself."

"I don't know that I agree with you," I said. "In fact, I'm sure I don't."

He smiled and said, "If you agreed with me, Your Honor, I'd be worried." Then he put his glass on the table and stood up.

•

"**Think about my offer,** Devora," he said. "You won't get a better one."

"Let's wait and see."

There was something annoying about his self-confidence. Attorneys who showed that kind of arrogance always made me want to rule against them.

"Yes, let's wait and see," he repeated my words.

Then he bent his entire body and kissed my hand. The kiss was longer and softer than the one he'd given me in the Tel Aviv apartment. And this time I didn't pull my hand away quickly, and felt warmth spreading from my hand to my arm to my shoulder. And from there to the roots of my hair.

●

Don't worry, Michael. I'm not a silly young girl. After Avner Ashdot left, I didn't watch him longingly from the window or call my best friend to relive every tiny detail of the meeting with her. That is not my way. That is not our way.

After Avner Ashdot left, I did exactly what you would have done in my place: I tried to find out how, as he claimed, "our paths had crossed." And how he could have known that I was looking for an apartment in Tel Aviv. I went through all my records going back thirty years. When that didn't work, I called Mira and asked her to check discreetly whether any of the defendants in the trials I had handled was named Ashdot. She was wonderful, as usual, and asked no unnecessary questions. The next day, she called with a negative answer. Then I asked her to check your trials, just to be on the safe side. You, it turned out, had tried an Ashdot, not Avner, but Aharon. And not an employee of the Ministry of Defense, but an accountant for Egged buses who had been accused of embezzling money from his employer. In 1996. He was single, a Holocaust survivor. With no living relatives. Which severely limited the possibility that Avner Ashdot was connected to him in any way.

●

I miss you so much at times like that, Michael. Couples who truly work as a team share not only household tasks, but also memory tasks. Just as I remembered your childhood for you, you remembered the cases I tried for me: the defendants, the claims, the verdict, the sorrow and the satisfaction I caused, if any, to all the sides. I would have forgotten them. Wiped them from my memory so I could go to my next trial with an uncluttered mind. And when I occasionally had to remember a verdict I had handed down, the best idea was to ask you.

So now I am asking you. And there is no one there to answer me.

I went to sleep that night feeling sad (because you were not beside me) and troubled (because of Avner Ashdot).

●

Correct me if I'm wrong, Michael, but in all the years we were together, we never told each other our dreams. You said that dreams were meant to fill the gap between what is and what is desired, and that in both your personal and professional life, there was no such gap. You declared, *I don't need dreams, so I don't dream!* But I actually need them.

And I did dream. But I could never hold on to the dream before it dispersed in my wakeful consciousness.

I don't even remember clearly what I dreamed the night after meeting with Avner Ashdot. Most of it is gone. Nevertheless, for the first time in many years, I managed to hold on to one image and document it in my recipe book before I forgot it. I'll read you what I wrote, word for word, and hope that answering machine beep doesn't cut me off in the middle:

> *A group of doctors, Adar in their midst, is standing over my bed in the hospital discussing the operation they are about to perform on me. I understand from their discussion that they are going to remove an organ, but I don't know which one. I try to ask them, but no sound comes out of my mouth and they continue to ignore me and talk about me as if I can't hear them. I take a piece of paper and write on it: "According to the patients' rights law, you are obliged to provide me with the information I ask for." I hand the piece of paper to the tallest doctor, and he reads it, bursts out laughing, and shows it to Adar, who is also smiling. The doctor says to him, "See? That's exactly why we've decided to remove her suprego."*

•

You probably would have understood from the first minute. Your general knowledge was always more accessible than mine. I wasted half a day combing through medical encyclopedias until I realized that there is no organ called a suprego in our body, and that my dream apparently referred to the "superego," the term Freud coined as part

of his topographical theory that divides the psych
three floors.

The *Encyclopedia of Ideas* helped me remember that the
first floor, which he called the id, contains all our impulses
and urges. The middle floor is the ego, which tries to
mediate between our desires and reality. And the upper-
most level, the third floor, is the domain of His Majesty, the
superego, which calls us to order sternly and demands that
we take into account the effects of our actions on society.

I hear you asking in that tone of yours, which hints that
you know the answer quite well: *Is there any proof whatsoever
of that theory? Has it been tested, proven scientifically?*

No.

If not, then what validity does it have?

It doesn't.

Scandalous, you say. Can you imagine a verdict without any documented proof? A medical diagnosis that does
not take into account the symptoms? Only in psychology
can a theory without any factual basis take over the professional discourse!

I nod, seemingly in agreement, but can't help thinking: It's all a defense mechanism that your ego has acti-
vated, Michael, because psychology and everything else
related to Adar, your only son whom you did not love,
arouse such powerful impulses in your id.

•

All of a sudden, it's hard for me to speak, Michael. Something is blocking my throat. I'll pour myself a glass of
water and try again soon.

•

A few days after his first visit, Avner Ashdot called and said he wanted to invite me to see the apartment in Tel Aviv. I told him I wasn't sure I was interested.

But he insisted: "You don't have to do anything. I pick you up. You see the apartment and then I take you back home. *C'est tout.*"

"Still, Mr. Ashdot, there is something we have to talk about before that."

"Go right ahead," he said.

"You said that our paths have crossed. How did they cross, if I may ask?"

"It's not for the phone."

"Why? Is our line tapped?"

"Not as far as I know."

"Not as far as you know?!"

"I'm kidding, Devora. You have nothing to worry about. I left the Ministry of Defense three years ago. They're not listening in. You can rest easy. My intentions are good."

"The path to hell—"

"—is paved with good intentions, I know. What time would it be convenient for me to come tomorrow?"

"I'm busy tomorrow, meetings in the tents on Rothschild."

"So the day after tomorrow. You shouldn't wait too long. Apartments get snapped up quickly here."

•

I used the time I gained to do two important things.

The first: I broadened the inquiry on Avner Ashdot. You always said that it's better not to ask people for favors so as not to be in their debt. In our position, you said, it was better to be extra careful and not owe anything to anyone. That was accurate, of course. Accurate at the time. But my status has changed, Michael. The sand of my life is running out, and what I don't ask for today, who knows, perhaps I won't be able to ask for it tomorrow.

A few phone calls to our friends in the police and the Defense and Interior ministries helped me to piece together the following picture: Avner Ashdot served in the Mossad and retired three years ago. He went into business, mainly real estate, and has been quite successful. He's a widower. The father of a daughter who lives on a cooperative farm in the Arava. He has no other children. He contributes a great deal of money to charity. No criminal charges have ever been filed against him, and except for a driver re-education course he had to take a while back, he has never been in trouble with the authorities.

•

And no, there is no pregnant woman, not even among his most distant relatives, who was run over. Really, Michael. Give me a little credit. Did you think I wouldn't check something like that?

•

The second important thing I did was buy clothes. Since you went away, I haven't bought myself anything new, Michael. I had nothing to get dressed up for (you were the ideal partner as far as that was concerned: noticed every earring, every ring, never hesitated to give a compliment), and even now, I want you to know, I didn't get dressed up for Avner Ashdot. I can't even say I liked him. At that point. But the elegant way he dressed made me feel frumpy when I was with him. And I wanted us to be on an equal footing while we were negotiating. That's all.

So I went and bought myself a new dress. And I didn't enjoy the experience at all. The saleswoman suggested, tactlessly, that I buy a black dress. I told her I didn't want a black dress. Even if it was slimming. I'd worn respectable, buttoned-down black and white for years, and now the door to the cage had been opened and I wanted to wear something colorful. But when I tried on various colors in the dressing room, you weren't there and there was no one to sneak in (remember when we were young and I used to push you away, then press up against you and whisper a threat to call the police?) and the dress I wanted was too expensive, even considering the permissive financial policies I was practicing at home, and the only way I could bring myself to buy it was to think of it as the first purchase of many that I would make with the money left over from the apartment-selling and -buying deal Avner Ashdot was setting up for me.

•

But there is no deal, I reminded myself as I waited for him in front of the building the next day. There's still no deal and you're not obligated to do anything. There's still no deal and you're not obligated to do anything.

"What a beautiful dress," he said when I got into the car. And he bent down to kiss my hand.

I pulled it away before he could and said firmly, "I want to make it clear that the fact that I'm going to Tel Aviv with you doesn't mean I've agreed to any deal or part thereof!"

He smiled that annoying smile of his and said, "I never thought otherwise." A moment later: "There's an almond croissant in a bag on the backseat, if you'd like it."

I said, "Please stop the car."

He kept driving.

"Stop the car immediately!" I demanded. And this time I spoke in the tone I used in court instead of banging my gavel.

It worked. He pulled over. It's possible that his thin arms even trembled a bit.

I interrogated him: "How did you know that I like almond croissants?"

In a perfectly innocent voice, he said, "I had no idea. It happened to be the last one in the bakery."

"Pu-rely by chance," I said sarcastically.

"Yes, purely by chance."

"I'm not sure I believe you."

"But it happens to be the truth, Devora. Can I keep driving?"

•

The apartment he found for me was wonderful. Top floor. With an elevator. A quiet street. Close to Rothschild Boulevard. No parking spot. But I didn't have a car anyway. Three clean, large rooms. A living room, bedroom, and a room for a young guest.

"Young guest?"

"It's a project I'm promoting now," he explained. "To revive an arrangement that was once common — to have poor young people stay in the apartments of older people who live alone. It's good for both sides. The differences in lifestyles aren't as great as they were in previous generations, and it's possible to agree on a few dos and don'ts that will make living together easier."

"Such as, for example?"

"We're still working on it. Mor, the girl with the braids who brought you to me, and your humble servant, are setting up an Internet site that will match up the people from both age groups. That will lay the foundations for that natural alliance. Mor told me how much you've helped the protesters, so I thought you might be interested in being the first to implement the idea — and become the inspiration for others." I didn't say anything, and he quickly added, "It's not a condition for buying this apartment, God forbid."

"To tell the truth, I like the idea..."

And I think that was the moment I allowed myself to relax slightly.

•

I was vigilant, Michael. I was constantly vigilant. After all, both you and I have sent smooth-tongued, nattily dressed scoundrels to prison after they exploited their victims' naïveté in all sorts of scams. I don't remember the specific details of every single case, but I remember the principle very well: even when the scammer was sent to prison, the victims never regained their money. Or their self-respect.

I didn't forget that for a moment as we walked around the apartment.

Right, left, trepidation, left, right, suspicion. That was the rhythm of my steps as I walked beside Avner Ashdot. And yet, when he told me about his young guest initiative, I had to admit that my inner scale tipped in his favor. I thought, A man who comes up with an idea like that cannot be essentially bad. Nevertheless, I said to myself, he's still withholding the secret of our crossing paths. Why? What does he have to hide?

●

We went up to his apartment. To discuss details. He offered me wine. I asked for water. And then the same thing happened again: instead of getting down to business, he chose to shift the conversation to a different subject.

He told me that the apartment we were in was the one he had shared with the wife he had separated from, the wife whose death had made him a widower. He hurried to explain: "It sounds strange, separated and widowed, but that's how it happened." He and Nira had been married twenty-five years. Loving, but not always happy. His work, the many trips that sometimes kept him away for months, took a toll on their married life. Travelers become accustomed to the freedom they have when they're away and the ones remaining behind become used to managing alone. And when they are back in each other's arms, it's difficult for them to re-establish their shared rhythm. Sometimes it would take a week before they relearned how to be flexible with one another, and then a call would come that sent him abroad once again.

Nevertheless, they didn't separate. Their love did not fade, despite everything. And they had their Maya to raise together. She wasn't an easy child, Maya. They had to move her from one school to another very often. Something had gone wrong in her relationship to the world. An ongoing misunderstanding, chronic, heartbreaking.

"That sort of demanding child can drive parents apart," he said.

I nodded.

"But she can also strengthen the bond between them, and that's what happened to me and Nira."

•

But it was then, after they had survived all the difficult years and their Maya was studying agriculture at the Weizmann Institute, having finally found her place in the world—it was then that Nira left.

Avner Ashdot sipped his wine. There was a struggle taking place in his expression, particularly around his lips: His mouth wanted to open, but his teeth clamped down on the flesh and prevented it.

I waited expectantly for the outcome of the battle. But even if he stopped now, he had already been extremely frank. He didn't belong to this generation, which revealed its secrets to one and all in the middle of Rothschild Boulevard. He was from our generation, which had a PRIVATE PROPERTY sign stuck to its chest.

And yet, to my surprise, he began speaking again. "They gave me a retirement party," he said. "People don't understand why the defense budget is so large—they should go to one of those parties. Tens of thousands of shekels spent on one evening. Singers, catering, imported liquor."

I clucked in agreement. "Yes, scandalous."

"You get tipsy at those events, not enough to be drunk, but enough to loosen tongues. It happened toward the end of the evening. A few of the guests had gone. And then Gadi Tessler came up to me, and in front of Nira, blurted out, 'How come you didn't invite that Swedish guy's family? What's his name again? Holstrom?' And he laughed loudly and slapped me on the back. Then, pretending his hand was a gun, aimed it at his own forehead, shot, then started laughing again. When he'd gone, Nira asked, 'What was *that* all about?' I said, 'You don't want to know.'"

•

Avner Ashdot poured himself more wine. Slowly. Swirled the liquid in his glass without bringing it to his lips and asked, "Are you sure you don't want a drink too?"

I said, "Come on, finish the story!"

He swooped down on my "come on" as if it were a treasure: "Ah! You see, Devora, that's exactly the problem with secrets. If you don't know about them, they don't bother you in the slightest. But the minute you get a whiff of one, you have to know it all."

"So did you tell her?"

"The commander of the cadet course told us in our first lesson, 'I'm warning you before you even start, the profession you're about to learn here is the loneliest one in the world. And the temptation to share the burden placed on your shoulders with someone close to you will be enormous. But every time you want to reveal secret information to them, remind yourselves what happened to Bruno Schmidt.'"

"Bruno Schmidt?"

"A CIA agent. In East Germany. His wife told her friend something he told her. Unfortunately that friend was, by chance or not by chance, a Stasi agent. Schmidt and his wife rotted in separate prisons for twenty years and weren't released until the wall fell."

"So... Nira... She just accepted your silence all those years? She didn't object?"

"It was a different time. Today men place a camera in front of them and blabber about their private lives, but then? Men didn't talk so much. Men went out on missions and came back, and the women didn't ask questions. That's how it was."

"Even so, I find it hard to believe that she never asked..."

"Maybe she felt more comfortable that way. In any case, suddenly, after twenty-five years, she wanted to know everything. Not wanted—demanded. I had no choice. Do you understand?"

"You could have stayed silent," I said.

Avner Ashdot put his wineglass on the table. His hand, I noticed, shook slightly. It occurred to me that this might be the first time he was telling this story to someone. I wondered what I had done to deserve that honor.

He smiled more with sadness than happiness and said, "You clearly didn't know Nira. It was very hard to say no to her. That's why she was such a good school principal. And to tell the truth, it was also hard for me to resist the temptation to confess and be purified. To be purified by the confession. So I said to myself, one story, that's all. But after she heard the story of Holstrom, which had been a real disaster, a terrible mistake in identification, she demanded to hear the rest of the stories. I talked and talked the whole night, and she listened and listened, new wrinkles forming on her forehead. In the morning, she acted normally. I figured that everything was still okay. But that night, she slept at Maya's place, and a week later, she came to get her things."

Avner Ashdot emptied his glass of wine in one sharp gulp and said, "'I don't know who you are anymore.' That's what she said before she left—'I don't know who you are at all.'"

•

And then, Michael, while I was talking with Avner Ashdot, a wave of longing for you passed through me.

Since you left, I've felt ripples of longing for you that come and go. But sometimes something happens in the world and the ripples only come and don't go, accumulating into a large wave. Throughout that conversation about lies and secrets, I felt that it wasn't only to Nira that Avner Ashdot hadn't told everything. He hadn't told it to me either, and that made me suddenly feel a fierce yearning for the truth that had always been between us. It hadn't always been paradise with you, Michael. I will never stop resenting you for what happened with Adar. But even that was out in the open. We didn't always talk about it, but it was out in the open. And I don't understand how it's possible to live differently, how it's possible to live with someone for twenty-five years without knowing what they do at work.

If anyone were to ask me what love is, I would say, The knowledge that, in a world of lies, there is one person who is totally honest with you and with whom you are totally honest, and there is truth between you, even if it isn't always spoken.

•

Avner Ashdot didn't sense the longing that flooded me. He was in the middle of his monologue. And from his tone, I could tell that he was coming to the point he wanted to emphasize.

"And then," he said, "she incited Maya against me. She went and told her all of my sins in great detail, and ever since, the girl has been estranged from me. Her mother reconciled with me before she died. During the last months of her illness, I never left her bedside. But my daughter still won't forgive me. We see each other, yes, but there is a Berlin wall between us, and she's my child, the girl I cherished and looked after for more than twenty years—"

"Except for when you traveled," I felt obliged to be accurate.

"Yes, that's also what Maya said. That I was never really there for her. That she could never rely on me completely. That she didn't need a father who told her stories, but a father who was with her. Who would simply be with her."

I thought, *The girl is right.* But then I thought, *It doesn't matter who's right. This is not a court here. And you are not being asked to judge.*

Avner Ashdot said, "So now I'm there for her. And I do things for her. Even this young guest project is actually for her. So she knows that her father can do good things too. It's terrible when there's a rift between you and your child. We shouldn't just accept it."

He spoke in a tone of finality and sipped his wine, looking into the glass. And then, all at once, he raised his glance and looked hard at me. I tried to extricate myself from the trap of those eyes, and his words echoed in my mind—"It's terrible when there's a rift between you and your child. We shouldn't just accept it"—and I thought, no, it can't be that he...

The thought that he knew about Adar was so chilling, Michael, that I immediately had to change the subject to something more concrete, so I asked, "So what do we agree about the apartment, Mr. Ashdot?" But I couldn't control the quaver in my voice.

Avner Ashdot took a piece of paper and a pen out of his pocket and said, as he filled the paper with numbers, "Let's see. I'll buy your apartment. With the money you receive, you'll buy the great apartment I just showed you, and with the difference, you'll redo the bathroom to look like mine."

He handed me the paper. I held it in my hand without looking at it and said, "I want to make it clear that the young guest matter is crucial to me."

"It's crucial for me too, and as soon as you sign the lease, we'll start looking for a suitable candidate."

"The young people on the boulevard," I explained, "they have fired my imagination. I want to help them any way I can."

"I take that completely for granted, Devora."

I couldn't decide whether his tone was admiring or disdaining, so I gave him back the paper and said, "I assume you'll want an agent's fee?"

"No," he said and smiled.

"No?"

"No. Instead of a fee, I want to ask you for something."

(To be honest, I thought his request would be of a sexual nature. The lingering kisses on my hand. The compliment when I got into the car. His attempts to get me to drink wine. The quick glances at the neckline of my dress. The extreme frankness. Everything pointed in that direction. And I was already preparing a firm refusal. Not that I wasn't interested in some physical contact. The long, warm hug with Hani had left me yearning for it. But I didn't like or accept the idea that sex would be part of a business deal.)

Avner Ashdot stood up and began pacing the room. Slowly. In measured steps. He went to the window and opened it slightly like someone who plans to light a cigarette and exhale the smoke through the crack. His right hand moved very briefly toward his shirt pocket, as if he were about to take out a pack of cigarettes, but came away empty.

I suddenly remembered that Adar did the same thing after he'd stopped smoking.

•

Finally, he said, "I want you to drive somewhere with me."

He was still facing the street.

"Drive?"

"Let's call it an excursion."

He turned around to look at me.

"But where to?"

"I can't tell you, that's part of it."

"And how long will this excursion take, may I ask?"

"What with all the new roads, less than three hours."

"When do we leave?"

He looked at his watch. "Now."

I also looked at my watch and said, "I can't. I have an appointment with the protest activists this afternoon. They're waiting for me."

"Then tomorrow at the latest."

"What's so urgent?"

"It's urgent, Devora, believe me."

"I need to think about it."

"Okay. But don't take too long."

"You know something?" I smiled. "I think best in the bathroom."

•

During the entire conversation with Avner Ashdot, my body seemed drawn toward the bathroom. If a camera had been documenting my responses, it would not have captured it. My eyes didn't move. My knees didn't turn. It was an internal shifting of my body, concealed but adamant, toward the thing that would give it pleasure.

And yet I was quite surprised by the words that came out of my mouth.

But Avner Ashdot did not look surprised. He looked as if my request was the most normal one in the world, the natural result of everything that had been said in our conversation so far.

He said, "Gladly. There are fresh towels on the rack."

I remembered the velvety feel of his towels very well.

I've had so few moments of undiluted pleasure since you left, Michael. You have to understand. Can you understand?

This is me talking to you. Your Devora. Still.

But that kind of death, the death of a spouse...you have to understand. Can you understand?

It changes something in you. It can't leave you unchanged. Do you understand?

Every time I had to give up something in my life and remain in the cage, I consoled myself: Never mind, there will be other opportunities.

And that kind of death—do you understand?

It makes you think that perhaps there won't be. Other opportunities, I mean. To do what you want to do. And that changes something in you. Sharpens something. You have to understand, Michael. Can you?

•

The buttons and the water pressure that increased and decreased at my command, the cosmetics and bath oils and natural soaps, the scented candles—I lit two of them—and the colored lights and the soft towels—all of that made me forget the sad fact: I hadn't taken a change of clothes with me this time either.

But Avner Ashdot didn't forget. When the sound of running water stopped, he assumed that I'd finished and asked from the other side of the door, "Do you need clothes?"

"Yes, but—"

"Open the door a crack. I put some of Nira's clothes in a bag for you. You can choose what fits you. You're about the same size."

I thought, Okay, I've had it. This is sick. I was about to say in a no-nonsense tone: Never mind, I'll manage.

But he beat me to it. "I have only one request, Devora. If you can, after you get dressed, walk straight from the bathroom to the front door. I'll wait in my study. Nira's clothes on another woman...I...It's too soon for me."

And that's what I did. I dried my hair and combed it and put on a green dress of hers that fit me perfectly. After one last look in the mirror, I opened the bathroom door and walked straight to the front door.

Right before I opened it, I stopped and said, "Thank you."

His voice answered me from another country: "You're welcome."

"And...Avner," I said, "I've thought about it and...pick me up the day after tomorrow in the morning."

•

I wonder if, at this point, you've already guessed the nature of the trap that had been laid for me. You were always faster than I was at analyzing evidence. More than once, just from listening to partial, fragmented stories about trials *I* was presiding at, you handed down a verdict. And most of the time, the right one.

But only most of the time. That lightning speed of yours also made you err. And all those errors tormented you during the weeks before you died. You dredged up the image of the parents of Rivi Magal, whose rapist you found innocent by reasonable doubt. Again and again, you recalled her father coming up to you in the corridor outside the courtroom, grabbing your arm, and saying, "Your Honor, forgive me, I am just a simple man, but can you explain to me why you just released a defendant who confessed to his crime?"

Lying on your sickbed, you said to me in a crushed voice, "Maybe you wouldn't have been in such a hurry to pass judgment as I was, Devora, and maybe the people in the courtroom did not regard you in awed silence when you entered, but look at your record. Thirty years without a single injustice."

I consoled you with soft words, of course. That's what you do when you love someone. I said, "It's only a minor incident." I said, "You never took a bribe, Michael, never fixed a trial. The prosecution was negligent in the Rivi Magal case, and we both know that the rules of evidence sometimes compel us to rule according to law and not according to justice…"

But that small spot of arrogance in my chest flashed with joy as we spoke.

It's natural for a couple who have the same profession

to be jealous and competitive and to have different viewpoints. Especially if one was originally a prosecutor and the other a defense attorney. And in truth, I'd been jealous of you many times over the years. You were a more gifted and successful judge than I. Your minority opinions were accepted time after time in the Supreme Court. You were promoted and given high-profile cases, while I stayed where I was, keeping a low profile. And now it turns out that I scored at least one victory over you.

So what do you think at this point, my dear, beloved Michael? Do you already know what Avner Ashdot was hiding from me? Have enough hints been dropped?

If they have, I didn't see them. Not at all. And the reason I didn't see them is terrible. No mother would admit to it. In fact, I can only admit it to the answering machine. So I'll take a deep breath and say—damn it, it's hard—

It never entered my mind that Adar had any part in this story because, as the years passed, Adar entered my mind less and less often.

The first year of the estrangement, a minute didn't go by without my thinking about him. Where was he? What was he doing? What was he eating? Remember that you suspected that I had a lover then? That I "wasn't with you" when we made love? Now I can finally tell you: I really wasn't with you. I was with him. I'd close my eyes while you lay on top of me and try to imagine where Adar was sleeping. In what bed. Did he have warm blankets?

I tried to dig up information. From his old friends. On the computer. But I found nothing. The first year, I'd walk in the streets and fantasize that I'd been diagnosed with cancer and Adar had no choice but to end his boycott of us and visit me in the hospital.

The second year, I kept thinking about him, but a bit less. You refused to talk about him. And what isn't spoken doesn't solidify. Just as you said in our last conversation in prison. "A complete break." And so a year passed. And another year. And then you became ill. And I retired to take care of you. You were the focus of my life (Adar would say: So what's new?).

Right before the funeral, I wondered whether he knew and would come, and when he didn't, I wondered if he'd come to the shivah, and every time I looked up to see who was at the door, I hoped it was him. But he didn't come. And I wondered once again if what had happened really justified this terrible anger of his, and repeated what you always said in reply: No, no, it doesn't justify it. Absolutely not.

•

But today I would answer: What difference does it make what justifies what and who is right? This is not a court of law. And you are not being asked to hand down a verdict.

•

After I dreamed that my superego was being removed, I ordered a full set of Freud's writings on the Internet and paid extra for an express delivery—I could have waited and saved the money, Michael, I know, but my id refused to control itself! Twenty-four hours later, the seven volumes were at our door.

You would clearly give me an I-told-you-so nod if I said that I found dubious ideas in Freud. Penis envy—come on. I liked your penis very much, Michael, it was a fine example of the organ, but I never wanted it to be mine. On the contrary, it always seemed a great bother to have to walk around with something like that between one's legs.

Nevertheless, I must admit that Freud also had some interesting ideas. The sort that reverberate in the world. For example, the way the subconscious sometimes pops up in our daily lives: someone uses a wrong word, and the mistake reflects what he's really thinking. How many times did we hear defendants or attorneys have slips of the tongue, exposing exactly what they didn't want to say. (I remember Armond Bloom, the defense attorney who claimed you went to school with his client's brother-in-law and demanded that you "accuse" yourself.)

It's a shame that you can't read Freud with me, Michael, I would have been happy to argue loudly with you about him. You would say, for example: The only thing you can judge about a person is his overt behavior, the tip of the iceberg. The seven-eighths below the surface is irrelevant. And I would have replied: But you can't claim that they don't exist. Then you would say: Freud idealizes the destructive impulse, and that's dangerous. I would reply: What are you talking about? Not recognizing that a particular impulse exists is much more dangerous!

Later, as we loved to do, our bodies aflame with the righteousness of our claims, we would make love, at first continuing the argument using different devices, and in the end...not arguing at all.

•

So why am I mentioning Freud for the second time? (I picture you pulling your earlobe the way you used to when an attorney was bothering you with details you thought were not relevant to the case).

At the meeting I had with the protesters the next day, one fellow came in late. I looked up to greet him, and for a fraction of a second I thought it was Adar. At second glance, he looked completely different from Adar: long hair, long limbs, straight nose, thin lips. I didn't understand how I could have thought he was Adar.

But now I think it was my subconscious. It guessed what was about to happen.

The meeting itself, by the way, was annoying. The protesters argued bitterly even though they agreed in principle on most of the issues on the agenda. I thought that their instinctive suspicion and hypersensitivity, which I did not share, were making the atmosphere ugly. Someone left the room, and when he returned a few moments later, everyone looked at him as if he'd committed a serious crime while he was gone. "What?" he asked. "What's wrong?" No one answered. I think their exhaustion had further strained their nerves. Spending a month in a tent on a noisy street isn't easy. It isn't easy at all.

I tried as hard as I could to mediate, I made compromise suggestions, but they were all rejected out of hand. It seemed that although everyone there wanted cooperation in principle, their greatest desire was actually to be differentiated from the others. To say: I'm not like everyone else. I'm different. I'm a bit more right than they are.

In any case, I left that meeting less euphoric than I had been going into it, but no less convinced of the importance of trying and imagining a different reality. A new one. But at least they all agreed that the young guest project was a great idea.

●

How little time we apportioned to imagination in our conversations, Michael. Imagination is not important in a court of law. Only the facts are important. And so we became used to ridiculing imagination. Ignored it. Exiled it to a penal colony.

●

Avner Ashdot was listening to Richard Strauss's *Thus Spake Zarathustra* on the disc player of his car when I got into it. The first sounds of the third part were playing, and right after I buckled in, I said, "*Von der grossen Sehnsucht.*" Of the Great Longing.

Avner Asdot nodded and lowered the volume of the music.

I asked him not to lower it, and he raised it again.

We drove in silence as the wonderful sounds (sorry, Michael, they are wonderful) of the oboe and violins filled the air.

When we merged with the road to Beersheba, the last section began: *Nachtwandlerlied.* Song of the Night Wanderer. And I suddenly thought, how can I allow myself to go on an excursion when I could be sitting and writing verdicts? Then, like someone awakening from a nightmare to discover with relief that it's only a dream, I remembered, there were no longer any cases waiting for my verdicts. And there never would be.

"Michael," I said, "I mean, my husband—"

Avner Ashdot lowered the volume and turned his head slightly toward me, a small, almost imperceptible movement, but it was enough for me to know that he was listening.

"My husband wouldn't allow us to listen to Strauss at home. 'The house I live in will not play works by the president of the Reichstag music bureau!' That was his position."

"That extreme?"

"He would get angry every time there were arguments on the news for and against playing Strauss, and he'd shout at the screen, 'You boycott Wagner?! He died in the nineteenth century. It's Strauss you should boycott!'"

"Your husband, he was a second-generation Holocaust survivor, I assume."

"Actually no. It was a matter of principle with him."

"So he was a man of principle."

"Absolutely."

"Wait a minute. How do you know this piece so well if you never heard it?"

"On Wednesdays, I'd finish work before him, go home, and listen to Strauss. I hid the record in the sleeve of a Bach record. It wasn't right. But I love Strauss so much. For me, his music is . . . a joy."

"I agree with you completely. Should we stop for something to drink?"

•

Are you surprised, Michael? I'm sure you aren't. I'm sure you knew what was concealed inside the Bach sleeve and decided, in your wisdom, to keep silent. To grant me that small thing and many other small things, so that when the day came, you could ask me to return the favor and grant you something big.

•

Strauss's music must have softened me. Otherwise, I can't explain the conversation that developed at the roadside stop. In retrospect, I thought that everything was planned. I was a puppet—and Avner Ashdot was pulling my strings. The offer to buy my apartment. The apartment in Tel Aviv. The premature, generous confessions about his private life. The music in the car, that music of all possible choices, Strauss of all composers. It was all a long, slow seduction. But not the seduction of a lover who wants intimacy. The seduction of a spy. Who wants information.

He said, "You never talk about your children, Devora."

There were hardly any people at the roadside restaurant. At a nearby table, an ultra-Orthodox man was reading the newspaper sports section, a family was sitting at a table farther away from us: a father, a mother, and a baby in a carriage. The smell of a vegetable omelet was in the air.

I said, "What is there to say?"

A waitress came to our table, wiped it with a cloth, and then put down a salt-and-pepper-shaker stand that held only a salt shaker and asked, "What'll you have?"

Avner gestured with his head for me to order first. I asked for tea and an almond croissant. He ordered a double espresso, and when the waitress was out of earshot, he asked, "So...how many children do you have?"

I liked that he waited for the waitress to walk away. I liked that even though she was very attractive, his eyes didn't follow her but remained focused on me.

"One. I have one son."

"What's his name?"

"Adar."

"That's a nice name."

"I agree."

"And what does Adar say about your intention to sell the apartment?"

"He doesn't know about it."

"He doesn't?"

"We're not in touch."

Avner Ashdot nodded understandingly. And said nothing. That was clever of him, giving me a short break. As it was, I was frightened by my own frankness. Relatives, close friends, colleagues—they were all careful not to talk to us about Adar. Even at the shivah, no one mentioned him. I wanted them to. I was prepared for it. I was afraid that there was a stockpile of words in my subconscious just waiting for a question that would dig down to the right place. But everyone kept silent. Of course, I could have spoken. Raised the subject. But until the last day, I was waiting for Adar to come in, walk with those clomping steps of his to the living room of the house he grew up in, and sit down beside me.

•

Avner Ashdot didn't ask me anything else about Adar. Not even when we went back to the car and began driving again. *Thus Spake Zarathustra* reached its minimalist ending, so different from the Odyssean beginning: the final four bleats of viola and flute. Avner Ashdot waited for another two beats of silence, then asked, "More Strauss?"

I nodded. I thought he'd remove one disc and insert another. But he pressed a button, and the changing of the guards took place inside the player, invisible.

I heard the first familiar sounds and thanked him silently for choosing that particular piece. I thought, That too is a gift, knowing how to choose the right soundtrack. I closed my eyes and let the music flow toward me and the taste of the transgression — Strauss twice in one day — spread through my body.

When I opened my eyes and looked out the window, I was startled to see that I had no idea where I was. I thought in alarm, I'm driving with a man I barely know to a place he refuses to name, and I have no idea where we are. So what if he also likes Strauss's *Metamorphosis*? Perhaps that, just like the almond croissant he bought me, is no accident either?

•

And then, as if he sensed my urgent need to know where I was, he said in a tour guide's voice, "On the right you can see the Goral Hills. This is where I taught navigation to soldiers in military command courses. It looks like a wilderness, doesn't it?"

"Yes."

"People and animals live in the crevices of those hills, and you can even drink water from the wells here."

"Wells?"

"It's hard to believe, but there are no less than nine active wells in the Goral Hills. The Bedouins tie a big pail, which once held olives, to a rope beside the well, drop it inside, and pull it up again filled with water from the depths of the earth."

"And what does the water taste like?"

"Paradise."

I agreed. Yes, it really is hard to believe. The idle talk, sightseers' talk, calmed me down a bit. I looked out the window and searched for wells among the crevices.

But then he asked, "So why...aren't you in touch with your son, Devora?"

"Ah...it's...a long story."

"We have all the time in the world."

•

Do you remember that Saturday in Sde Boker, Michael? A good friend of yours lent us his cabin. We drove down there to celebrate the end of your internship. We left our backpacks in the cabin and went right out to hike before the sun set. We walked to a spring you knew about and I didn't. We walked hand in hand between the yellow walls, the space growing narrower all the time. I wondered, There's water here? It's hard to believe. You smiled and said, "Wait and see." And then we saw ibexes. We saw them before they saw us, so we stopped. Silently, we watched them for a few moments until they climbed up from the wadi to the hill in a small procession. I said, "Their movements are so aristocratic." You kissed my neck and said, "Aristocratic."

We kept walking until we reached your spring. There was no one there but us. We weren't judges yet. We still weren't asking ourselves twice before everything we did whether it was normative or not. We simply took off all our clothes and walked naked into the cool water. Then we spread a thin blanket on one of the flat rocks and made love on it. We'd known each other only a few months—and I was still surprised at what a passionate, uninhibited lover you were. At home, it sometimes frightened me. At home, I sometimes felt anger in your touch, felt that you were angry at me or at someone else. But out in nature, it was...natural.

I remember that a wasp landed on your rear end after it was over and I drove it away by shouting at it, "Out damned wasp," which made us both laugh. When our laughter died down, I said, "What if I just became pregnant?" You stroked my hair and said, "A child with your eyes? That sounds wonderful."

•

After a long, heavy silence that Avner Ashdot heroically maintained for many kilometers, I said, "He's not in touch with us. Three years ago, he told us that he wanted no further contact between us. And we haven't heard from him since then."

"But what happened?"

"Many things. It's...complicated."

"Even so?"

"He...got into trouble and expected us to help him. When we didn't, he...lost control."

"What kind of trouble did he get into, if I may ask?"

"He went out one night with friends for some fun. On the way back in the morning, he ran over a pregnant woman who was crossing on a crosswalk. He was driving fast. Much faster than the city speed limit. She suffered a blow to the head and died on the spot. The fetus had no chance either. She was in her fifth month. They did a breathalyzer test on him right there, two breaths into the device one minute apart. That's what they do. They found elevated levels of alcohol in his blood. Extremely elevated. He...was charged with...manslaughter."

●

I remember your face, Michael, after we had him released on bail and took him home. All your features became exaggerated into a caricature: Your strong chin became completely square. Your thick eyebrows became even thicker. Your nostrils flared with rage.

"Idiot," you said to Adar. "You're just an idiot. I can't believe my son is such an idiot."

●

You know, Michael, in retrospect things become clearer: there was no love under your anger when you said that. If you listen carefully, you can usually hear the love under a parent's anger. With you, there was only anger. All those years I had persuaded you to restrain yourself with him after his escapades, and that anger had festered and grown in your mind until it blocked out any positive feelings you had. All the school principals you'd had to ingratiate yourself with — after we discovered that you were better at ingratiating yourself than I was — so they wouldn't throw him out of school. All the rebukes we had to endure from other parents, all the patronizing advice they gave us, all the times we couldn't meet with friends who had small children because they were afraid that Adar would do something nasty and unexpected to them. All the times we told him that this was the last time, next time he'd be punished, the time you put him on trial (because you genuinely believed it was the way to help him, I know) when he was eight, and the way he laughed when it was over and you decided on the punishment — to be sent away to boarding school on probation. All the times that followed when he was given educational and noneducational punishments that only made him laugh, all that ongoing failure to understand him, to placate him, to bring him closer to us, all that self-flagellation — maybe we were the ones who...maybe we missed something that, if we had seen it, if we had stopped it in time, we might have been able to shift the course he was on.

All that mutual flagellation, which we never spoke of out loud, but thought about constantly: *He's like that because of you, Devora, because you deserted him when he was three months old.*

Because of me? You didn't desert him, Michael, because you were never there for him, you gave up on him from the beginning.

I gave up on him? You're the one who gives in to him, Devora, you're the one who lets him get away with things all the time.

All the whispering swirling around you in the court-house corridors after the first time he was charged, Michael, and the time you went into your office and your interns stopped talking abruptly and you knew exactly what they were talking about, or the time you repri-manded a parent who began shouting during a session and told him that if they had educated their child prop-erly he wouldn't have been there, and the defense attor-ney whispered loudly enough for you to hear, "Look who's talking..."

It all came to a head that evening. You kept hurling painful insults at Adar and he didn't answer. His entire body shook from the effort not to answer. Only after you stopped talking did he say, "I know I'm a piece of gum that got stuck to the sole of your beautiful shoes, Dad, but what can I tell you, the gum needs help now."

•

Avner Ashdot was silent for a long time before he asked, "But what exactly did he want you to do for him? It sounds like a lost cause. A speeding driver under the influence, a pregnant woman—what is there to talk about here?"

A lone soldier raised his thumb for a ride at the raw concrete station for hitchhikers as we were about to drive past him. A soldier. Alone. In the middle of the day. We should stop for him. We had room in the backseat. If we pick him up, I promised myself, I'll stop talking. As it was, I'd spoken more than enough about things better left unsaid. And what if Avner Ashdot was recording me? Suspicion began to gnaw at me again. His phone rested in the center console between us, next to the bottle of mineral water, and it flashed constantly. Could that rhythmic flashing be a sign that the phone was recording?

Avner Ashdot drove past the hitchhikers' station without slowing down at all. He didn't even consider slowing down. On the contrary, he deliberately drove faster. That pushed me against the back of my seat, and the blood-chilling thought passed through my mind that he didn't stop because he didn't want the soldier to get in the way of his kidnapping me.

"Why didn't you stop for him?!"

"Who?"

"The soldier!"

"I thought you wouldn't want to, I mean, that you wouldn't want anyone to join—"

"Ask me next time. Ask me before you decide what I want."

"I can go back and pick him up if it's important to you, Devora. Should I go back and pick him up?"

I exhaled.

I exhaled a very long breath. The way you exhale into a breathalyzer.

•

I didn't ask Avner Ashdot to go back for the soldier. But I did ask him why his phone was flashing all the time. He picked it up, looked at it, and said, "I don't know."

It sounded as if he really didn't.

"Is it bothering you?" he asked. "If it is, I can try to figure out how to stop it."

"No. It's okay."

Signs saying DANGER: FIRING RANGE, fixed in concrete posts, lined the right side of the road. I heard myself say, "He...I mean Adar...wanted us to pull strings. To get him out of it. He said we could question the reliability of the breathalyzer test in court. That there were precedents."

"I understand. And what did Michael say about that?"

"Michael...told him the truth. That it was impossible. The unequivocal results of his test made it impossible. Adar wanted him to sit down with the lawyer and try to find a loophole or at least do something behind the scenes, talk to his best friend, the court president, and have the case referred to a more sympathetic judge. Michael told him that the only thing that would help him now was to show remorse. To run over a pregnant woman and not to be upset about it at all is—but Adar said, 'Why don't you at least tell the truth, that you can help me but you don't want to?'

"And that was it. That was when Michael exploded. He yelled at Adar, 'Wait just a minute, what do you mean, tell the truth? Are you calling me a liar?' Adar said, 'Yes.' Michael demanded that he apologize immediately. But Adar hissed, 'Are you kidding? You're the one who should apologize.'

"It was like that every night for an entire week, with me shuttling between them trying to mediate, to conciliate, to explain one to the other. And you should know that when I was a judge, I was a champion mediator, mediating between Kramer and Kramer, between Rose and Rose, and now—"

"You were stuck between a rock and a hard place," Avner said.

I nodded and turned my glance to the window.

•

We drove through total desert. Sand and more sand, not even a single tree to hang on to. Not even a bush. Occasional streambeds wound around the hills, but they were dry. Dry as a bone.

"Water?" Avner asked.

"Water."

He took the bottle out of the center console, put the cap to his mouth, and opened it with his teeth.

I drank. Almost the whole bottle.

Finally, I resumed speaking—I felt that I was talking because I had to talk, not because I wanted to: "One night Michael was in the middle of one of his admonishing speeches when Adar suddenly leaped up. I think Michael used the phrase 'It serves you right.' He said, 'You killed a pregnant woman. As far as I'm concerned, you can rot in prison. It serves you right.' Then Adar grabbed the chair next to him and threw it at him. It hit Michael in the head, and when he fell, Adar kicked him in the stomach, screaming, 'It serves you right, it serves you right.' He kept telling me to move away or else I'd get hit too. When it was all over, he raced to his room, threw a few things into a plastic bag, and left."

I know, Michael. I know I promised you not to talk about that night. I bandaged your wounds and said, "We'll tell people you fell on the stairs." You said you wanted to file a complaint with the police. That he couldn't get away with such an act without punishment. You used the word "act," I remember. I begged you not to go to the police. The boy had been charged with manslaughter as it was. I said, "I'm asking you, Michael. How many things have I ever asked you for?"

For twenty-four hours, you raged about your injured pride and shattered principles, and in the end, you agreed. You said, "I'll do it for you. Only for you. But on one condition: If we don't report it to the police, then as far as I'm concerned, everything that happened here didn't happen. We will never speak of it again—not to each other and not to other people. Ever."

•

A herd of white goats crossed the road. It wasn't clear where they had come from. It wasn't clear where they were going. A shepherdess with a baby strapped to her body hurried the last goat along, a black one. A refuse-nik. Avner Ashdot turned his whole body around to me and said, "You must have been in shock. I mean, that's not something you expect from your child."

"Yes and no," I admitted. "Adar was sixteen the first time he was charged by the police. He punched a security guard who wouldn't let him into a club. And a month before the accident, he ran away from home and joined a gang of thugs who harassed tourists on the promenade in Eilat. The police there told us to come and take him before things got out of control. So . . . the signs had always been there."

"But still, he was his father."

"Yes, his father."

The last goat finished crossing the road. The shepherdess and her baby had also left the asphalt, and we began driving again.

After a few moments of silence, Avner Ashdot asked, "So after that night, there was no more contact with him?"

I didn't answer right away. A makeshift, handwritten road sign tied to a traffic light pointed to Uziel's Farm, and a dirt road led from the main road to the curves of the hills. I wondered whether we would turn onto it. I hoped we would. I hoped that doing so would put an end to our conversation and I wouldn't have to speak anymore. Somehow, all the sudden frankness made me feel worse, not better.

•

We didn't head toward Uziel's Farm. We kept driving toward an unknown destination.

Avner Ashdot looked at me expectantly.

Finally I said, "At that point, we were still in touch. I visited Adar in prison the entire time he was there. Every other week I traveled two and a half hours to bring him sheets and underwear. Michael knew, of course, but never went with me. He said, 'First let him apologize.' And Adar said, 'First let him apologize.'

"Then Adar went into therapy. The opportunity is offered to prisoners the system believes it has even a slight chance of reforming. After three months of therapy, he decided that we were responsible for everything that had happened in his life. He said to me, 'You set impossible standards at home, there was no way I could come up to your expectations: "that is not our way," "that is our way"—how could I find my own way in that situation?'

"We sat across from each other in the visitors' room on metal chairs that were screwed to the floor. It was very noisy. That's how it is there, all the visitors and all the prisoners sit in a single room and talk at the same time. Total cacophony. A visit lasts only forty-five minutes. That might sound like a lot of time, but it's nothing.

"He said, 'What kind of father puts his son on trial in the living room, tell me? And why? Because I took a few shekels from his wallet? I was eight, Mom, eight! And he forced me to stand on the stool and asked me what I had to say in my own defense. You think that's normal? You think it was normal for him to threaten to banish me, an eight-year-old, to boarding school?'

"I said, 'Dad wanted...I mean, we...we wanted to get you back on track. Our...our intentions were good.'

"Then he said loudly, almost shouting, 'The hell with your intentions, the results were shit!'

"The guards turned to look at us. One of them came over and stood close. I tried to calm things down: 'We can talk about all this at home, Adari. You'll be released soon.'

"And he said, 'I'm not coming home, Mom. I thought about it and decided that my relationship with you poisons me. If I want to be happy, I have to cut myself off from you for the time being. Build myself alone.'

"I said, 'You're punishing yourself? Is that what you're doing? Where will you go?'

"'I'll manage.'

"'I don't think so.'

"Then he said, pounding a fist into the palm of his other hand, 'It'll end badly if I go back home . . . Dad and me — it'll end badly.'"

•

Avner Ashdot sighed. He took his right hand off the wheel for a moment, as if he planned to caress me. Then he put it back. Without a caress.

I pulled the sun visor farther down for more protection against the sun. And also so I would have something to do with my hands.

He asked quietly, "So what . . . what did you say to him, Devora? I mean, what can you say in a situation like that?"

"I told him, I mean, I asked him to keep a channel open with me. At least that.

"He said, 'I'm sorry, Mom, but it won't work if it's not a complete break from both of you. At least for a while.' And that was it. He just stood up and left. Prisoners never leave before visiting time is over, and we still had another ten minutes — ten minutes! But he took the bag I'd brought him, and without even saying goodbye, went back to his cell.

"When I got home and told Michael about Adar's decision to cut off all contact with us, he said it was manipulation. That 'for the time being' would come to an end soon and he'd be back in touch with us. Because he'd need money. And he'd have no choice. But six months after his release, when Adar still hadn't called us, Michael said, 'You know what? Good riddance. Look at how much better our lives are without the . . . constant fear that he's about to get into trouble again.'

"I shouted at him, 'He's your son!' That was the first time I raised my voice to him in all the years we'd been together.

"'Good riddance,' he said again in a quiet, steady voice.

"I said, 'I plan to fight for him. I won't give up on him so easily.'

"'You'll have to fight that war without me.'

"'Don't do me any favors, I'll do it without you.'

"'You don't understand, Devora, I kept quiet when you went to the prison to grovel in front of him after he ran over a pregnant woman and struck me so violently. But now I'm telling you this in no uncertain terms: if you stay in contact with him, you will have no contact with me.'"

●

Then I told Avner Ashdot other things about you, Michael. I had to tell him other things so he would understand what kind of person you are, what kind of person you were. I had to counterbalance that "Good riddance" of yours, which sounded so terrible when I repeated it. So I described how you went to see your father in the hospice three times a week to sit beside him and hold his hand, despite all the scars he'd left on you. I told him about your generous annual contribution, given anonymously, to My Body, the organization that promotes harsher punishment for sexual abuse (I know that by doing so, you violated ethical rules and it should be kept secret, but I just had to speak). I told him about the court reporters—other judges were always condescending toward them, but you always treated them respectfully. And not only them, but also the cleaners, the clerks, the paralegals, the guards—you always went over to each one of them before the holidays, wished them a happy holiday, and thanked them for their excellent work. And if there was a new guard who didn't recognize you and asked for identification, you didn't roll your eyes, but took out your identification card patiently.

I told him about your generosity as a husband. About your ability to praise. No woman in the world has ever received as many compliments as I did. And I don't know many women whose husbands continued to bring them flowers every week for thirty years, on a different day each time so it wouldn't become too routine. I told him about the notes. I didn't quote them, don't worry. But I told him that every Saturday morning, you'd get up before me and write me a short love poem on a bit of paper and paste it on the fridge.

Only after I told him all of that did I feel that I could also say, "Yes, he was as stubborn as a mule. And when you live with a stubborn person, you gradually learn that if you don't want to spend all your time fighting, you have to learn to give in."

Then I said, "But in this case, I would have fought" — as the words left my mouth, I felt the bland taste of a lie on my tongue — "but there was nothing I could do. Adar vanished as if the earth had swallowed him up. I didn't hear from him for three years. He didn't even bother to come to Michael's shivah.

•

There might not be another opportunity. If I don't tell the answering machine the cruel truth *now*, I might never have another chance to say it. So here it is:

I could have searched harder for Adar. I could have hired a private detective. I could have overturned every stone until I found him. After all, we're in Israel: how many hiding places could there be on the head of a pin? And when I found out where he was, I could have persuaded him to call. At least me. He *did* say he was sorry that he had to break off relations with me. And he said "for the time being." A normal mother would have made great efforts to find him, to change his mind. But I didn't do that. I didn't do that because your warning echoed in my mind: "It's him or me." And I knew you well enough to know that you would carry out your threat if you had to.

That isn't a choice a woman should have to make, Michael, to decide which bond is stronger — the one between her and her husband or the one between her and her children. But I did make the choice. Every mother's court would find me guilty, of course. And have me executed. A mother who gives up her son — is there a greater sin than that in the nation of Jewish mothers?

On the last day of your shivah, there were already fewer people in the house. After they left, only Hava Rosenthal and I remained in the house. As she helped me load the dishwasher, she said, "It's nice that all of his court reporters came. Very touching."

"He treated them exceptionally well."

"Yes, he was a true gentleman, your Michael."

"Yes, he was."

Then she said, "Adar wasn't here today."

"Adar wasn't here yesterday either. He's not in touch with us."

"I never really understood what exactly happened between you. Was it because of…the accident he had?"

"We don't like to talk about, Michael and I."

"Okay."

It was actually because she didn't pressure me that I told her. Standing in the kitchen wiping glasses. It just came out of me. And the more I spoke, the less sympathetic she looked. She stepped back from me toward the wall until the back of her neck almost touched the bulletin board that used to be covered with pictures of Adar until you destroyed them, and now only bills were tacked on it.

When I finished talking, she didn't console or support me, she only said coolly, "You made your choice, Devora." And I never heard from her or the other members of our book club again. She must have told them. And they must have thought I should be stoned, or at least not invited to the next meeting, when Elsa Morante's *History* was going to be discussed.

Truthfully, I have nothing to say in my defense except

that I didn't believe I could live without you, Michael. And without him, shameful as it is, I knew I could.

·

Avner Ashdot turned the wheel and we drove onto the bypass road. Like Hava Rosenthal at the shivah, he shifted his body away from me.

Freud was right, I thought, as I turned away from him too, to look out the window. All men are actually searching for a substitute mother, and I'm not a good enough mother. I was never a good enough mother. When he was three months old, I handed Adar over to a nanny. I couldn't bear my own powerlessness. I had graduated from high school with honors and from college with honors (right behind you on the dean's list), and with Adar—from the first moment, all I felt was failure.

You tried to encourage me. You'd say: It's not you. It's the child. He's difficult. And at first, when I was still sure of it, I'd say, There's no such thing as a difficult child.

·

Through the window I saw clusters of Bedouin tin shacks crowded together. In one of them—I couldn't help imagining it—a mother must be calling to her children to come and eat lunch. The heat is blazing inside the tin shack, and her galabiya is black and thick, but she feels comfortable inside her body. The role of mother comes naturally to her. She gives them food, a tin plate for each child. Her movements are effortless. The tin plates slide naturally from her hands to land in the right place in front of each child. The smells coming from the plates are good. Let's say, rice with cooked carrots. The children arrive. Laughing loudly. Something is making them laugh. She laughs with them.

And if I had been a natural-born mother—the thought passed through my mind—would it have helped?

And if you had been a natural-born father, Michael?

•

Avner Ashdot pressed up against the window with the entire weight of his shoulder on it.

I can feel when an act of judgment is taking place where I am. And I knew he was judging me now. And finding me guilty. I thought, I can forget about compliments. About his hand on mine. Maybe it's better that way. It was too early for me to open my heart to someone anyway. The conditions weren't right yet.

•

Another sign pointed to a farm. This time it was Azrikam's. I remembered what those farms were called. Isolated farms. I think you once ruled in favor of an NPO that represented Beduoins in a dispute about grazing lands between them and the owner of one of those farms... Or did you rule against them?

Avner Ashdot pressed the button that opened the window. Hot, dry air blew into the car. His right hand once again moved for a fraction of a second toward his shirt pocket as if reaching for a pack of cigarettes, and once again returned to the wheel.

"When did you stop?" I asked, rescuing us from the strained silence in the car.

"Stop what?"

"Smoking."

He smiled. "Five weeks and four days. But who's counting?"

"I imagine it must be hard."

"I'm doing it for her. For Maya. She hates that I smoke. Always did. So I'm trying...for her...to improve. But yes, breaking any habit is hard."

"You know, Avner"—I called him by name for the first time—"I think that after I've been so open with you, you should be open with me and tell me, if you would be so kind, where we're going."

"To Noit, a cooperative farm in the Arava," he said. "She lives there. My daughter."

●

As if in response to his words, a tornado of sand and dust suddenly swirled at the side of the road and then settled.

Why in the world does he want me to go to see his daughter with him? Am I supposed to advocate for him with her? How? Is he going to introduce me as his escort? His girlfriend, heaven forbid? And why is he suddenly willing, after saying it was impossible, to tell me where we were going?

I didn't know. But I decided to do as he did: not to ask directly for answers, but to clear a bypass road leading to them.

I asked, "So how did she end up here...in the Arava?"

"She took an undergraduate course in desert agriculture and it fascinated her. While she was still at school, she told us that that's what she wanted to do later. But we didn't take her seriously. A girl who grew up in cafés, how could the desert possibly interest her? Right after submitting her final paper, she got on a bus and went to the Arava. Before she left, she arranged jobs she would do in exchange for room and board and told us that we couldn't even imagine the huge expanses down there."

"She's right," I said, and looked out the window. From the car all the way to the horizon, there wasn't a single house, only acacia trees, endless acacia trees.

Avner went on, "She was so happy there. The first time since she was born that our little girl was happy. So we were happy for her."

(Adar had his golden age too—remember Michael? The vacation between ninth and tenth grades. He got a job at the Safari in Ramat Gan. Do you remember suddenly noticing what a beautiful smile he had? For the first time in ages, I saw a flash of hope in your eyes. And then—money went missing from the cash register. And the internal investigation they carried out found that Adar was guilty. He claimed he hadn't done anything. He screamed and cried. But even we didn't completely believe him. With great effort and much sweet-talking, we persuaded that pig of a manager not to report the incident to the police. But Adar never set foot in the Safari again, and that beautiful smile disappeared as if it had never been.)

•

And if we had believed him? If we had believed him with all our hearts and taken his side, would it have helped? Was that the moment we still could have saved him, Michael?

•

"For three years" — Avner continued his story — "Maya went from hothouse to hothouse, from farm to farm. Dates. Tomatoes. Cherry tomatoes. Cucumbers. Green peppers. Red peppers. Melons. Eggplants. And then, after two years of fieldwork, she went to the manager of a farm with an idea of her own. You know those little peppers that sometimes grow inside the big ones?"

"Yes, of course."

"It seems that they sprout naturally, without any fertilization. It's called parthenocarpy."

"How is that possible? How can a plant sprout without fertilization?"

"To this day, no one has been able to explain exactly how it happens. But my daughter claimed that she had been studying the phenomenon and believed that with the right temperature and hormones, she could cause it to happen — and also control it, that is, intentionally grow large peppers that have small ones inside them. And she could make sure that the small peppers weren't misshapen the way they are sometimes, but they would be as beautiful and perfect as the large ones."

"Don't you think that was a bit…presumptuous of her? Forgive me for saying — "

"It's all right. That was exactly how the more experienced managers of farms in the area reacted. She asked them for a piece of land where she could do her experiments, and they told her, amiably and with a lot of pats on the back, to forget it. They explained that it wasn't realistic—why would she succeed where great scientists had failed?—and reminded her that they only gave land to sons of residents and she didn't even have a family. But she didn't give up. She showed them data and proof and calculations, and told them that consumers would love the idea. You buy one pepper, she said, and for the same price, you get a small pepper as a bonus. It's like a Kinder egg. In the end, she managed to persuade the manager of Noit to give her some land and a shack to live in on the outskirts of the farm. When she showed us her tiny piece of land right at the border with Jordan, Nira and I . . . Let's say we just looked at each other. And on the way back, we agreed that if that's the land they gave her, they wanted her to fail. But she succeeded. That girl, who didn't have a single report card without a D in conduct, who had been thrown out of every group she'd been in and every job she'd had, from school to youth movement to waitressing, because she'd fought with everyone, that girl established the first hothouse in the world for babushka peppers."

"Babushka?"

"That's the commercial name she gave them."

"They're already on the market? Why haven't I heard about them?"

They're still trying to improve the taste of the small peppers. And make production more efficient. Only a year ago, they discovered that a particular bee, the *Bombus,* is especially effective in pepper pollination . . . That's how she met the quiet boy who runs the Noit apiary, whose name is Adar."

●

The tape ended, Michael. That's why I haven't left messages for two days already. It wasn't deliberate. It's not that I wanted to torture you by stopping the story at the most suspenseful moment. Not that you don't deserve to be tortured a little, but that wasn't my intention. The tape simply ended. And it wasn't easy to find a new one for this machine. They don't sell them anymore. No one uses answering machines anymore. I went from store to store until someone finally sent me to a place on Allenby Street. There, among the stores that sell stamps, was one that sold electrical appliances whose glory days were behind them.

The salesman, who looked like a refrigerator, tried to hit on me. He apparently likes his women, like his merchandise, to have been around for a while. He wanted to know if he could take me out for a cup of coffee.

I used the same reply I'd heard a tall, stooped girl use with a psychologist when she came to the tent for some support: "I'm still stuck in a relationship with my ex."

●

The second thing I wanted to do after I understood that we were on the way to Adar was to call you (the first was to slap Avner Ashdot). I wanted to tell you. So you would know. Not so you could grant permission, God forbid. I've already said that I don't need your permission. But I thought it was only fair to let you know. I wanted to call you and press on the loudspeaker button so you could hear everything Avner Ashdot told me later.

His daughter went to Adar's shack and he opened the door, a look of alarm on his face. Instead of being alarmed herself, she showed him the babushka pepper she'd brought with her. He went silently to the fridge and took out some honey and apple slices for her. She asked him whether beekeepers like bees. He didn't answer her. She wasn't offended, but understood right away that this was a case of extreme shyness. As they worked together in her hothouse, she managed to create a picture from the rare bits of information he gave up: Since arriving in the south a few years earlier, Adar had only had contact with animals. At first, he worked with wild animals, then on the alpaca farm, and then he heard that Noit was looking for a beekeeper. No wonder, she thought, that he has no idea how to act with people. And then, one evening after they'd finished hanging another few *Bombus* hives among the babushka bushes, he asked if she wanted to join him on his walk, and when they reached the emergency reservoir and stood watching the ripples caused by the wind, he said to her, "You don't know who I am, I'm trouble, I hurt people whether I want to or not. You should run away from me now while you still can." And then he kissed her, taking her completely by surprise. She hadn't even been sure that he liked her until that moment.

That kiss broke a dam between them and within a few weeks, a flood of emotion swept them off to a wedding, without a rabbi, on the lawn next to the basketball court, and he moved into her shack. Because, of course, houses are given only to sons of residents, although we can only hope that the fact that they were a couple definitely improved their chances for one in the future.

The monastery of silence — that's what the people on the farm call their shack. That's how they are, Michael, your son and his wife: They believe that words cause only misunderstanding. That we should do and not talk.

•

I should also tell you the ending, Michael: They had a son a month ago. They insisted on giving birth at home, and there were problems. Maya was taken to the hospital in Eilat. They saved her life. But she still hasn't recovered from the operation. She can't stand on her feet more than an hour a day. She's not allowed. The surgical incision is infected. Stitches still have to heal.

When Avner told her that he met me in Tel Aviv, she asked him to bring me to them. To help. And warned him that Adar must not know. Because he wouldn't agree.

•

We have a grandson, Michael. Do you believe it?

•

"Put on some music for us," I ordered Avner Ashdot. "I need music urgently."

"More Strauss?"

"No! Something calmer."

"Chopin?"

"Chopin is good."

The sounds of Chopin's Piano Concerto no. 1 filled the car. The long introduction by the strings, and then the piano, which I usually found sentimental, now sounded hesitant. Stammering. A bit anxious.

●

I felt the stents. After Adar cut off contact with us and the chest pains started, you insisted that I go for a checkup. And you were right. For the second time since we met, you saved my life (the first time was when you rescued me from my parents' house). To this day, I tremble at the thought that my arteries were completely clogged then. That if I had waited a bit longer, my heart would have given out. And you, Michael, you never moved from my bedside after the angiogram. You canceled all your sessions. You held my hand. You bought me tea and almond croissants from the café in the shopping center next to the hospital (I know that you know all this, but I'm not telling it for you, Michael. I'm the one who needs to remember now, at this particular moment, that you also had good qualities).

You're not supposed to feel the stents after the angiogram, but I always felt them. I still feel them. Especially when I'm overwrought. They dance. Stab me with pain.

After a long few moments with music the only sound in the car, Avner Ashdot said, "We're getting close to the farm."

I asked him to stop at the gate.

He pulled over to the side of the road, a few meters before the gate. It was open. The guard booth was empty.

Beside it was a rusty sign that said WELCOME TO NOIT COOPERATIVE FARM. Avner Ashdot turned off the engine but left the Chopin on.

He put his hand on mine.

I jerked it away. As if his fingers were a scorpion's claws. I spoke without looking at him: "We're not children, Avner. If you wanted to arrange a meeting between me and my son, you should have told me that was your intention."

He said, "You should know that it was Maya's idea. After you showered in my apartment the first time, I told her about you, about the impression you made on me, and she was the one who suggested—"

"It doesn't matter who suggested it."

"I'm sorry it had to be like this, but—"

Once again, I interrupted him: "It didn't *have* to be like this. *You* decided that this is how it would be. Underhanded. Devious. You set me up, Avner. And I don't like to be set up."

●

I'm used to the way we argued, Michael. That's why I expected Avner Ashdot to flatten my claims with his counterclaims. I expected well-founded justifications based on proof. I expected new information to be revealed at the critical moment that would shed new light on the facts. I expected precedents that would support his position and prove that he had acted properly, or at least find him innocent based on reasonable doubt...

Instead, Avner Ashdot merely sighed and said, "Maybe you're right. And after a long silence, he added, "It's hard to change bad habits. Deception is the only way I know, Devora. I practiced it for thirty years."

A pickup truck drove out of the farm carrying some Thai workers in the back.

Avner waited for it to pull away—as if there was a danger that the Thai workers might hear him—and then said, "I was afraid that if I had told you where we were going, you wouldn't have come. Or that you would have asked for time to think about it. And we don't have time. The situation here is not good, Devora. But you're right...I'm sorry."

"I'm not a pawn on your chessboard, Avner."

"I understand."

"And I'm not Nira either," I said. "You can't hide things from me for twenty-five years."

"That's clear to me."

I warned him, "If you trick me one more time, that will be the end of our relationship."

He nodded. "Agreed."

The stents continued to hurt me. There wasn't much water left in the bottle, only the last few drops. Tilting it into my mouth, I trapped them with the tip of my tongue.

I said, "We'll wait here until the Chopin is over. If we go in now, I don't think my heart will be able to take it. When the Chopin ends, call them and tell Adar that I'm at the gate. I won't force myself on anyone. If he doesn't want to see me, we'll turn right around and go back to Tel Aviv. Understood?"

•

During the last minute of Chopin's Piano Concerto no. 1, the music swells. The piano, the violins, the oboes, they all crescendo at once. At first it sounds as if the instruments are arguing with each other about which ones can play louder, but during the final seconds, they all blend, you can no longer hear each instrument separately, and the only clear thing is that the end is approaching...

•

Nevertheless, I want to separate the details from each other, Michael. Since you weren't with me at those moments (as you *would* have been if you hadn't been such a stubborn mule), you can at least picture the scene:

First of all, Noit is much greener than I expected.

Meadows, bushes, palm trees with fronds large enough to shade you from the sun. Window boxes filled with blooming plants. Low, simple houses. And between them, paths wide enough only for bicycles.

But no one is riding a bicycle in the blazing heat of the noonday sun. Everything is utterly still. No one comes into or out of the row of houses. There is no movement. Even the hammocks are motionless. We keep driving. Slowly. The front yards here, I notice, are full of the pieces of junk that are typical of backyards: the backseat of a car without the car, a couch with torn upholstery, a rusty scooter. Abandoned.

At the end of the row of houses and front yards—a temporary shack. Without window boxes. In front of it are laundry lines filled with clothes and clothespins—proof that people actually live here—and beside them, a pickup truck, its bed covered with yellow canvas.

We stop. The wheels of our car crunch the dirt. The hum of the engine stops abruptly. Avner Ashdot turns to look at me to check that I am all right.

At almost that exact moment, two doors open—the car door and the door of the shack. I emerge from the car door. Your son's wife emerges from the door of the shack. Delicate, that is the only word to describe her. Soft bones. Long blond hair. Small wrinkles around her mouth. A certain affront in her upper lip which, at first, reminds me of something, but I can't remember what, until I realize: it reminds me of the affront in Adar's upper lip. He follows her out. Bearded, expression grim, holding a baby. He suddenly stops moving, as if he wants to maintain a safe distance from me.

His delicate wife, however, doesn't keep a safe distance. She walks toward us, her hand on her waist, pecks her father on the cheek, takes his hand, and says, "Thank you Dad, for bringing Devora." And then, without adding a word, takes me to see the baby.

The stents are hurting me very much, but I follow her. Already at first glance I can see: Your grandson, Michael, looks like you—the devil's work. The high forehead, the nose, the slightly folded ears. The coloring is Avner's, but the features—yours.

•

I asked her what his name was. I wasn't sure I was allowed to ask. I wasn't sure I was allowed to speak at all.

"Benyamin."

"Can I...hold him?"

She looked at Adar for permission.

And he, without looking at me, said no. Then he turned on his heel and went back into the shack.

His wife hurried to put her hand on my shoulder. "Don't be upset," she said. "He's a little bit in shock right now, that's all."

So am I, I wanted to say. So am I.

•

For two days your son didn't say a word to me, good or bad. For two days we were all action. And action was definitely needed there, in their shack.

It seemed that the fear of making mistakes paralyzed them and that their anxiety spread to the baby. Maya couldn't breast-feed. She had no milk and her body still hadn't recovered from the difficult birth, so the baby drank formula. He suffered from gas pains, and they suffered along with him. I'm not at all sure they understood that he was screaming because of gas pains. They were so...lost. It's hard to believe that someone could be so clueless in this age of the Internet. But they had no Internet connection. And they didn't even have a changing table for the baby. I'm no expert in this either, right? Years had passed since I had cared for a baby. Even so, I felt like an expert. Adar always had good hands, so I asked Maya to ask him to build a changing table. It was ready in a few hours. He asked with a glance where to put it, and with a movement of my head I indicated where the best place was. I sent Avner to Beersheba to buy a different brand of formula, a rocking cradle, a bath seat, and some toys. Adar had to take Maya's place in the babushka hothouses and at the same time, collect honey from the hives, and during the many hours he wasn't home, there was no one to help ease Benyamin's gas pains. Maya couldn't hold him for more than a few minutes without her stitches hurting her. I asked her to ask Adar to let me hold the baby when he was out of the house. He was only a few meters away from me when I asked. He was washing dishes in the small kitchen, and I was wiping down the new changing table with a rag. I could have spoken to him, but I was afraid he wouldn't answer, so I asked her to give him the message. With a brief movement of his beard, he agreed to let me hold Benyamin. I thought that was a good sign.

•

When Adar left for the hothouses, I picked up the baby and put him on my shoulder, patted his back lightly, and sang him the songs I used to sing to Adar when he was a baby. After a while, my arms hurt, so I put him in the cradle Avner had brought from Beersheba. He cried. I picked him up again. He liked being in my arms. I liked that he liked it. It gave me confidence. When Adar was a baby, he didn't like anything I did. I always thought he wanted something else. I sent Avner to Beersheba again to buy a baby carrier. He drove there for the second time that day, anxious to please. I bathed the baby, and when I saw that he liked it, that it soothed him, I bathed him again a few hours later. Each time I soaped his folded ears, I smiled inwardly, thinking of you, Michael. I was sorry that you weren't with me, that you would never know what it was like to hold a grandchild. And I was furious at you. For locking Adar out of your heart and entering into a pact of silence with a part of me that had grown tired, that wanted to believe you when you said that even if there had been a moment when we could have saved him, we had missed it.

I was furious at you for having the nerve, after all that, to die before me. And leave me alone. Completely alone. My fury at you was so intense, Michael, that it would have scorched your flesh if you had been beside me. And I was sorry that you weren't beside me. To be scorched.

Avner came back from Beersheba with the carrier. He glanced at Maya, making sure she saw how hard he was trying. He brought me an almond croissant. I managed to take two bites of it, no more, because just then Benyamin woke up. I put him into the carrier I'd harnessed to myself and went out to the yard with him to get some air. I needed air. The sun was setting and it wasn't so hot anymore. His tiny head protruded above the straps of the carrier.

He seemed to be smiling at me, and I thought that was another good sign.

Then Adar came back from the hothouses. And walked right past me. Without looking at me. As if I were a stranger.

●

You weren't in court, so you didn't see, but that's exactly how he walked past the husband of the woman he ran over: as if he didn't exist at all.

●

Benyamin woke up at night. That's just how it is—babies wake up at night. Maya went to him. I got up with her and we made him a bottle. She held him and I fed him. When she got tired and started having pain again, I took him, wrapped him in a blanket, and went out to the yard with him again.

Nights are different in the Arava. There are more stars in the sky. The air is drier. Wind chimes tinkle gently in the distance. Which means there's a wind.

I walked along the empty paths of the farm, rocking Benyamin in my arms and singing a lullaby to him. He liked that, and his long lashes had already fallen by the end of the second verse. I used to sing that lullaby to Adar too, but without success. Yasmina, the nanny who replaced me after three months, used to sing him songs in Ladino, which he actually did like. I asked her to teach them to me, and she agreed. She even wrote the words down on a piece of paper so I could practice singing them. Can you believe it? I practiced songs in Ladino in the car on the way home. But when I sang them to him, he kicked his feet in the air in frustration.

It wasn't the songs—I understood that. It was me. He was pushing me away.

I went back into the shack with Benyamin, put him in the cradle, and covered him with a thin blanket. I covered Maya with a thin blanket too because she had fallen asleep on the couch, and I noticed that she had six toes on her left foot. I lay down on my mattress, controlling a strong urge to go to Avner Ashdot's mattress on the other side of the room and check how many toes he had. And then—I'm sorry, Michael, it's the truth—to sleep beside him, to lie in his arms. To feel the heat of his body enter mine through our clothes. To be consoled for all the mistakes I'd made in my life, including the one I was making by finding consolation in him.

•

"Thank you, Devora," Maya said the next morning. "You really saved our lives."

Avner said, "Yes, well done, Devora, you performed miracles here."

Adar was just installing a new shelf so there would be somewhere to put the toys. I thought he was too focused on his work to listen to our conversation. But then he turned around and said in my direction, "Tell me, when do you think you'll…?"

•

I couldn't answer him. The most painful blows are those your body is unprepared for. And I—I just doubled over with pain. Adar, for his part, didn't even wait for my reply. He finished putting up the shelf, folded the ladder in two quick, matter-of-fact movements, and told Maya he was going to the hothouses.

The slam of the door woke Benyamin up. Maya put a hand on her lower stomach, looked at me, and said, "Please, as long as you're here, you pick him up."

But I gave her a look that said, Sorry. I have another child to tend to now.

•

I walked out of the shack and Avner followed me. I told him to stay there.

"But—"

"This is between me and Adar," I said firmly.

I started walking toward the hothouses. Avner remained standing where he was. My first steps were angry and purposeful, but after a few dozen meters, I had to acknowledge the sad fact that I hadn't the slightest idea where I was going in the sun. I recalled Avner saying that the plot of land they gave Maya was near the Jordanian border, so that meant I had to walk eastward. That is, to go as far away from the Arava road as I could. I turned east on the first dirt road it was possible to turn east on. The air was getting hotter and I began to perspire under my clothes. Drops of perspiration crawled down me like ants. Part of me wanted to give up. But another part was absolutely unwilling to do so. I passed a few houses and a kindergarten, and then I saw the first hothouse. Then another hothouse. And another and another. Dozens of hothouses spread across the desert. I shaded my eyes with my hand, thinking that I had no way of knowing which of them he was in.

•

Where are you, my son? I spoke to him silently, the way I used to sometimes after you had fallen asleep and I was no longer afraid you would hear my thoughts.

•

From where I stood, I could see the flash of the sun's rays as they hit the windshield of the pickup parked near one of the hothouses. I recognized the yellow canvas that covered the bed of the pickup.

●

When I opened the door to the hothouse, I saw rows and rows of green bushes with red peppers sprouting from them. There were drip irrigation hoses on the ground, and every few meters, hanging from poles, were white cardboard boxes that had holes on their sides. From the buzzing coming from them, I guessed that those were the *bombus* beehives.

For the first few seconds, I didn't see Adar. But then I heard branches moving and saw him emerge from between them.

I cleared my throat.

He turned to face me. I saw the surprise in his face. And then the attempt to pretend he wasn't surprised. He came a bit closer to me and asked, "What are you doing here?"

"I came to see the famous babushka peppers."

"So now you've seen them."

I wanted to say not really, because I hadn't seen the small peppers hidden inside.

But he looked at his watch and shifted his weight from one foot to the other, so I said, "I also wanted to see…you, Adar. I thought we should talk."

He rubbed his beard for a few seconds. "What is there to talk about?"

"Tell me, do you *really* want me to leave?"

He didn't answer. For a long moment he stared at a nearby branch, and then finally said, "I'm not like you, Devora, I'm not good with words."

•

That was the hardest thing, Michael. The fact that he called me Devora. More than his ignoring me, and honestly, even more than the fact that he said nothing about your death. Denying me the title of mother—that was just unbearable. And he didn't do it to hurt me. There was nothing hostile about the way he said "Devora." Just the opposite. He spoke my name naturally. As if that was exactly what I was to him now. A woman named Devora.

•

I needed more than a moment to swallow my pride before saying, "Even so, Adar, I'd like to know if you want me to stay or not."

He was silent again. Pulled a leaf off a branch. Rubbed it between his fingers.

I thought: Spaces are different here in the desert. Between one person and another. Between one sentence and another.

After a long while, he said, "It's too fast for me. I've built something new, and all of sudden—all of a sudden you come. Unannounced. Changing things. It's too fast for me."

"So let's do it at your pace," I suggested. And I sounded like I was pleading. Almost groveling. I thought, when have I ever groveled?

He shook his head (with disbelief? Refusal? Pain? I didn't know. That boy, the fruit of my womb, was as unreadable to me as a stranger).

"Listen, Adar," I said, "Avner will take me away from here now. If you want me to come again, just ask."

He tossed the leaf onto the ground and said, "Maybe I'll ask and maybe I won't. Things should happen when it's time for them to happen."

•

I gave Benyamin many goodbye kisses on his chubby cheeks. I gave Maya a gentle hug goodbye because strong hugs hurt her. I didn't say goodbye to Adar. When I got into Avner Ashdot's car, he was still in the babushka hothouses. Do you understand? He made sure to stay in the hothouses so he wouldn't have to say goodbye to me.

For the first hour of the trip, we were silent, Avner Ashdot and I. As if our children's silence had stuck to us. We drove past army bases and monuments to fallen soldiers, and I wondered why I hadn't noticed them on the way down to the desert.

We stopped for gas. The fellow who filled the tank cleaned the windshield with a small squeegee, and Avner Ashdot gave him a generous tip. You never tipped at gas stations. You didn't like being forced into spending more money.

When we were back on the main road, he said, "I'm sorry, Devora."

It was clear to both of us what he was sorry about. There was no point in pretending otherwise.

"Your intentions were good," I said, sighing instead of crying.

"Yes. But the results—shit."

He put his hand on mine. This time I didn't move it away. He said, "You were hurt. That wasn't my intention. Adar didn't tell...I mean, I only heard the details for the first time when you told them to me on the drive to Noit."

"Are you saying that you knew I liked almond croissants but you didn't know the story with Adar?"

"The croissant was a coincidence, believe me. And Adar—he didn't say much about you. As you saw, he's not a big talker...We knew you were estranged. We even knew there had been a shivah and he didn't go. But we didn't know why. We didn't know that the story was so..."

"Serious? Yes, Avner, it is definitely a serious story."

He looked at me with compassion, then returned his gaze to the road and said, "He's a good boy, do you know that?"

"I never noticed that he was bursting with goodness."

"Look, he...he's a hard nut to crack. It took me time to get used to him too. During the first few visits I made to them, he didn't say a word to me. It was insulting. Infuriating. But then, all of a sudden, on the fourth or fifth visit, before I left, he put a jar of honey on the hood of my car. Do you see? That was his way of communicating with me. Also, he's taken over for Maya in the hothouses now—do you know how hard that work is?"

I thought, He didn't give me anything when I left. But I said, "That's all well and good...But still...There's something in Adar...There was always something...cruel. Did you know that he never said he was sorry to the husband of the woman he ran over?"

"No. I didn't know."

They sat a few seats away from each other in court. Adar never turned around to face him even once during the entire trial.

●

I told Avner about the space-filled conversation with Adar in the babushka hothouse. And as I spoke, he began to move his hand on mine. To stroke it.

When I finished, he said, "The situation isn't as bad as I thought. He left an opening. Both of them, Maya too, have left us an opening."

"But Adar's anger and resentment are so deeply rooted in him," I said.

"We have to take a long breath. Both of us. And be patient. People usually lose each other because one of them doesn't have the patience to wait for the other one to be ready."

"I don't know, I wish I were as optimistic as you."

Avner Ashdot was silent. Slowly, he spread my fingers and laced them with his.

●

It's all because of that hug with Hani, my neighbor. Until that hug, I didn't know how much I yearned to be touched. That's when the countdown began. Internal. Silent. But the kind that could end only one way.

I invited Avner Ashdot to come up to the third floor. For coffee. Even though we both knew very well that

I drink only tea and water. I won't go into details about what happened later. There's a limit to what I can ask you to listen to. I will only say that I discovered that he too had six toes on his left foot. And that after he left, I felt unbearably lonely.

I want it to be clear, he behaved like a gentleman. He made me a light breakfast. An onion omelet and a salad. He sat down to eat with me. Complimented me endlessly during the meal. Caressed my cheek once. Asked over and over again whether it was okay for him to go. He would have liked to stay, but he had a meeting...

I told him it was all right, perfectly all right...

But after he was gone, I don't know, Michael, everything weighed down so heavily on me. All the events of the last few weeks. I was filled with such an intense desire to talk to you and so deeply sad that it was impossible.

Our apartment suddenly looked like an isolated farm. Four rooms surrounded on all sides by hills devoid of love.

●

You know how I am at such moments. I have to find something to do. So I started packing for the move. Sorting: winter clothes, summer clothes, tableware I wanted to take with me, tableware it was time to give away or discard. Old letters. Newspaper clippings. Photo albums. It took much longer than I thought. Even though it was not our way to collect things, we'd lived in that apartment twenty-five years. You'd be amazed at how many tchotchkes we accumulated.

I left your study for last. It took me a week to gather the courage to go inside. My heart pounding. I started with the easy things. First the shelves with the binders and the books, and only then your desk, with its many drawers that had always been closed to me. It turned out that they didn't conceal dark secrets or letters from clandestine lovers (really, Michael, all those years and not even one court reporter?)—only two Rolex watches you received as gifts and never wore because you thought they were too ostentatious, and fragments from your professional diary that you apparently thought would one day become a book, but you never got to write it (which is a good thing, if you don't mind my saying so).

I found this answering machine in the bottom drawer. I connected it to the phone. And then—your bass voice asked me to leave a message.

I suddenly realized what I had to do. And since then—I've been speaking to you.

It's ridiculous, I know. Talking to a machine. A normal person would not do that. But if I've learned anything in the last few weeks, it's that there is no such thing as a normal person. Or normal actions. There are only actions that a particular person, at a particular time, must do.

•

For the entire time I've been leaving you messages, I never expected you to reply, Michael. I didn't believe you'd give me a signal or appear in a dream with answers to all the questions. I wanted to talk to you because I knew that to you, I could speak only truth. The whole truth. And nothing but the truth. That's what forces me to do the hardest thing of all: remove all the masks and look at myself—this is my face, these are the choices I've made and these are the results, for better and for worse. And for the very worst.

Sigmund Freud, you understand, was a very wise man, but last night, after I finished the last volume in the collection and put it on my night table, I thought that he made one mistake. The three floors of the psyche do not exist inside us at all! Absolutely not! They exist in the air between us and someone else, in the space between our mouths and the ears we are telling our story to. And if there is no one there to listen—there is no story. If there is no one we can tell our secrets to and sharpen our memories on and find consolation in, then we talk into an answering machine, Michael. The main thing is to talk to someone. Otherwise, alone, a person has no idea which of the three floors he is on, and he is doomed to grope in the dark for the light switch.

•

Yesterday I took part in the million-person march in Tel Aviv. This time, unlike at the earlier demonstration, I went by train and a rickshaw was waiting for me when I came out of the station. Yishai, the young man who is going to live with me in my new apartment, was the driver. A charming fellow. A law student. He dreams of setting up an office for environmental justice to protect nature against those who want to exploit it. An idealist. You would like him.

We managed to reach Weizmann Street in the rickshaw. There the activists I'd helped over the past few weeks were waiting, along with several people from the psychology tent and Avner Ashdot. We marched together slowly—Avner can't walk quickly—until we reached the square. We stood facing the stage. Not too close, but not too far either. There was a nice breeze blowing. I was wearing clothes that were inappropriate for a judge, but perfect for a woman at a protest rally: loose pants, a comfortable blouse with a slightly scooped neck, sneakers. I knew that this time I wouldn't faint, but if God forbid something happened to me, Avner Ashdot was beside me. The square gradually filled up with people: some carried large, well-designed signs, some had small, makeshift signs. On the sidelines, I noticed, ordinary things were happening: French kisses, a short line in front of the ATM, a child falling and starting to cry. The usual human dance. Nevertheless—I thought—there's something unusual going on here: so many people who are no longer willing to accept things as they are, who believe that change is possible, had come there to say so. This was something special.

At ten that night, the first speakers came onto the stage. Others followed. Some said smart things, some said less smart things. But you could hear the thread of sincerity running through their words.

Singers and groups I didn't know performed between speeches, and when during one song, Avner asked me to dance, I said yes. It had been so long since I danced in public. And you know how much I love to dance. Since Avner Ashdot's legs were as heavy as tree stumps, we couldn't really dance to the rhythm of the music, so we danced a slower waltz in the middle of the square. My head almost touched his chest, his breath ruffled my hair, our feet moved in a circle.

•

Before midnight, we sang the anthem with three hundred thousand other people. And I truly felt that hope was not lost, as one of the phrases of that song says.

I knew the feeling would pass, but for one moment, I held onto it, Michael, for one moment it was mine.

•

The movers are coming tomorrow. And the day after tomorrow, in the morning, I'll wake up for the first time in a house that is not our house. In a bed that is not our bed.

I think this will be the last message I leave you. I'll take out the tape and keep it in one of the bottom drawers. Maybe Benyamin will find it one day after I'm gone. And listen to it.

On Saturday, I'm going to Noit again with Avner. Maya called. Said that the boy misses me. And that Adar doesn't object to my coming. Not strongly, in any case.

You would probably say: *What's the rush? First get organized in your new home.*

You probably would say that I should wait until Adar explicitly asks me to come. That it's not our way to force ourselves on people.

But from now on, my love, my joy, my disaster, it's no longer our way.

It's my way.